HOLDING LIES

HOLDING LIES

A NOVEL

John Larison

SKYHORSE PUBLISHING

Skyhorse Publishing books may be purchased in bulk at special discounts for
sales promotion, corporate gifts, fund-raising, or educational purposes. Special
editions can also be created to specifications. For details, contact the Special Sales
Department, Skyhorse Publishing, 307 West 36th Street, 11th Floor, New York,
NY 10018 or info@skyhorsepublishing.com.

www.skyhorsepublishing.com

10 9 8 7 6 5 4 3 2 1

Library of Congress Cataloging-in-Publication Data

Larison, John.
Holding lies : a novel / John Larison.
p. cm.
ISBN 978-1-61608-255-0 (alk. paper)
1. River life--Fiction. 2. Fathers and daughters--Fiction. 3. Fly fishing--
Fiction. 4. Murder--Investigation--Fiction. 5. Northwest, Pacific--Fiction. I.
Title.
PS3612.A6484H65 2011
813'.6--dc22
2011007834

Printed in the United States of America

Especially for Navah and Naomi

At times when man is overcome by the horror of the alienation between "I" and "world," it occurs to him that something might be done.

—Martin Buber, *I and Thou*

Fare you well,
Fare you well.
I love you more than words can tell.
Listen to the river sing sweet songs,
To rock my soul.

—Robert Hunter and Jerry Garcia, "Brokedown Palace"

Chapter One

HERE HE WAS straddling an alder limb above the Ipsyniho River, the bluegreen currents melting by, and through the shimmering tension of the surface, a gray space sliding back and forth from obscurity—the opalescent back of a steelhead. This was it: suspended between the worlds of water and wind and being paid for the privilege.

And yet Hank Hazelton couldn't shake the nagging sense that despite a lifetime of living right, of caring for his friends and his watershed, he'd nevertheless fucked up something crucial, something a better man would have gotten right. He was fifty-nine years old now but only half as sure as he'd been at thirty. Could it be, *this was it?* Because it sure felt like this moment and this river and this lifetime had been severed from their proper place and sentenced for all eternity to flow in circles.

"Right there," he again called to his dude, who was casting from the bank. "Along that seam."

Those fish and this river were inexplicably linked—any thought of one conjured images of the other. His clients thought of them differently; the fish were the trophy and the river the field of play. Maybe that was part of the problem.

Steelhead. Their recovery had been a grim prospect even thirty-five years before, when he'd turned down the insurance job in Portland, bought his first boat—that grungy *rapid Robert* that wanted nothing more than to stall in a rapid and flip—and registered with the state marine board as a fly-fishing guide. He'd known even then that it would be a life of endless battles and increasing hardship. Though he also knew this campaign to save America's last salmon would require that much and more, from him and everyone else. But what did it say about him, about how he'd used his life, that those fish were closer to extinction now than they'd ever been?

What would she think, his daughter Annie, when she arrived next week, thirty-one now, twenty-six years since they'd last lived together, fourteen since they'd last seen each other, since she'd said, "You mean nothing to me." She was so cosmopolitan now, so removed. She wouldn't understand.

He couldn't forget standing on the bank of this very pool with her as a four- or five-year-old, when she still went by her given name of Riffle, when she still looked at him like he possessed something worth knowing. The sun was setting, and her hair was damp from swimming, and she was barefoot and gripping his fingers for balance as they negotiated the rocks. He had gestured toward a white sail above the water and explained that it was called an osprey and that it had naturally polarized vision and that it could dive deep into the river to capture fish. She raised an arm to block the light and said, matter-of-factly, "Catch him, Daddy. I want to ride him."

"Am I reaching them?" the dude called. Stan Burke, a regular, came up from San Francisco twice a year for a long weekend, three times if his construction business was doing well. Married, four children, two of them married themselves, a granddaughter on the way. To him, the river was a lighthouse on which he could take a bearing; every dollar earned brought him a step closer to the Ipsyniho's protective harbors, to his retirement along the water. They'd first fished together in the early nineties, right after the movie, when Stan decided to "make the switch" to fly-fishing. Like so many of Hank's clients, Stan seemed to think the most pressing ethical concern was which type of tackle you cast. "I can't believe they let people fish indicators on this river," he was prone to quip. "I mean, where's the sport in that?" Despite this fervency, and a half-dozen half-baked theories on politics and religion, Stan wasn't a bad guy to spend the day with. And he tipped well too.

"They're on the far-side seam," Hank answered. "You can make the cast. Sweep deeper into the D-loop, and come over the top. Let the rod do the work."

The fish always chose that ledge over the run's other holding lies. The migration route up the river, the fish's path of least resistance, delivered them right to its protective lee. In the early years, or *his* early years, the late sixties, before the headwaters were logged, the tributaries dammed, the hatchery built, fish would be scattered all through this run they called Governor. The biggest fish would often sit on that ledge, the smaller ones dispersing to other lies in the pool. He'd even caught them in the knee-deep bucket on the near side, before the silt from the new road filled it in. Back then, forty thousand native steelhead spawned in the watershed. You could find a fresh fish or two in most pools most months of the year. Which, according to the old-timers, was nothing. "They're practically extinct," Mickie McCune, the river's first guide, was saying then. "My first year, back in twenty-five, the cannery gillnetted eighty thousand out of the estuary and I still landed two hundred fish!" These days, the young guides were relieved when eight thousand natives returned.

It was an even sadder story across the Northwest, with most salmon runs completely gone and the few that remained returning at 1 or 2 percent of their historic levels. The Ipsyniho, with its rugged headwaters and vicious whitewater, was one place where there was still hope.

The young guides. They were different, too hopped-up on proving themselves to see the whole picture, to appreciate the gravity of what was happening around them. The river to them was a basketball court or a half-pipe—a place to demonstrate how "badass" they were. "Chargers," his longtime friend and fellow guide Caroline Abbot called them. "Just listen to them," she said. "When they land a few in a session, they 'slaughtered them.' When they get skunked, they had their 'ass handed to them.' It's the language of evisceration. It's the language of war."

Hank didn't know about that, but he did know that he couldn't stand their phony regard for the fish. They preached restoring the habitat, preached safeguarding the gene pool, but then they didn't do shit to help. They didn't help drop logs in the spawning tribs, count redds, fight the State's new broodstock program, nothing. They talked like they were the most pious on the river, more pious than you, but they didn't *do* anything. Except allow their clients to catch too many fish.

For as long as Hank had been working the river, there had been an unwritten rule among the guides: two fish and you're out. Once a client had caught two fish, the guide was to ensure he didn't get another one. Sabotage on a steelhead river was an easy thing. Hank knew a dozen runs that looked greasy but never held a fish. And he must have known a hundred submerged boulders or ledges that even to the most experienced eye looked ideal—walking-speed current and foam dotting the surface—but that had a secret upwelling or swirling eddy or some other glitch that ensured no fish would ever hold there.

It was a speed difference, really, between the generations. These young guides rushed everywhere. They talked like they oared like they fished: too fast. Like if they didn't say it or do it now, somebody else would. Maybe the humbling thirties would slow them down, teach them the truth about living, that it is better savored than devoured. And if not the thirties, then definitely the fifties, when their balance wavered, their bladders contracted, and they became invisible to the girls in town.

Poor Annie: these were the men of her generation. He only hoped they had deeper regard for women than they did for watersheds.

The worst of the new breed was Justin Morell. "As in the mushroom," he'd said when they first met at a ramp three years back. Justin was a body counter. Like all these young guys, he had a website, and he posted how many fish were caught on each trip, as if that was the

He imagined Annie in a big city apartment, one of those with sprawling wood floors and wall-sized windows. He imagined her taking her coffee in the morning, watching the rain slide down the glass and the antlike people scurrying far below. She would be used to a certain ease of life, a certain level of affluence. She wouldn't be used to freedom.

Stan's tenth or twelfth cast landed right, the waker immediately chugging toward the bank. The fish came fast, swatting at it with its tail and throwing a wall of water. Stan jerked the fly away and said, "Holy fuck."

"Loosen your grip on that rod," Hank called. "Don't set the hook." She wouldn't be comfortable here. She'd leave early. She wouldn't be glad she'd come.

This time, the fish took solidly, and Stan did nothing, perfectly. The reel was screaming, the rod bucking, and the fish somersaulted over the lip of the rapid and out of the pool.

Stan was yelling, "Do it to me, baby! Yes, yes, YES!"

Hank lit a cigarette. It was moments like these that made him feel like a pimp.

*

THEY WERE ROUNDING the last oxbow, having just run Whitehorse Rapid, drinking ale at Stan's insistence in honor of the two fish he'd caught, when Hank spotted the boat broadside on the midstream gravel bar. It was a low-sided ClackaCraft, orange guide stickers. Only two people had a boat like that around here; he hoped it was Danny Goodman's, owner of the fly shop in town and a longtime guide. Always a good guy to share the water with.

"I've never had a fish take like that before. I mean, Jesus!"

There wasn't a run to swing on either side of the bar, no reason to stop the boat there. Maybe Danny had found a new spot. Danny was always finding new spots.

As they drifted closer, he noticed an oar was missing and the anchor was up. He studied the banks, then the water around them. Someone had lost that boat. Someone had gotten thrown.

"That boat looks abandoned," Stan said. Then with more urgency, "Hey, that boat *is* abandoned!"

He was still a double-haul away when he spotted the Fish Fear Me decal. It was Justin Morell's boat. And a minute later, as he dropped anchor alongside it, he saw the smear of blood across the oarsman's seat.

Chapter Two

HANK MET SHERIFF Carter and the fire department's search-and-rescue team at Millican Ramp, a mile down from Whitehorse Rapid. He'd called them from Stan's cell phone, just before Stan drove his rented Camry back to his motel in town. Only now did Hank realize Stan forgot to tip.

"I stopped at Morell's apartment on the way up," Sheriff Carter said, catching his own reflection in a passenger window, adjusting his badge. "His boat wasn't there."

"That's because it's on the bar." Carter could be a bit distracted sometimes, especially when he expected reporters to show up.

"Called Danny at the shop," Carter said, repositioning his belt and holster now. "They didn't give Morell a trip today."

Hank helped drop the search-and-rescue sled in the river, buckled on the fire department's thick red PFD, and took a seat near the bow. The boat drifted back from the ramp, then tipped deep into the pool as the four-cylinder roared to life. Two seconds later, they skipped out on top, planing now at full throttle. It was a different river from a boat like this, a staircase of jumps, a place where current didn't matter and landmarks blurred; it was just another highway.

He'd been on the body boat before: the acrid smell of gasoline mixing with river water, the roaring splash of that engine chasing up behind them—it felt now as if he'd never quit searching.

The ClackaCraft was right where Hank had left it, anchor down.

"That's blood," Carter shouted.

"Like I told you on the phone."

＊

ALL THE GUIDES converged at Millican Ramp, fourteen trucks towing boats, and highway traffic slowed to a crawl because of the rigs parked half on the shoulder, half in the lane. Everyone who could be reached was there. The new guys with their fish tattoos and stubby beards. The old guard including Walter Torse, who needed a wading staff just to navigate dry land these days. Caroline was there, pulling rods from her boat, locking them under her Tundra's canopy. Andy Trib was the first one to the ramp—he hadn't had a client that day.

This was what they did for each other. They might bicker and shit-talk, might even backstab a little, but if a guy went missing, everybody dropped everything and committed.

"Listen up," Sheriff Carter bellowed. "You probably heard—we found Morell's boat on the bar, blood on the seat."

Walter placed a hand on Hank's shoulder, nodded his head. He'd been a tall man when he first took Hank in, or at least that's how Hank remembered him, but now Walter was looking up. His eyes were sunken and gray as if he'd not been sleeping much, but with them he was asking a question basic enough not to require words: *You all right?*

Hank spit: *We'll find this kid, this time we'll get it right.*

They'd converged like this three other times in the years Hank had been working the river. Once when Mickie McCune's heart gave out and he tipped headlong into Liberty Run. They'd pulled the body of the valley's first guide from a sweeper four miles downriver sometime after midnight. A sad day, but an end that Mickie would have approved of, as happy probably as John Brown. There had been the client of Malloy's, the radiologist, who'd drowned in front of his daughter. A tragic day, for sure. Malloy had fled the valley after that, gone. And of course there had been Patrick O'Connell, which never should have happened. His body didn't turn up for a week, until a joe from Eugene spotted it wedged against a submerged boulder.

Danny was on a cell phone, his thick shoulders turned against the crowd, his eyes on the twins scraping pictures into the pavement with stones. Even from here, Hank could tell Danny was trying to arrange child care. He and his ex traded weeks, half the time in Eugene, half up here. When the twins saw Hank coming, they waved him over. Miriam and Ruben, six years old now, and coming up riverfolk, sandal tans and water blisters. Hank took a knee, and Miriam explained what he should see in the faint sketches. "This is a bear and this is a salmon and the bear is swiping at the salmon—"

Ruben finished the thought. "But he's missing and the salmon is ducking between his legs. See?"

Hank pointed to a circle a few inches over the bear. "What's this?" It was pride he felt when near these kids, so bubbling with enthusiasm and creativity, pride for Danny because he was doing it right, despite that messy divorce. And there was gratitude too, because Danny wanted Hank involved. The twins called him uncle, and once not that far back when Danny was in a bind, he'd called, and Hank had dropped everything and rushed over to finish up dinner and put the kids to sleep. He'd read them *The Emperor's New Clothes* until Ruben was sawing under the covers and Miriam was breathing slow and even, her head on Hank's shoulder. He'd stayed just like that, unmoving, until Danny returned home—two hours of perfection. "What's this?"

"Ruben drew that," Miriam said. She was always the first to speak.

"It's a . . . ," Ruben was deciding, "a moon."

"Uncle Hank," Miriam asked, "do you have any elk jerky?"

He grabbed what was left in the Bronco, and they were reaching for the ziplock before he could even get it open.

11

There was Caroline leaning against her truck. Their eyes met above the sea of sun-bleached baseball caps, and she lipped, *You okay?*

Caroline knew him better than anyone. Even from this distance she could probably sense the tightness pinching in again. It was starting, like it always did, in his throat, and soon it would be in his chest too, pressing in, suffocating him. Tonight he wouldn't sleep a minute; there would be the panic of drowning every time a dream took hold. He—no, they—had been living with this too long. He might have four or five nights of clean sleep, a break every two hours to piss, of course, but dreamless, and then two or three nights of endless drowning. Booze helped some. Pills didn't.

He needed to get past it. He needed to put Patrick O'Connell to rest.

But his voice was still there, lonely and haunting, like it'd been in that first message on the answering machine: "Been dreaming about the Ipsyniho since I was a boy, and well, after my buddy passed on last summer, figured the only way to be sure you'll get your trip of a lifetime is to take it presently."

O'Connell had come for a week of fishing from Flagstaff, Arizona, where he had worked fifty-hour weeks as an appliance repairman. Rented the cheapest motel in town and borrowed a car from a friend of a friend. He'd never hired a guide before; only flown once. Forty-seven years old, he was that summer; he should have turned fifty-one this year. That first morning on the water, he'd admitted, "I'm spending my savings this week. Putting it to good use, I figure." It was then, or maybe even before that, that Hank found himself taking a little pity on the guy.

Most of Hank's clients where regulars. Guys for whom four hundred bucks equaled maybe a half-day's wage. These were "sportsmen"; they owned shotguns that cost more than Hank collected in a year, talked of investments and dividends like they were rivers or friends. He had no trouble taking a check from these folks, or keeping the relationship distant and businesslike. But O'Connell was different.

The first day he rose two fish, but didn't hook either one. At the ramp, he said, "I've been told that forty dollars is a fair tip." He was counting out five bills on the hood of the truck. Hank surprised himself by saying, "Save the tip until we've found you some fish."

A south wind arrived that night, the evening air actually warming from dusk to dawn, and the next day, the high temperature soared over a hundred degrees and the fishing went to shit. Hank found a dozen fish holding deep in tailouts and high in rapids, but not one that would so much as flick a fin at a passing fly. Normally, Hank would have subtly trimmed back the client's expectations until eventually the day would be spent drifting the river and talking of fish as much as actually casting to them. But with O'Connell, Hank rolled up a bandana as a sweatband, cut the popper off the single-hander, and rigged up an indicator. He oared for hours in the hot sun, digging deep to slow the boat above holding fish and give O'Connell time for a few dozen presentations. This was steelheading at its dirtiest, and yet they still couldn't turn a nose. He had other trips the next two days; otherwise he probably would have taken O'Connell out for free. He did lay out a program for O'Connell to follow the next couple of days, all warm-weather spots, and said, "You'll get one, I'd wager anything."

It stayed hot all week, and the night before their last trip, O'Connell admitted he'd yet to hook a fish. "I knew steelheading would be hard, but damn, this is something else." Hank could hear the disappointment in the guy's voice, the disenchantment. Was *this* worth it?

As a guide, he'd long ago learned how to temper a client's hopes so as to keep the person as satisfied as possible. This meant offering the person some sort of narrative that explained it all, giving them—on a silver platter—the story they would tell their friends and colleagues. There was the "fish haven't been grabby" story, the "hardly any fish in the river" story, the "lots of other anglers pressuring the fish" story. All of them usually ended with, "We'll be lucky to get one." Then when they got two, the client would be glowing with joy. That's when Hank would turn on the praise and write the story's end. "Took some real skill to raise that last one." "Only one in ten anglers could have made that cast." "Wasn't any luck in that." Hank did this now without thought. It was a crucial part of the job, maybe more crucial in terms

13

of tips and repeat bookings than tying on beautiful flies or fishing the right water. And he didn't feel bad about it, not in the least.

But O'Connell wasn't a sport. He was just a regular guy who really wanted to catch a steelhead. He confessed on that first day that he didn't like the idea of guides—"no offense"—because to him fishing was all about learning a river, discovering where the fish held and what they took. A guide dished all that up in easy servings. "Wouldn't normally do this. But figure I'll need all the help I can get fishing the Ipsyniho."

And so for O'Connell, Hank broke his routine a second time. Instead of fishing first light to midafternoon, they fished first light to midmorning, midafternoon to dusk, and that way maximized their low-light casting. He hated working late, especially when he had a trip to run in the morning, but he couldn't have this guy going home fishless.

And yet the river would offer them no slack. It wasn't raining or cloudy or even cooler the last day. Instead, the high temperature rose to 108 degrees. Come 6:00 p.m., Hank told O'Connell to reel in. This was ridiculous. "I know a spot," he said. "It's bit dangerous, but the fish will be there, and it won't have seen another angler all day." He'd never taken a client to Froth, never even fished it with Danny or Walter or Caroline. But the time had come to play his ace.

Froth was the hidden step between upper and lower Nefarious, one of the river's most feared rapids. It couldn't be accessed on foot because of the barrier cliffs upstream and down. And guides didn't fish it because no one wanted to run their boat through Nefarious. The whole river pinched down to ten feet across, then dropped six or eight feet, widened over a boulder field, only to pinch together again and drop eight or ten feet more. What made this spot so dangerous was exactly what made it so fishy. The steelhead would tire in the first rapid and hold for hours or days in the boulders before attempting the second. During hot weather, the fish were in no hurry to leave because of the little ice-cold creek that converged just below Nefarious's upper drop. When the flows and water temps aligned, as they had that day, Froth produced a fish about ninety percent of the time, a fact Hank would have withheld from most clients, but divulged to O'Connell.

They ran the rapid first, after Hank tied down the gear and cinched on his own life vest: two big backstrokes to position them, then a series of tight forward strokes to balance them over the wonky hydrologics at the base of the drop. Steelhead scattered as they went over the boulders. O'Connell cracked his nose on the gunwale during the second drop and, despite the blood staining his T-shirt, swore he was fine. "Let's get those fish!" he said in a high nasal whine.

They started by resting the run for thirty minutes, then swung a Lady Caroline through. Nothing. Then a two-ought Green Butt. Nothing. Then a fourteen Partridge and Orange below some T-14. Nothing. Rested it over an hour until last light. Tried three more approaches. Nothing. Hank handed O'Connell the single-hander, onto which he'd looped a glow-in-the-dark balloon as an indicator. *If Caroline or Walter saw me now . . .* "Stand on that ledge and dead-drift it through. Do or die time."

There was something else about O'Connell, something Hank could hear in his voice. Deference, that's what it was. He'd said when booking the trip, "If you'll take me," as if others had refused, "If you'll take me," as if he might not be *worth* taking.

He shouldn't have put him on that ledge. It was wet and mossy and dangerous as all hell at high noon, let alone at midnight. And O'Connell wasn't exactly agile. Hank should have known better. He had known better.

What exactly happened, Hank never knew. One minute O'Connell was there, high-sticking the flies through, the rapids loud as hell, and Hank turned to light a cigarette. The lighter blinded him for a moment, and as his vision returned, he slowly became sure that the ledge was empty, that his client was gone. "Are you there?"

*

By dark, the search for Justin Morell had turned up nothing. The fire department kept at it until 11:00 p.m., then called it for the night. "We'll be back at dawn," Sheriff Carter said.

The guides, young and old, regrouped at the ramp, drank a beer, said this didn't mean shit. A guy could get lost hiking up from the water, or take a swim and huddle on shore until morning, or a dozen other scenarios. Plenty of people had disappeared on the Ipsyniho only to be found hiking up the road the next morning.

Walter leaned on his wading staff and said, "It's all a matter of grace, of whether you're in good with the river or not."

Eyes flashed to Walter, and there was a long silence. A beer opened. "What's that supposed to mean?"

It was one of the younger guides, maybe the youngest, a guy Hank had met before but whose name was as memorable as his personality. Most of the youngsters came and went with the summer, here one season and gone the next. This punk was on the river come spring, Hank would invite him for a fish and buy him a beer. Until then, he was just another joe. A joe who was calling Walter out. "Watch yourself."

"It means," Walter said, "if you're clean with Lady Ipsyniho, you got nothing to worry about. Am I right?" Walter was asking Hank.

Hank snuffed his cigarette. "Sure as shit."

Caroline was there too. She popped the cap off her beer with Hank's lighter, then slipped it back in his pocket. They shared a glance, and for once he could tell what she was thinking. *That boy is not coming back.*

"By that measure," Danny said, sitting on the tailgate, the twelve-ounce bottle shrunk to eight by his big hands, "we're all angels."

If Hank hadn't broken his routine and taken O'Connell to Froth, the man would still be alive right now, and in the half lunacy of this long search, Hank felt sure that if he hadn't been hating so hard on Morell just that afternoon, the kid would still be up and pissing people off now. He knew Morell's disappearance wasn't his fault, but it sure felt like he'd caused it. He tried for a full breath. Took two small ones instead. "Angels fix things. We don't fix shit."

The last time he'd seen Morell, he'd had him by the neck against the side of the Bronco. Morell had deserved it, but still, that was no way to treat a person. And now, from the darkness, he thought he heard that gagging sound Morell had made. Hank turned toward the sound, but there was nothing there.

"It's late," Caroline said. Somebody had to.

Jimmy, an older guide, said, "Ain't doing the kid no good here. I'm gonna get forty winks. Fresh eyes for dawn."

And then the guides started peeling away two at a time. Walter, Caroline, the others over fifty. Their trucks leapt to life and they shouted their good-byes from afar. Old fishermen weren't built for late nights.

In his mind's eye, Hank could see O'Connell's corpse clear as if he'd just touched it, see it ragged and submerged, its back pressed to a boulder, a limb jammed tight against its neck, its arms outstretched and flailing in the current, its mouth gasping for air. He'd called out to O'Connell that dusk, "Are you there?" He sure felt here now.

"Fuck this," Danny said. "I'm going back out. Who's with me?" He was already pulling the battery from his truck to rig up a spotlight.

All at once, the young guides finished their beers. Nobody was going home with Morell still out there.

Hank heard his own voice, distant and strange in the darkness. "I'll row."

Chapter Three

THE NEXT MORNING, as Hank arrived at the diner just after dawn, he saw the town paper: "Local Guide Missing." There was a picture of the fire department racing upriver on their sled when it was still new and didn't have the gouges—a file photo. The paper was in the yellow circulation box outside the door, on the table near the waiting area, in everyone's hands.

He had stayed on the water all night, taking turns at the oars and on the spotlight, and he had worn out his voice calling the boy's name. To see this paper now stunned him in his sleeplessness: How had the news made it all the way to town already? He hadn't even been home yet.

Caroline was eating huevos rancheros at the counter, a second order steaming beside her, and she looked up from the paper when he neared. He hadn't said her name or even cleared his throat. She must've sensed him nearby. That was her way in this world.

"Ordered for you," she said. "Figured you'd be hungry. They say you 'acted quickly in calling 911.'"

"Not quick enough."

They didn't kiss—they rarely kissed in public, or touched each other for that matter—but he took the seat beside her, and thanked her for the eggs, though he pushed them aside and ordered a coffee and a large milk instead.

"Can't be hard on yourself, Hank. This isn't your fault."

"I know." He lit a cigarette. "I was wishing he'd leave. Move to Alaska, be a body counter up there." He pulled hard on the Camel, wishing now he hadn't said "body counter." He looked around. Only truckers within earshot, nobody looking.

He reached for the ashtray; it wasn't there.

"I hope he doesn't have any family," Caroline said. "Damn that phone call."

Tommy, the server, poured Hank's coffee. "Got to ask you to snuff that, Hank. New state law. Smoke-free workplace and all that."

Hank dropped the cigarette in his coffee.

Tommy flipped over the clean cup at the next setting and filled it. "Sorry Hank. Ain't my rule, you know that."

Caroline's fork dashed at the eggs. She was wearing a black tank top, her back and shoulders lean and striated from years at the oars. Her skin wore a permanent tan, mahogany in summer, fading to oak in winter, a Z perennially stenciled on her sandaled feet. She'd been a raft guide for decades before the big-money nineties convinced her to switch to guiding fly anglers. But well before that, she'd been an insti-tution on the fly water, "that woman" who appeared from the forest, stepped in above you, and rose a fish where you'd found none. Which shouldn't have been all that surprising, seeing as she was the only child of Malcolm Abbot, the valley's most legendary guide.

Hank's forearm brushed the side of Caroline's—he wanted nothing more than to touch her, to be touched by her. That's what he needed right now, the warm wash of her body against his, the pulse of her breathing in his ear, a moment of contracting reality so intimate not even the Ipsyniho could budge its way in. Only there could he take a full breath.

She reached for her coffee. "Not here, sweet."

It'd been like this between them for a while now. Hank assumed Caroline was just being cautious. She'd carved a career for herself—a traditionally male career—not in small measure by avoiding becom-ing fodder for the rumor cannon. Guiding, or really scoring clients, was all about reputation, and hers was carefully calibrated. Strength, competence, self-reliance, all things that a romantic relationship might undermine. Just look at how she behaved when they moved through town together: she opened her own doors and carried her own groceries. Hank knew the truth: that under that coarse veneer she was as fragile as anyone, and as lonely too.

"I take it you're not working today?" he asked.

"Half-day trip, rearranged it for the evening." She finished her coffee, tossed him a glance. The glance.

"Tommy," Hank called, as Caroline walked out the door and climbed into her truck. "Can you wrap up these eggs?"

*

HANK FOLLOWED CAROLINE up Steamboat Creek, crossing the small tributary of Echo, then another called Sunshine, where they turned up a thread of a county road, roaring up the ridge to a hanging valley. This was hers, all of it.

He'd met Caroline years before, when he first arrived in the valley. She'd been a college girl then, spending the year down in California and returning to run splash-and-giggle trips during the summer months. He remembered seeing her, before he even knew she was Malcolm Abbot's daughter, cinching down her raft at a ramp or joking with friends at Upstream Runs, the guide's preferred bar at the time. She was a mystery to him then, that girl with the bellowing laugh and the strong arms, the one who never wasted an oar stroke in even the wildest rapids. Her hair was brown then, and she kept it back in two cute braids. You could recognize her by those braids a couple pools away, enough time to lose your confidence and bumble the hello. There were plenty of women on the river then as now, but none who seemed so at ease on the sticks. Hank had been taken by her instantly. He'd never had trouble starting conversations with women—he'd been raised the little brother to two older sisters. But this woman was different. She seemed at peace with herself then, and it was hard not to be intimidated by a person like that,

21

man or woman. His infatuation became near obsessive one August day some thirty years back when she called from her raft, "Keep the fly broadside through that bucket." She was running a group of clients and he was fishing on a day off. He hadn't realized she knew anything about fishing. "With this light, the fish can't see your junk." Only later did he figure what she meant: the sun was slightly upstream, and the fish couldn't see the thin profile of the fly with so much light in their eyes. Keeping the fly broadside would, and did, make the difference. He'd asked Walter that night and discovered the mystery girl's name. "Ah, Carrie? She caught her first fish when you were still shitting in your drawers."

Then one June, the same year Annie was born, Caroline didn't return to the Ipsyniho. He heard through the grapevine that she'd married some rich guy and gotten pregnant. For once, the rumors were true.

"When men go looking for a wife," she had quipped once about that marriage, "they're really looking for real estate."

They passed along the fence with a No Trespassing sign nailed to every fifth post, then turned into her driveway. She held open the gate for him, and as he pulled through, her two Rottweilers leapt at the open window, roaring and biting. He blew each a kiss and pulled around the back of the house, where Caroline liked him to park. By the time the dogs came racing around the corner, he was on one knee, a hug for each of them. They licked his eyes and mouth and beard savagely.

This property had been Caroline's grandparents'. They'd bought it after the First World War when western property values, like so much, plummeted. Now, she had two thousand acres all to herself. The house sat a hundred feet or so above Sunshine Creek, its patter the familiar sound track of her deck. To some—to most, maybe Hank included— living here as Caroline did would have been a desolate prospect. An entire valley with no one else in it. But Caroline wasn't made lonely by being alone.

From the outside, the house looked weathered and a generation past its prime. A look, Hank figured, she had cultivated. On the inside, she had opened the ceiling, constructed a loft (which was where they cuddled and watched movies on rainy nights), wired track lighting and surround speakers, revamped the kitchen, added a bathroom. Hank's favorite addition was in the corner, a two-hundred-gallon aquarium complete with a current, which the trout dodged with cobbles Caroline had hand plucked from the river. He stood before the aquarium now, and watched Charlie, a four-inch cutthroat, rise and take something on the surface.

For years Caroline's free hours had been devoted to improving this house, but for the past weeks she had been devoting those hours to Hank's place, helping him ready it for Annie's arrival. "Can't have your daughter staying in squalor."

"It's going to be a hot morning," Caroline said now. "I might take a look at the creek."

They descended the trail, leapt the two logs that had fallen last winter, and emerged in the morning sun along the clear steam. A moss-drenched cliff towered against the far bank, while just downstream the land fell away at the edge of a waterfall. If they walked over and looked down, they'd see the blue hole twenty feet below, and maybe an otter lounging along the edge. Upstream, the water descended the serpentine vertebrae of the valley, polished boulders gleaming in the early sun. Hank knew of few places on this earth that felt more removed than this one.

And yet, he'd brought them with him. "Do you think Morell lost the boat in Whitehorse?"

She took off her sunglasses and tossed them into the shade. "I don't think we'll ever know."

"But what do you think happened?"

She pinched him. "I dreamt about you last night."

"Dreamt?" He'd forgotten that she'd come home and slept. "What did you dream?"

She unzipped his pants. "This."

They ravaged each other there on the sunbathed beach with the wet passion of young idealists, or the newly grieved.

Afterward, she tiptoed naked onto the top edge of the waterfall, peered over quickly, and turned to face him. She was backlit, and her body seemed to be steaming there, a creekside apparition. It was a mossy world, a world of ferns and firs and dank little nameless mushrooms, and yet there she was against all this, glistening like an olive, refined and salty. He could still taste her, like he could still feel the bites she'd left, and even though she was all the way over there, she was right here with him, her moans in his ears, her heels on his ass. He shut his eyes so as not to lose her. "Shake it, sugaree."

"We should bring Annie here, when she comes," Caroline called from the edge of the waterfall. "Wouldn't she love it?"

And it was gone, all of it. Replaced by a surge of sobering regret: first the girlish image of Annie as he last saw her, then of a male corpse contorting in the merciless current. He sat up and gasped, "Come back over here I'm not done with you."

A light wind was blowing up the creek now, and she pulled her silver hair from her eyes and smiled at him. She was still smiling when she backflipped off the edge and out of sight.

*

HANK AWOKE IN the bedroom, where they'd napped the midday away, to find the sheets bare. In the kitchen, Caroline was busy making the boat meal for her trip that evening. She was listening to some Spanish guitar, a CD she'd snagged at a show in Portland. Hank preferred buying a sack lunch from the diner, picking it up on the way to meet the clients, but Caroline said she didn't mind the twenty minutes of extra preparation. It gave her a chance "to tighten her knots," which was her way of saying screw her head on straight.

"Mind if I crash here a little longer?" Hank asked. The exhaustion hadn't abated with the sleep. In fact, if anything, it had become as destabilizing as a sudden fever. He needed to stay here and sleep, watch the aquarium, be away from all that awaited him at home. This is what he told himself, and it was true enough, but there was something else too.

Despite all that had happened last night, she'd pulled her arm away this morning at the café. As if anyone would have seen. And so what if they had?

He'd had enough sneaking around; it'd been years of this now. Either she wanted him outright and in total, or she didn't want him at all. "Just need another hour or two."

Caroline didn't look up from her sandwiches. "I'd rather you go, if it's all the same. Just simpler."

"Simpler?" He turned to Charlie in the fish tank, watched him tuck into the lee behind his favorite cobble. "How about I take Samson and Delilah for a walk? I could do these fucking dishes." He hadn't meant to swear. Now she'd know what was really going on. She could read him with a glance, like she could the holding lies in a tailout. And yet, try as he might, he could rarely decipher a damn thing about her. "I can have dinner ready when you get home."

"I'd rather you go, sweet. You know how things stand."

What did that mean? "No, I don't think I do. One minute we're loving and the next—"

"Hanky." She looked up now, pulled a tendril of hair from her mouth with a pinky, and said, "You really want to do this now?" Then, after a long moment, "You're pulling at your beard again. You only pull at your beard when you're feeling trapped."

"I'm about as trapped as a . . . as a leaf blowing around your pasture up there." He looked around for his pants and shirt. He'd been standing here this whole time in his skivvies.

She was looking out the window. "I kinda like that image."

He stepped into his pants and tightened his belt. "You know what, Carrie? I guess I am trapped."

"You have exactly what you want. You're perfectly free to do whatever."

He hipped open the front door while pulling on his shirt. "Guess that's what I mean."

Chapter Four

GOING HOME WAS the last thing Hank needed. So, while still towing the boat, he turned right on River Road and came up to speed. He would go pay a visit to Walter, who would probably be sitting at his picnic table, tying up some flies for the evening fish.

If it wasn't for Walter, Hank would never have stayed in the valley. It was Walter who'd taught him to run rapids, to keep clients happy on fishless days, to skate dry flies. They'd first met on a run called Time Traveler when Hank had just moved to the valley. Walter had cursed at him, told him to cut his hair and get a real job and "hire a guide 'cause that's the only way a joe like you will ever find fish." The next time they saw each other, Walter threw a rock at his water, told him to go home, take up golf. But the third time, Walter asked to see his fly box, then said, "Why you wasting your life casting this bullshit? I'll show you a steelhead fly."

Hank passed the turnoff to Rennie's Landing and looked in time to spot Justin Morell's truck and trailer, that champagne Tacoma and the galvanized Baker. The pair sat in the sun where Morell had left them the morning before, all alone, forsaken, awaiting a driver that would never return.

Hank turned up the music.

It wasn't that Justin Morell was all that different than Hank had been at the start. Once upon a time, Hank too had been consumed with proving he could catch more fish than anyone else. It was strictly a game of numbers then, of fish caught versus hours angled. He considered that the definitive proof of ability, and ability was everything in this world of too many people. But eventually his egotism had ebbed, then faded, drawn out by the gravitational pull of maturity and better sense. Catch rates were a concern of dudes; if the river taught anything, it was that economy is a delusion for those who can't see ecology. Justin would have—would still—arrive at that conclusion too. He would regret all this posturing, this aggression, those articles. But would the older anglers forgive him as they had Hank? Or would the fallout, from those articles especially, haunt Justin and relegate him to a second-class status among the river's more senior keepers?

The river had appeared in print countless times, dating all the way back to Zane Grey's *Rivers of a Forgotten Coast*. Since then, luminaries like Roderick Haig-Brown and Trey Combs had written about it. And Hank had a stack of no less than twenty-two magazine articles that had featured the Ipsyniho. Maybe Morell's largest sin had been assuming himself qualified enough, seasoned enough, to speak for the river.

Of course, Morell's articles constituted the largest stride over that thin red line separating public and private knowledge anyone living could remember. Not only did Morell reveal the secret flies of several local guides, no small sin, he included the river's most guarded pattern, one that had been passed down and enhanced like an old-world song through four generations of career guides. This was the fly they never fished with clients, the one they cut from their lines when mixed company approached. And Morell had included the recipe and photos with his first article. Who had given him the pattern remained a mystery.

More than this, though, Morell had included photos of the river's best runs with color-coded circles and ovals revealing where, precisely, the fish were prone to hold. Some of these spots weren't exactly secrets, the bucket in Raspberry for instance. But others, the invisible ledge at Fox Creek or the forgotten seam in Middle Williams, were among the guide's most treasured, most guarded confidences. Morell hadn't found these places on his own. He'd been shown them.

There was also the new style of flippancy among the younger generations. When Hank was young, he'd worked for years proving himself before the older guides would even toss a nod his way. It wasn't the time spent fishing that mattered, though that was part of it; it was the risks taken protecting the fish. Walter didn't take him in until Hank snuck into the hatchery by the cover of darkness and poisoned the smolt tanks. It was this selfless act, an act aimed at protecting the river's wild fish, and that earned Hank acknowledgment—tenure, really—among the old guard. Walter had, a generation prior, earned his own tenure by detonating the irrigation channel built by the State, a crime he repeated three times until the State grew tired of rebuilding. But now, the Morells of the world were granted entrance into the circle simply because of their technical proficiency: They fished custom rods, built innovative lines, tied new flies—and caught fish. Morell had proved his devotion to steelheading, but had he really proved his devotion to steelhead?

It was the Internet, Hank knew, that had catalyzed the shift in guide culture. Whereas river knowledge used to be seen as the product of years of on-the-river observation and experimentation—and hence, the valley's most valuable commodity—now it was seen as just a few mouse clicks away, its value on par with all the random facts available on Wikipedia. These young kids had divorced information from the time required to gather it. To them, information wasn't passed between generations, it was passed between computers.

The guides of Danny's generation were responsible for letting Morell in too soon. They were the transition generation; they'd learned the secrets the old way (Danny, that hothead, had firebombed Cherry Creek Timber's regional office), but some of them had failed to keep those secrets properly guarded. This infuriated Walter. Just a year back, he put a brick through a young guide's window. Hank and the other senior guides were done sharing their secrets—and they still had plenty—with anyone who couldn't remember where they were the day Kennedy was shot. Except with Danny himself of course, who had been more or less raised by the guides and so had proper appreciation for a secret's incalculable value.

·

WALTER WAS RIGHT where Hank expected to find him, sitting on the picnic table out back of his small one-story home, spinning moose hair. He lived here alone, and had since his wife left him some twenty years back. When Walter saw Hank approaching, he opened the cooler at his feet and produced an IPA from the Salmon Tail Brewery thirty-two miles downstream. Walter still traded with the brew master, flies for cases, trips for kegs.

"Figured you'd drag your ass up here at some point." A small pair of reading glasses hung from the tip of Walter's nose. He clipped a clump of hair, and the hot breeze carried the loose fibers over the lawn. There, in the grass, sparkled fragments of tinsel and floss and pink hackle, a summer's worth of trimmings. "Were you out all night?"

"Didn't do a lick of good."

"I heard." Walter clipped another clump. "Bet you ten he's a floater and they find him in tidewater next week."

"Not much of a gamble at this point. Seems the real wager is in how he lost it."

"Natural or artificial causes?" Walter had yet to look at Hank. They often spoke to each other like this, as if they were speaking to themselves. "You're the only one of us that got a look at that bowl of glass he oars."

Hank picked up one of the finished patterns on the table. A sphere of tightly packed moose hair at the front, a red floss body, a half-dozen strands of silver tinsel streaming back an inch past the hook. "Still fiddling with it?"

"Mostly a matter of getting the thing to fish right now. Course, that's all it ever is."

Hank chuckled at the old man singing his old songs, and swigged his beer to hide it. Once, to prove that fly tying was an overglamorized and overemphasized craft, "yet another way for somebody to swipe dimes from your pocket," Walter had tied a stick to a hook and rose a steelhead four casts later. As if this wasn't proof enough, he switched to a leaf, caught another. Now, Hank said what Walter was about to: "A bloke can't make a fly a fish won't take."

"That's it."

"But they take some patterns more than others. Can't deny that, old man."

Walter looked up this time, cold faced. "Is that so?"

"God's truth." Hank dropped the fly on the table. "Read it in an article."

Walter whip-finished the fly, pulled it from the vise, and put a file to its point. "Didn't realize God was writing again." He tested the point's sharpness against his thumbnail. "And what's your two cents?"

Hank shrugged. "You know me. Fish now, think later."

"No," Walter said. "About Morell. Natural or artificial?"

Some of the blood had smeared, like he'd dragged something—a hand maybe—through it before going overboard. He could have been looking for fish when the oar hit a rock and clocked him. Stranger things had happened. Hank himself had been struck nearly unconscious by an oar some years back, though he'd been fighting heavy water at the time. Or, it was possible, someone smashed any number of objects—the oar, a rock, a beer bottle—against his head, lifted his feet, and dropped him overboard.

But this was all overthinking the situation. What mattered was the boy was missing.

Overthinking was a recipe for getting skunked, Hank knew that much for sure. Fishing had trained him to be a student of precedent more than theory, to trust what had happened before rather than somebody's eager deductions to reveal what would happen next. "This would be the first murder in Ipsyniho. Well, if we're not counting Mrs. Forman." Who had stabbed her prick of a husband in the neck after he, again, took a hand to her. She'd been convicted and locked away for twenty to life. "Self-defense ain't murder, no matter what the State says."

"Not true. Well, true enough about self-defense, the State doesn't know an ass from an ear, but not true about the first murder. You're forgetting your history there, lad." Walter was pinning the finished patterns in his box. "Sixty-three I think it was, or sixty-four. The spring after Kennedy got it. Earnest Jackson, shot to death at Altitude Ramp."

Hank didn't know this one.

"Let me see if I can recall." Walter finished his beer and looked to the ridge, summoning what must have been a nearly forgotten memory. "So Jackson was working the upper river, way high, taking clients to the redds."

"He was fishing the tribs?"

"No, back then we still had the mainstem spawners. Probably about a thousand fish, winter fish, used the gravel around Altitude. They were some of the run's biggest. Gone now, course. But then, Jackson was taking his clients up there, fishing big bare hooks in the tailouts. Killing a half-dozen a day. I saw him once, posted up on a rock, telling his dude to throw it long. There was a pair of spawners out in the middle, twenty-pounders if they were an ounce. Told the sheriff at the time, Dick 'Cowboy' Bullhouser. Did you know him? Bridge's daddy. Good guy. Anyway, word got around what Jackson was up to. Didn't take long until there was a fight between him and a few of the old guys, Abbot's boys. Next thing you know, they find Jackson with a bullet hole in his throat. Assassinated."

"Jesus."

"Jesus didn't have anything to do with it. That schmuck was exactly the kind of trash we should've run off his first season. Could've called it. Had photos of a dozen big dead fish, knew he was a wanker from the get-go. If he'd lived, who knows, the run might be extinct by now. Not that I'm saying he should've been shot, just that he deserved it." Walter nodded at the cooler. "Grab that. It's move-on time. I'm driving."

They drove Walter's '77 Chevy, which he'd painted sometime in the eighties to look like a Royal Coachman, upriver, all the way past both bridges, above the falls that all the magazine articles and books ever written about the river said stopped the fish, to a side road that climbed the ridge. They followed that for a quarter mile, until the rig was out of sight, and parked. Walter said, "You're fishing. I'm sitting."

This place had been named Red Gate by the *old-timers* precisely because it was about as far as you get from the red gate. If a joe or young guide heard them talking about the place, decided to go looking for it, they'd only find the shabby pocket water near river mile 84. Many of the river's best runs were named in this manner. Upper Bridge was fifteen minutes from any such overpass. Cougar Creek wasn't near the creek with this moniker; it was near Boone Creek, where Mickie McCune had been chased by a tomcat. Misdirection was an essential strategy on the river.

They waited until no cars could be heard, then hurried across the road. Once at the shoulder, a steep slope down through a thicket of poison oak, Hank offered the old man a hand—at which Walter swung his wading staff. "Keep your pity."

They didn't speak about where they were going, how they would fish, which fly to use, or any of the things anglers usually discuss on the way to the water. They'd had those conversations decades ago. Now they were talking rods, as they had been most of the forty-minute drive, ever since Walter had surprised Hank by selecting from his vast quiver the seventy-one fifty-three, a fifteen-foot three-inch seven weight.

"Sure," Walter admitted now, "I'll take the seventy-one thirty-three or the eighty-one thirty-four if I'm looking to cast a line, but *Christ Hank*, do I look like the kind of man who's covering miles in a day? When you get to be my age, and god forbid you make it this long, you'll learn. The bayou bait-chuckers, they got something figured right. Fishing's best when you post up, flip out your junk, and crack a can. You can't find a better flippin' and crackin' rod than the seventy-one fifty-three. Quote me on that."

"You just got to know where to post up." Hank stepped into the water, about to wade onto the center rock.

"Hold up there, eager beaver." Walter opened the cooler that dangled from his neck like a creel, and passed over a new beer.

"I'll wait on that," Hank said, thinking about the deep wade separating him from the midstream boulder that was this run's established
casting point. "Feeling a bit light-headed as it is."

"Shit. Where'd you buy your Subaru, Mr. Joe?"

Hank took the bottle and tucked it down his waders, to the slot
between fly boxes and belt, as was the custom among off-duty guides
out fishing the evening light.

*

DRIVING BACK HOME, Hank nursed a bottle of water. The lack of sleep
and the afternoon buzz had gotten the better of him, and now he
made liberal use of the fishing pull-offs to allow the hurried lines of
RVs and motorcycles and minivans to pass.

From the road, he saw anglers in most every run, though he didn't
recognize but a couple of their rigs. It must be a Friday. Fucking
weekends.

For locals, real time—the personal and intimate metering of life—
was recorded in large swaths, sprawling intervals that corresponded to
specific and essential movements within the river. The New Year began
in June, when the last of the winter fish had finished their spawning
and were either rotting on the bank or gorging on sand shrimp in the
estuary, and the early returning summer fish first began appearing in
the fly water. The fish were few and far between, but always aggressive. This period was known as the "long and far" time, meaning if
you wanted to catch fish, you had to throw your flies long and oar
your boat far.

Then came the summer routine, fresh fish trickling in with every
freshet just as the older fish slipped up their natal tributaries, the
number of steelhead in the fly water remaining more or less constant;
this was also the steady sweating sprint of peak tourist season, when a
reputable guide could work every day if he wanted. The fishing during
"the sprint" tended to be best during the day's tired shoulders, meaning guides got very little sleep unless they went to a four-and-four

sleep schedule, four hours between 11:00 and 3:00 a.m. and p.m. Then came the fall cooling, when the last of the summer fish arrived, usually in a big wave, and the chilly nights and warming days ensured the fish remained aggressive all day. These were the "glory days," when the scenery was perfect, the fishing easy, and the clients perpetually in a tipping mood.

The first blowout, usually within a week of Thanksgiving, marked a profound shift in the watershed, and began the "low and slow" period, as in to catch fish, you needed to fish deep in the water column and swing the fly as slowly as possible—a metaphor for winter life. With every freshet would come a new wave of fast-moving and large winter steelhead, their numbers few but predictably placed. Seven days from the freshet's start to reach the fly water. Twelve days to reach the upper tributaries. Count the days, and fish accordingly.

Last came the spawn, or the "holy days," usually when the spring weather arrived and people donned their short sleeves for the first time since September. This was a favorite time for clients, and Hank probably could stay busy for two or three weeks straight if he had no scruples. But he, like all the river's guides, left the fish during the holy days to their most essential business. Instead of running clients, they patrolled the spawning tributaries to ensure no dirtbags were snagging.

Work time—what to joes and civilians would be the Monday through Friday workweek—was to Hank and the guides, a simple string of dates. Trips scheduled the fifth, seventh, eighth, ninth, tenth, twelfth, sixteenth. Whether these days were Mondays or Wednesdays or Sundays hardly mattered. What did matter was if one of these dates was a Saturday.

Come 3:00 p.m. on Friday and continuing more or less through dark on Saturday, the highways along the river slowed with honking traffic. During the summer, they were river enthusiasts mostly, anglers and rafters and those bizarre and largely aimless people in khaki who called themselves "bird watchers." During the fall, they were blaze orange deer and elk hunters and tie-dye mushroomers. And during the winter, they were skiers and boarders and snowmobilers on their way to the resort in the headwaters. It seemed the whole world decided to spend their Saturday on the Ipsyniho. If Hank had a client scheduled, as he did tomorrow, the crowds would force him to change his routine, to run a different pattern. Walter had taught him a few tricks for beating the crowds when he was young, though what constituted a crowd then would constitute a Tuesday lull now. Hank had learned a few more of his own, and had, in turn, passed those onto Danny.

Fairview, his home run, was empty, and he considered spending last light there, but instead turned right up his driveway and climbed the ridge to his cabin. He was too exhausted to back the boat under the carport and so parked the rig in the turnaround.

Given the trip tomorrow, he needed to restock his fly boxes, lace up some new leaders, order lunch, call his sport—an hour's worth of work and all he wanted to do was tip headfirst onto the couch and fall asleep to *Cornell '77*. He'd attended a few dozen Dead shows in his twenties, and still had a pretty serious collection, but that show, more than any other, cut to the heart of it all.

Hank's house could have been a fly shop, had the carpet been clean and the air not smelled of wet waders. One entire wall held strung fly rods: single-handers, two-handers, switchers, their pieces held together by hair ties, which he bought in bulk from the beauty supply store in Eugene. There was also the fly-tying desk he'd built of salvaged oak, its shelves climbing the wall above. Another wall held five hundred years of literature, everything worth reading, from *The Compleat Angler* all the way to *The Habit of Rivers*. Any book ever written about steelhead, any book that had even contained a chapter on steelhead, was there. He'd spent years tracking down the volumes, and only after the emergence of online book sales was he able to locate the rarest titles, like Enos Bradner's *Northwest Angling*. There were more books and tackle in back, but these were things he kept in the front room, the things that kept him going on windblown days.

He'd never owned a television, but there was a laptop, which he opened now to check his bookmarks: the weather sites, the river levels, the current fish counts, Speypages. Sometimes he'd pull the computer from its home on the bookshelf to the coffee table and watch a DVD he'd rented, and he was considering doing just this when he saw the posting in a forum: "An up and coming star, lost." It was about Justin Morell. Fifteen people had posted their own remembrances, their tributes. Hank read each of them, the ones from clients, from friends, the one from Danny. Some people anyway really liked this kid. Or maybe they were just being kind.

He closed the window and turned on some tunes and was about to pick up the phone to call his sport when his fingers guided the cursor to the file named "Annie Now." He'd seen these photos hundreds of times, and he knew each well enough to recall even the peripheral details, yet he fished out his reading glasses and spent two or three minutes studying the images, imagining what she would look like in this very room. Then he changed the file's name, in case she used this computer, to "A.N."

It wouldn't happen; she'd call him tomorrow or the next day and offer some airtight excuse. She couldn't come. Work required she stay. A friend was going through a messy divorce and needed her. He should expect it. He shouldn't get his hopes up.

He checked the answering machine, two messages, but neither from her.

It was a simple house, a cabin really, and she would feel uncomfortable here. He'd never spent much money updating the place—in fact, the total retail value of the rods on the wall probably equaled the house's worth. But he had spent considerable time and expense perfecting the cooking arrangements, and maybe she'd appreciate that. He would explain that he'd paid for an external tank and piped in the gas specifically for the stove, which he'd found used in town. The vent hood and its lighting had come new from Eugene and they cost more than the refrigerator but were worth every cent. Dinner, like fishing, was too important not to do right.

But tonight he didn't have the energy to cook, so he found some water crackers and sliced some cold elk roast and unwrapped the wheel of aged cheddar he had asked the co-op to order special and poured a splash of cab. But he only managed two bites before stepping onto the porch for some big, slow breaths.

Annie would hate the house. There was little he could do to help that—she would be used to so much more—but he could distract her with the cooking. He'd already spent a trip's profit in wine and ingredients. Each meal was mapped out in the back of his fishing journal. They'd start rustic and simple, salmon with sweet potato au gratin and a chilled salad of spring greens and blue cheese and filberts and huckleberry vinaigrette. A shiraz seemed the right choice, or a zinfandel, he hadn't yet decided. When she raved about the complexity of flavors, the crisp freshness of it all, he'd tell her every ingredient had been grown right here in the Ipsyniho Valley. There would be elk tenderloin the next night, bear burgers the night after. Malbecs, pinots, a bottle of tawny port. He'd show her there was more to this place than clear water and big mountains.

He called his sport to confirm, then ordered the man's lunch, and finally packed his own cooler. He kept it pretty bare out there on the river, so as not to be distracted by the flavors: string cheese, almonds, an apple, a bag of jerky, and a beer for the ride home.

And coffee, of course, which was as important as his fly box. He measured a thermos-plus-a-cup's worth of water into a pan and put a lid on it. Then he measured six tablespoons of his own homemade roast into the French press and cleaned his travel mug. In the morning, he'd turn on the burner first thing and would be drinking steaming brew ten minutes later on the drive to the ramp. Nothing perked up a predawn morning like a cup of mud.

One benefit of Annie not coming would be that he wouldn't miss any mornings on the river. If she came, they'd stay up late and sleep in, and he'd miss all those dawns, the orange and pink pastels on the glassy tailouts, the secret promise of the day to come, the sipping rise of the unharried steelhead. Dawn offered its own rewards, and the year was too short as it was.

She'd call him tomorrow and cancel, and he'd be glad for it.

Chapter Five

HE'D MET ANNIE'S mother, Rosemary, in '77, on Bakke Island, a slab of forested land on the middle reach of the river.

He'd just dropped his client at the ramp above, finishing his half day of work, and was pushing down to the island and a run called Barrier just below, a place that shifted to the shade just after 2:00 p.m., the first run on the whole river to find reprieve from the afternoon shine. Rosemary had pulled her kayak into the cove on the island's bottom end, where she was sprawled out in the sand, nude.

She was more than a bit surprised to see a boat, as was he to see a pair of breasts. She held her shirt to her chest and crossed her sandy legs, and called, "Guess there's no place private on this river anymore." He recognized the face—he'd seen her around town and on the river a time or two—but those were her first words to him.

"Guess not," he called back. "Sorry."

The problem, though she didn't know it, was that he needed to anchor here, on that beach where she was now waiting for him to leave. If he pushed on, he'd be drifting over Barrier and would be forced through the rapid below, rendering him unable to wade back up to give the water a proper fish. He pondered his options. Quickly determined he didn't have any.

"I hate to be a bother, but this is where I need to be."

"Here?"

"I hate to be a bother."

"Then push on."

"Sorry, I don't have a choice." He pointed to Barrier, explained the situation.

"Fishing is always a choice," she said.

He turned his head to give her privacy, considered what she'd just said, realized they had fundamental disagreements. He muttered, "You can sun yourself anywhere."

But this is where she wanted to be, and she wasn't moving. If she wouldn't bend, neither would he. He anchored, grabbed his rod, and leapt over the gunwale. "We can share the place then. I'll be down there for an hour or more. I'll holler when I'm on my way back up."

She just stared at him, her hands still strategically placed. He spied the wet filaments of her armpit hair, the bulge of her underbreast. Maybe fishing was a choice.

"I'm not a painting," she bit.

There was a strong run of fish that year, and he rose one in Barrier where they always rise if they're going to rise at all. The fish came once, missed the fly, came a second time, missed again, then wouldn't return. He fished his way through the run, then returned to that lie and tried for what must have been an hour, switching flies, switching casting positions, resting, trying again, but the fish wouldn't budge. This was the kind of fishing he loved, the run to yourself, an eager fish out there somewhere, and yet he found himself fishing poorly. His casts landed in piles, his flies kept ducking underwater. He wasn't immersed in the water's reality like he should have been. He kept glancing upstream, all the way up near the boat, at the golden shape on the beach.

When he returned, she was emptying a trap-load of crawdads into a bucket, clothed now in a tank top and a pair of cutoff jeans. She banged clean the trap.

"Hi," he said meekly.

"You were down there a long time not to be coming back with a fish." Her hair was back and drying and leaving a wet patch on her shirt like sweat.

"Never seen a woman trapping crawdads before." He'd meant it as some variety of compliment. She took it as some variety of insult.

"Men don't have a monopoly on meat procurement." She pointed at his empty hands. "Do they?"

"Didn't mean to suggest they do."

And there began eight years of minor misunderstandings, some of which ballooned into major ones, which ballooned again into full-blown wedges, one of which would drive her to leave him. They were never right for each other. But in that moment, they were two late twenty-somethings on a hot summer day, the Ipsyniho a potent if one-sided aphrodisiac.

"I'm Hank."

"I know who you are. I live near Marcy."

During his few years in the valley, he'd developed—accidentally—a little reputation for himself among Ipsyniho's unattached ladies.

"Oh." Marcy, a woman he'd holed up with last winter, was a baker in town who would in the years to come open Ipsyniho's first gourmet restaurant, Spindrift. Things between them had gotten, well, messy.

He pointed at her bucket, asked after her strategy. He'd tried catching crawdads during the summer lulls, to add to the Ipsyniho bouillabaisse that he'd been refining as his default first-date meal. Bouillabaisse, he'd found, possessed magical powers. When he served it, the evening more often than not resulted in a following morning. The meal's seductive force, he figured, lay in its contradictions. It suggested sophistication, that he possessed a certain cultural refinement, but at the same time it exhibited his "rugged" waterman skills; the salmon, the rock bass, the mussels, all could be procured in a day with a quick drive to the salt. Back then, romance had seemed as important an ingredient to a good life as the Ipsyniho itself.

She played like she had little interest in him, in his fly rod, in his interest in her crawdads. "Look," she said, holding up a hand to block the light, "I've got a party to be at this afternoon and I've still got four traps to pull between here and Susan Creek."

"Is this Bridge and Rita's party up Echo Creek?"

It was, and so on this connection, she acquiesced to his advances and allowed him to follow her downriver, allowed him to help clear the traps, and later, allowed him to drive her to the party. But she refused when he offered her a ride home. And later, she refused two dinner offers. It wasn't until they saw each other again on the river that she finally accepted his invitation—though she said, "No bouillabaisse." So, he took her for an evening boat ride and they grilled steelhead over a beach fire and there was a kiss but no next morning. There would be no next morning for months. But all her resistance only served to fuel his interest—he was sucker for hard-to-get. By winter, he'd fallen for her, and by spring, he thought she'd fallen for him.

Riffle Anne was born two years later, the surprise baby that sparked so many other surprises in Rosemary, in him. He took a month off work. He doted, he tended, he preened. After that month, he worked only seven trips a month, just enough to skimp by. He was going to do this right, to be the kind of father the world needed, even if it meant sacrificing what he assumed he never would.

He was a miserable guide that year, and frequently, his clients went fishless. There were fish in the river, and the flows weren't abnormally bad, but he was out of touch with the system, with its cycles and moods. He was half a step behind, his boat always low rod at the ramp. That bothered him. But not as much as Rosemary's disdain when he mentioned it to her.

She'd been a raft guide and waitress then and, in winter, a lifty at the mountain. She thought she understood the nuances of his career, what was required to keep clients happy. But no matter how carefully he explained, she still seemed to think the fish, like the rapids, were always in the same places. Really this tiff, which grew into a fight, was about Hank's need to stay connected with the ecology outside their home and its small domestic orbit. That connection was what made him feel substantial in the world, worth his molecules. Without it, no matter the joys at home, he felt adrift, untethered, petty. He said as much. But for Rosemary, this fight was about having a partner at least as committed as she, a partner as attentive as her own father had been. Maybe, Hank wondered, he'd been raised to fail.

Still, Rosemary surprised him one day by deciding she couldn't live on the river forever and she couldn't live with him. "Riffle and I will be healthier elsewhere." Her life had stagnated and needed a freshet: in her words, "I can't go on like this." What she needed, she said, was to start architecture school in Eugene. When he begged why, she glanced toward four-year-old Riffle, who was in the yard talking to pinecones as if they were babies. "You'll be glad to have the space again, don't pretend otherwise. You'll be able to do whatever you want."

"That's not what I want."

"We both know you, Hank."

So his time with Riffle suddenly became two days a week, which felt like nothing. She was taller and leaner and more sophisticated each time he arrived to pick her up. She was growing and becoming a person, a person he would just come to know again by the hour of her departure. He begged Rosemary to let Riffle spend the summer back on the river, to let him have a block of time with her. "You've made me into a joe with my own daughter." But Rosemary had an internship in some far-off place, and was hesitant to leave little Riffle with a father who worked five or six days a week in the summer. He said he'd take time off, but she called him on it: "You can't afford to take time off during the sprint." "What about the winter?" he asked. And she agreed that it would be good for Riffle to come spend a month during winter term. "I'll need that month to focus on exams anyway."

She was six then, and he took the whole month off, though there wasn't much work to be had then anyway. An ice storm locked them inside for almost two weeks of the visit, and they filled their days reading stories on the couch and, later, crafting their own picture books. She would draw the images and he would write the words, and together they would staple the pages together and glue them within a cardboard cover. Those were the most intimate days they ever shared. He wondered where those books were now.

A summer later, Riffle left with Rosemary for Michigan and some "opportunity" waiting there. Though they still saw each other for a few days here and a week there, the visits became increasingly painful. The moment she arrived, he'd already be shredded with the agony of her departure. And then she'd be gone, and an abyss of longing and regret would open beneath his feet, and he'd flounder there for weeks after. She was changing and he was missing everything.

The years passed, and her calls came less frequently. They were living in Chicago, and Riffle, on her summer trip to the river, begged him to "move home" with her. He considered it, he really did. He went so far as to call a client there to ask after work. "I once was offered a job in insurance," he said to the man, summarizing the entirety of his professional qualifications. The client was kind—he had daughters of his own—and a few days later a call came with the offer of a position in sales. "It's a solid job, with a chance to move up." But when the moment came, he couldn't. On the drive to catch her flight, he explained why he couldn't follow her east. "This is my home, Rif." But she only heard what lay under the words: that he was choosing the river over her.

The next time they talked, Riffle was going by her middle name, Annie. Then, she wasn't home when he called and she didn't return his messages. Somehow, he'd lost her. Or so it felt.

The last time they saw each other, Annie was seventeen, starting college in Maine in the fall. She was scheduled to come for a month, but left after a week. They hadn't talked since, that is until she called him out of the murky blue just a month before Justin Morell went missing.

*

HANK GASPED AWAKE before his alarm. It didn't help that his bladder had contracted to the size of a goddamn mandarin. He pissed off the porch and started the kettle and checked the river levels and the fish counts and the weather predictions but none of this succeeded in washing away the drowning he'd been suffering just before he awoke. He still couldn't pull a full breath.

He ground the beans and poured the hot water over them and went to his bookshelf. The bottom row was filled entirely with composition journals, organized chronologically, and he knew precisely which to grab without checking the dates. He carried it into the light of the kitchen and opened to a page he'd seen a thousand times before, a page dated July 21, 1982. Riffle would've been three. He had recorded his regular river data, temperature, flow, clarity, and the details from a trip he ran that morning: client went zero for one. It was a short entry, at least by his current standard. But below it, he'd rambled on for pages.

She doesn't like to eat much. Occasionally, we'll show her a piece of chicken or a cheese ball and she'll rush across the room to strike, but usually, she'll turn immediately back to whatever it is that she's doing, usually drawing. But no matter how steadfastly she refuses something, I can still get her to eat it. I move in close without distracting her and place the bite within inches of her mouth. If she sees it coming, she won't take. But if I can deliver it without her seeing it, she'll strike it, every time. She senses it there somehow, and her mouth does the thinking.

Two pages later, dated the next day:

I came in the bathroom and found her standing before the toilet, gripping the rim, her undies at her ankles. She was peeing all over herself. "What are you doing?" I said. She looked up at me and smiled. "I'm using my pee-nee."

He tucked the journal back in its place and was on his way to the coffee. Time to meet the client. His eye glanced across the lone journal on the top shelf, out of order and out of place, and even without opening it, he remembered its words verbatim.

August 7 1997:

Fished with Annie this morning on what I thought would be our first drift of many this summer. She didn't want to fish, so I took the rod and landed one, a fourteen-pound buck. Mint fish. Probably be the best I'll get this year. She really missed out. Day ended early, when she said, "You mean nothing to me." Teenager thing, I'm sure.

I'm not very good at this parenting thing. Trying but I'm starting to fear that I'm missing some essential ingredient. Checked out four books on the subject from the library. Next time she comes, I'll get it right.

Tomorrow, after returning from an early trip to the airport, I'll fish hard. At least there's something I'm good at.

Chapter Six

I **N THE DAYS** that followed, little was learned about Morell's disappearance. Search and Rescue at first expanded their body search, bringing in a helicopter from Roseburg. The Huey's chop, chop, chop could be heard echoing up and down the valley as if it were delivering marines to some battle upriver. Looking up at the passing roar, Hank could see three pink faces, helmeted and intent, peering down on his pool. But after a few days, the Search and Rescue coordinator announced the formal search for Justin Morell had ended. "We have little hope of recovering him at this point."

That same day, Hank learned through the grapevine that Sheriff Carter suspected foul play. He'd been interviewing people in and around town, but had been focusing on those folks who'd spoken to Morell in the days before his disappearance. Hank expected Carter's truck to arrive at his house any moment.

But today Hank was with Danny enjoying a morning off. Danny had this way about him, something that made Hank feel lighter, more agile even. Danny seemed to see the world from a place of fundamental optimism. And if anybody had reason to think poorly of this world, it was Danny. Nonetheless, he had once said that if a guy let go the oars and did nothing else, his boat would eventually deliver itself to the takeout. "Oaring only adjusts the view." That seemed to encapsulate it all for Danny: This life would be filled with good and bad in more or less equal parts, and either way you would arrive at the end—so why not use your energies to maintain the best vista?

Danny backed his boat through an eddy and to the shore and dropped anchor. The same move would have taken Hank four or five pulls on the oars, but it took Danny just one. He was easily the strongest man Hank had ever known, a logger by breeding, an oarsman by profession. "Your turn, old man."

They were at the head of Big Bend, a long and wide pool for this river, a place where a caster could really open up. A ledge on the far side held most of the fish these days, though twenty, thirty, forty years back they would stack up behind all the pool's boulders. Hank and Danny knew right where the fish would be, yet they still chose to fish the run the old way, from the top down, a cast to every lie. Big Bend had four generations of custom to guide its angling, and who were they to fish it otherwise?

"I'll follow you through," Hank said. "One more fish isn't going to make or break my life."

Danny bit through his leader. "Enough deferring. How'll I learn your secrets if I don't watch you fish?"

"I don't have any secrets left."

Danny chuckled. "Fuck you."

They both knotted on new flies, and Danny lit a joint and Hank fished out a cigarette.

It was true that in the last few years he'd become much less stable on his feet. Someday soon he'd have to carry a wading staff like Walter's, at least while negotiating fast water. "Mostly," Hank called, wading into position, "I'm afraid I'll fall in and you'll tell everybody at the shop about it."

"I will too," Danny said, "you know it."

Hank had known Danny since Danny was too small for waders. He could still remember the little red-haired kid chasing all the girls at those summer parties some thirty years back, pulling at his wanker and hopping around like an overcaffeinated jackrabbit: boy in its essential form. Danny's older brother, Joel, who had passed away as a teenager, was at those parties too, typically roaming the periphery with a small band of pranksters. Now Danny was definitively grown-up, a couple years older than Annie, his face seasoned by decades outside. Hank had known from the first time he took Danny in the boat that the kid would end up a guide. No doubt. Children divided themselves into two categories when in a drift boat—those who couldn't peel their nervous eyes from the shore and those who were all but climbing over the gunwales to swim in the water. Danny had taken the latter to a new level of enthusiasm. Three times, Hank had lifted that sopping boy out of a rapid. Danny's own father had little interest in anything but the bottle. Something else Danny and Hank had in common.

As a teenager, Danny became a fixture on the river. He would hitch rides between runs and often linger at boat ramps hoping to score an empty seat. Hank remembered one trip in particular, a dawn he had only one client and Danny was waiting with his bike at the ramp. The client said he didn't mind if this kid took the empty seat—probably because he figured no pimply-faced youth could outfish an experienced angler like himself. But at the end of the day, Danny had risen six or eight fish to the sport's one. Angling ability was one thing, class was another, and Danny had both, even then. At the ramp as the client congratulated this kid on his fish, Danny shrugged and said, "I had to get lucky eventually."

It had been Hank who'd lent Danny the money for his first boat, who'd called the marine board and helped him get legal as a registered guide. It had been Hank who'd taught Danny to oar, to pick a line through a Class V, to rig the ropes and recover a stuck boat. Hank who'd shown Danny the remaining spawning strongholds, the rearing areas, the staging pools. Danny didn't need Hank to teach him how to fish the runs, but he did need Hank to teach him the history of those runs, their customs, their particular etiquettes. All the things Walter had taught Hank those years before. That was how it was done on Ipsyniho, at least then.

Over the years, their relationship had evolved until the tutelage went both ways. They had for years traded secret lies, hidden seams and ledges that held fish but weren't fished. But now they traded strategies for spinning deer hair and splicing lines and chucking heavy winter flies. Hank was an old dog these days, but Danny was just coming into form. He was known throughout steelhead country as an innovator, and had become an esteemed gear designer for the biggest name manufacturers—Danny *was* the cutting edge of the sport. Most recently, he'd refined and shortened Skagit lines, and designed a special series of rods meant to tip-cast these short heads in tight casting conditions— something other guides had for years considered impossible. If Hank had a question about tackle or boats, he came to Danny. If Danny had a question about the fish or river history, he came to Hank.

In a world of secrets, they were one another's trusted confidants. It was an intimacy as deep and permanent as any Hank had known. He felt it with Walter, and he felt it with Danny. That was the magic of mentorship, Hank realized now. Each person received more than he gave.

Of course, they both kept some secrets for themselves, a long-established custom among the guides. Hank had the boulder field between Upper and Lower Nefarious, plus a couple other minor spots, and he knew Danny had at least two or three places just as good that he kept close to his chest. If Danny was talking about a fish he'd caught and didn't reveal the location, it was understood that Hank wouldn't ask where.

Danny didn't know about Red Gate, for instance, which was one of Walter's many dozen secret places. When Walter had first been diagnosed with cancer, he'd begun divulging his places to Hank, on the unstated condition that Hank not fish them with anyone else. He'd learned of Red Gate, of Ridge Back, of Tendrils, three places that could produce fish on impossible days. When Walter got word the cancer was in remission, the divulging stopped. But now, when they spoke, Walter would say he "rose two in Tendrils, a couple others in another spot I'll show you soon." When Hank passed away, he'd leave his shelf of fishing logs, and all their pool maps, to Danny.

They respected each other's secrets because they understood just how essential these secrets were. To love a river, as to love a romantic partner, a person needed to have the sense that the water had shared something intimate. Those confidences, and the promise of further discovery and insight, were the fuel that kept any romance alive. Walter, Hank, Caroline, Danny—they all understood this. It was those "chargers" who didn't, a generation of misfits who'd never learned to love.

But Danny had a dark side too; Hank couldn't deny it. There were rumors and then there were the truths Hank had seen himself. Like when Danny was eighteen and had called asking for bail. Hank had arrived to find Danny's fists swollen and his toe broken. According to the cops on scene, it'd taken five men to pull Danny from the choke-setter who'd picked the fight.

Hank didn't know for sure what had happened between Danny and his ex. He didn't want to know.

"Have you been exploring the lower river much?" Danny asked. He was standing on shore behind Hank, off to the side so as not to interfere with Hank's cast.

The lower river had been gouged by two serious floods several years back, its course drastically altered, the old runs buried and new ones uncovered. "In December and May and June. Trying to catch the waves of fresh fish. I got the impression they were blowing through that water. Why?"

"Just wondering," Danny said.

Hank stepped down; his next cast would land on the ledge. He dug deep in the cast and made sure the dry fly landed at the same moment as the line—the fly was skating the moment it alit. "I take it you've been spending time down there."

"I have," Danny said. Which said everything he wasn't. "Morell was too."

A step down, a new cast. Morell.

"He got into it pretty heavy with Andy there last week." Andy Trib, Danny's good friend, though it was no secret they'd had their own troubles a few years back; the rumors had been vicious—concerning

51

Danny's wife at the time, now his ex. "Andy told me he was sure Morell was the one that cut his anchor rope. I told you about that, right?"

A step down, a new cast. He had. Andy had been guiding some clients through a run—Hank didn't realize it had been on the lower river—when Andy saw his own boat come drifting by. He had to swim for it.

"Morell didn't tell me his side, knowing Andy and me are tight, so I don't have the clearest picture. But from what I can muster up, Andy cut him off at the ramp one morning, then low-holed him that afternoon. That was the thing about Morell, he kept a grudge."

A step down, a new cast. Guides guarded their grudges like they did their secrets. "I heard that Morell had undercut Andy's prices, got his client list, and called a bunch of them." Hank had heard that through Caroline a couple weeks back.

"That's what Andy has been saying," Danny muttered.

"You don't believe him?"

"No, I do. It's just, well, I'm not telling you this because I'm interested in the particulars."

A step down, a new cast.

Danny aimed his rod to a point across the river. "Strip out another five feet and throw it on the same angle."

"Really? All the way to the bank?"

"I swam that ledge last week. There's a shelf just off that tuft of grass. There was a hog on it."

"You're kidding." Hank pulled out the line and came around: The fly smacked the surface just off the grass, broad wakes behind it. Nothing, not today. "Not interested in particulars?"

Danny spit. "I've just got a bad feeling about this whole thing. Can't shake it, that his going missing was no accident."

"The guy wasn't quick to make friends." Hank took two big steps down, sent another cast to the spot Danny had mentioned. This time after the fly landed, he fed it slack, tugged it, gave it slack. Nothing.

"Times are tight, least for the younger guys. That isn't making the situation any more friendly. Bookings through the shop are way down."

"People know the fish aren't here like they used to be."

"Morell, though, he was staying real busy. Maybe it was those articles he was writing. Or maybe he was swiping clients. Whichever, he was too new to be top dog, if you get my drift."

Hank reeled in, offered the water to Danny, but Danny declined with a nod to the boat. They walked back up the shore. Danny said, "I bet he turns up sooner or later, a knife in his back."

* * *

AFTER FISHING WITH Danny, Hank couldn't stop thinking about Morell. Disdaining Morell, really, and then feeling shabby for thinking ill of the dead. There was something else there too, something maybe like guilt. Like he'd watched the punk inch to the edge of a cliff and, despite knowing better, hadn't warned him to step back.

What bothered him now was that he couldn't muster more than some trivial compassion. He could say, "What a waste," but then again, wasn't he glad the kid was gone?

Case in point, the first time Hank encountered Morell guiding the river. Hank's clients were fishing Sawtooth, one at the top and the other in the tailout. Morell came around the corner and made a showy display of moving his boat—and his clients who were fishing Montana-style, one in the bow and one in the back—to the far bank. They shared a nod as Morell passed, and that's when Hank noticed the earphones in the kid's ears. He was listening to music while blessed with the splattering aria of the Ipsyniho? As if this wasn't insult enough, in the center of the run, Morell pulled back offshore and instructed his clients to cast to the center boulder, precisely where Hank's client would be fishing in another couple minutes. They didn't move a fish, but that was hardly the point. Morell had low-holed him, and while listening to a fucking iPod.

Hank could have held a grudge about the whole thing, but Morell was young and relatively new to the watershed and Hank himself had made faux pas at that age. Besides, forgiveness was the highest end. So they say.

But this wasn't an isolated incident. After a while, Hank started referring to low-holing as "Morelling." The kid's lasting nickname came not long after: Poddy. Walter had dubbed him after watching him shout at a client over music only he could hear.

But now the kid was dead and Hank was looking for an empathetic reading: Morell was just a product of this up-and-coming generation, a whole tribe of youth that had come to expect entertainment at every turn, and of course he would listen to music on the river, because you can't text while oaring. It wasn't his fault. He was the product, not the producer.

But there was one memory that Hank couldn't soften, no matter how rigorously he tried to reinterpret it. There it was as fresh as it had been in the moment: Walter at Millican Ramp, two clients waiting on land, Walter working as fast as he could given the limp and the pain of the cancer to move the tackle and gear from the bed of his Chevy to the boat. Like all the old guides, who never made enough money to secure even a simple form of retirement, Walter was still working, despite his doctor telling him not to and his friends chipping in to buy him some recovery time. Under his baseball cap, he was bald from the chemo. Under his waders, he was emaciated from the vomiting. He'd had to mortgage his house to afford the treatment. And yet, there he was at 4:19 in the morning, loading his boat and standing straight. Morell, though, couldn't wait. He was next in line on the ramp, his client asking about fish size, fish strength, fish numbers. Hank had his own clients, a pair of quiet teachers from Portland, and he told them to wader up while he went and helped a friend. He was walking toward Walter and the ramp when Morell leapt from his truck, grabbed the remaining gear from Walter's cab, and heaved it into the old man's boat. Walter looked up, a bit struck by the suddenness of the whole thing, and Morell said, "Next time, maybe, you could do this in the parking lot." Then to Walter's clients, who'd surely heard the exchange, "Come on, guys, time to climb aboard." It was Walter's silence immediately after, his refusal or inability to defend himself, that prompted Hank to grab Morell by the collar as he came back up the ramp. There were clients watching, so he didn't knock the little fuck's teeth out or throw him headlong into the river, but he did jam an elbow to his neck and press him against the side of the truck. Morell gasped for air. In that moment, Hank had so much to say, so much he didn't know where or how to start. All that came out was, "Mind your manners."

In Hank's day, such disrespect for the river's elders would have been met with a broken casting arm, an injury feared second only to total paralysis. A broken casting arm would effectively end your season, and your clients would find a new gillie. Depending on the details of your sin and the sobriety level of the vigilantes, there might also have been some truck sabotage, a ruptured boat, maybe minor arson to home or dwelling. And the assault would have continued until the offending prick had packed his shit and found a new watershed. In the ethical code of the Ipsyniho, respect for the river and its fish came first, then respect for the river's old guard, then respect for the etiquette the old guard had established. Justin Morell seemed hell-bent on insulting all three.

Yet Hank found himself surprised now, not that the kid had gone missing, but that he felt so obligated to forgive him, just because he was dead. And what was this "kid" nonsense? Morell had been a grown man.

Morell had wasted a chance. That was it. He'd misused his time. He'd neglected this most spectacular gift the world had offered him.

There came a time for people like that to face what they deserved.

*

He drove to town for supplies: paint and spackle and whatever über-potent carpet cleaner he could find. He still had plenty to do before Annie arrived.

But once in town, he drove first to Morell's place, one of those sixties-era ranch homes that proliferate in the West, the ones seemingly built to emphasize their garages. He parked out front and waited to shut down the truck, humming along to *Cornell '77*. "Row, Jimmy, row." He was here to muster up some compassion, to find a reason to forgive this kid. "How to get there, I don't know."

The girlfriend answered, a beanpole of a girl, black hair, lip ring, swollen eyes—probably a couple years younger than Annie though she looked ten years more haggard. She was wearing hardly anything, tiny shorts or a bikini bottom (was there a difference these days?) and a muslin-thin tank top. If interested, he could've learned much about the geography of her dark nipples, which were barely concealed by the fabric.

"I'm stopping by to pay my respects," Hank said. He caught himself pulling at his beard, and forced his hands deep into his pockets. "I want to help however I can. This must be, this is . . . well, I can't imagine how hard."

She turned and walked inside, leaving the door ajar.

He followed her in. "Shut this?"

She didn't answer, and he decided to leave it open, an escape route. She was drinking and offered him a glass. He accepted, and watched as her bony arm tipped the vodka bottle like it was tonic. He guessed she didn't do much eating.

"His mom is coming out on Tuesday," she said. "It will be hers to deal with then. I'm so done being the one. I didn't sign up for this, you-know-what-I-mean? It's not that I'm a bad person or anything, but it's not like I was in this for the long haul. It isn't fair to stick me with this. We weren't tight like that, you-know-what-I-mean? I'm not a bad person."

"It's too much for anyone." There was a Bob Marley poster on the wall, another for Pink Floyd, the one with the nude women sitting beside a pool, their backs painted with each of the album covers. Bottles of hard liquor lined the windowsill, some sporting half-burned candles, wax dripping like frozen tears down the glass. The place smelled of cat, of incense, of unsmoked weed.

With a series of eye-watering gulps, she drank her beverage down far enough that she could add some ice cubes. "You're one of his coworkers?"

Hank considered this. Supervisor was more like it. "Yep, exactly."

Down the hallway, through an open door, he saw a fly-tying vise, a stack of fly boxes.

"Do you think he's dead?" she asked, while crunching on a piece of ice.

"Oh. Um." He reached for the wall behind him, to lean against it, but stumbled slightly into the open room. He could have sworn there was a wall there. "A lot of possibilities. A lot of room for hope still."

"I'm sure of it," she said. "To be honest. I told myself if he wasn't found by last night . . . This is just so crazy. It's not fair. Like you said, it's too much for one person." She looked toward the window as if she were considering issues of great philosophical weight. "It's too much for one person."

Hank pointed his beverage down the hallway. "Do mind if I have a look at his flies?"

The room with the fly-tying bench also housed all his rods, which were leaning with no apparent order in one corner. There was a laptop on a second desk—likely the site where he'd written those articles. On the small bookshelf nearby rested a single row of books, mostly where-to-fish books. The other two rows were filled with sideways stacks of magazines. All the fly-fishing titles, plus some snowboarding glossies he'd never seen before.

On one wall hung the famous Sage poster of the guy double-hauling across the tropical blue from the roof of that crashed plane. On another, two posters, one of a big British Columbia river on a snowy morning and the other Jeff Callahan's renowned image of the Ipsyniho at dawn. Images so common as to hold little or no interest for Hank. However, immediately above the laptop hung a slab of corkboard. There Hank found maybe twenty-five photos tacked. He was expecting to see Morell in each of them, holding a big fish, gripping and grinning like some weekend joe. But to his surprise, only a couple of the photos were of Morell. The rest were of the river, of certain runs, of unidentifiable anglers casting at last light, of an otter sitting on a rock. And then, to Hank's utter wonderment, there was a picture of Hank himself and Walter. They were standing on the shore near Kitchen, wadered up and laughing. Hank couldn't remember the day, but he was wearing last year's waders. Morell must have happened by and snapped this photo. But why? And why post it so prominently?

"There's going to be a service," the girlfriend bellowed. Her drink sloshed over the rim. "You should come. They say it will be healing." She elbowed the pile of rods in the corner. "You can have any of this shit you want."

He unpinned the photo. "Mind?"

She shrugged. "What the fuck am I gonna do with it?"

Chapter Seven

Walter and Hank met Danny and Andy at the Cougar Creek confluence pool, the river's primary staging pool, just past noon. Another truck was parked on the one-lane Forest Service road. A fading and tattered bumper sticker read, "Fuck spotted owls."

Walter said to Danny, "Rifle."

Danny folded down the seat in his old Cummins and produced a slender, rolled-up blanket. He cracked open the bolt-action and tossed the blanket back in the cab. Walter grabbed his .30-06 from the gun rack in his window.

Andy shook Hank's hand. "How you been?" Andy Trib, a compact little guy with bloodshot eyes, prematurely graying hair, and a baseball cap always pulled low. For what the guy lacked in social skills, he more than compensated for with a two-hander. Hank had met him first in the midnineties, when Danny started bringing him around. He was one of the first Great Lakes transplants. In the years since, a river of unemployed twenty-somethings had come streaming from the failing industrial center, salivating to be steelhead guides, their hunger fueled by the images of big rivers and big fish that now plastered the national fishing magazines. Most burned out or drifted on within a year or two. But a few, like Andy Trib, proved themselves and became respected—if steadily goaded—members of the circle.

"Hear you had a run-in with Morell," Hank said.

Andy spit. "You could say that. Won't talk shit on account of all that's happened, but did you hear that fucker cut my anchor line?"

Walter called, "You two finish your tea party. Danny and I'll take care of these Bubbas."

Andy and Hank leaned against the tailgate and watched Danny and Walter disappear over the shoulder, rifles in their hands. Walter, of course, had his wading staff in the other.

While they waited, Andy tucked a pinch of Kodiak into his lip and Hank sparked a smoke, and the nicotine got Andy chatty. He went on and on about how Morell had been swiping clients, low-holing, and, Andy suspected though couldn't prove, puncturing his truck tires. "Feel bad saying it, but the valley's a better place with Poddy gone. Just wish of course he'd left under different circumstances."

"Funny how death changes the way you think about a guy." Hank was thinking of that photograph he'd taken from Morell's corkboard, the one still in his shirt pocket.

"Didn't change the way I think of him. Once a douche, always a douche." Andy blew some snot from his nose. "What do you think, somebody kill him?"

"Just a matter of respect, really," Hank muttered. When a person died, they could no longer defend themselves; the living had a responsibility to give them the benefit of the doubt. And some of the living, the indebted ones, had a moral imperative to fight the dead's battles. That's how debts could be repaid. Of this much, Hank was sure. Or pretty sure, anyway. But why did he feel indebted to Morell? Was that what this feeling was? "He was doing the best he could."

Andy shook his head. "Maybe. But I think somebody killed him."

"No," Hank said. "Nobody killed him. He was just a kid, for fuck's sake." But to be honest, the more times someone asked him if he thought Morell might have been murdered, the more he began to think the answer could be yes. Had to be yes.

"Didn't realize you were taking this so personal."

"I'm not."

Andy shrugged. "O-kay, boss."

Hank was just about to apologize for getting snappy when two men, one nearly obese, the other as thin as a binge tweaker, stepped up on the road. Neither wore a shirt. They threw their fishing rods in the bed of their truck, and the thin one hollered, "Fuck all y'all. Fucking, fairy-faggot fuckers. Yeah, you heard me. You want some of this, bitch-fuck?" He was beating his fists now against his chest, hard enough to leave bruises, which to Hank seemed somehow emblematic of all this guy's problems.

The scrawny one had halved the distance between them and was still coming. "I seen you prancing around in your fly costume, stroking off your big ol' sticks. Well I'll take that big ol' stick and bust it over my knee and ear-fuck your skull with it, yeah, you heard me. My daddy's daddy been fishing this river since your kin was still learning to wipe their prissy eastern asses, and I'm done with y'all coming in here and actin' like we're a bunch of off-reservation Injuns. We own this place, who the fuck are you?"

The blimpy one threw a fountain drink at them, which exploded on the road at their feet. "Yeah, motherfuckers."

Hank cleaned some dirt out from under his fingernail. He really needed to clip these before Annie arrived.

"What? You too pussy to stand up for yourself?" Scrawny was just a roll cast away now.

Andy stood from the tailgate. "Why don't you get in your truck, and drive back to your cave, and beat your dog—or whatever it is you do."

"Whoa, whoa," Scrawny said, his hand into the air like he had a question. "You hear that, Pin?"

"Sure as shit."

"Low Blow here thinks he can big-dick us out of our own spread."

Andy was taking the bait. He'd already turned his baseball cap around and spit out his dauber and was walking up to the fight. Hank laid a hand on his shoulder to stop him.

Then, Hank walked up the road and right past Scrawny without so much as looking at him. He had his eye fixed on Blimp, who had never left the protective lee of their pickup, and as he expected, Fatty faltered at the sudden challenge and took a step toward the driver's seat. This is what Hank had learned in his years of observing machismo posturing, that if you came at them in just such a way that they couldn't determine whether you were about to throw a punch or a kiss, you could fracture their momentum. And then you had them reacting, and reacting is losing. Now he picked up one of their fishing rods from the bed of the truck and studied the terminal end. "Huh. You were fishing black corkies through there?"

No answer.

"Why the treble hook?" He was directing his questions toward Blimp, who was one foot in the cab now.

"It works," he muttered hesitantly.

"So you throw it upstream?"

Blimp nodded.

"And tickle the bottom on the dead-drift, then swing it around?"

"Don't talk to him!" the scrawny one shouted. He'd come rushing to the edge of the truck, and now he grabbed the rod from Hank's hand. "What game you playing, Big Beard?"

"Just talking fishing," Hank said. "What pound test is that leader?"

Blimp's eyes flashed between his buddy and Hank.

Between the hook and the weight was almost six feet of monofilament—enough to floss fish and drive the hook into the side of the face. "Will they move far for a black corkie?"

Scrawny threw the rod in the bed of the truck and shouted, "Fuck this, Pin. These fairies are afraid of a little round a' round." He climbed into the cab and slammed shut the door, and a moment later, the truck jumped to life.

By the time Walter and Danny made it back to the road, the pickup was throwing gravel and jumping up the hill.

"Snaggers," Hank said.

"Yep. Flossing. They had two wild fish on shore. Tweakers, it's like kicking at a rattlesnake."

Walter cracked a Pabst while Hank, Andy, and Danny pulled on their wetsuits, spit in their masks, strapped on their weight belts. By the time they were double-checking the leashes on their spears, Walter had finished the can.

"I'll honk if Johnny rolls up," he said.

Danny grabbed his fins. "Don't fall asleep on us, old man."

"Haven't slept in years. Don't figure I'll start now."

They did it like they always did it. At least once a month during the summer and fall they came to this staging pool to clean it of hatchery-bred fish. The wild steelhead had for millennia collected in this deep pool, awaiting ideal ascension conditions for the tributaries nearby, where they would spawn come early spring. But for the last thirty years, the State's hatchery program had been releasing genetically deficient clone fish into the river. Now those steelhead gathered here too. If they weren't removed, they would end up spawning with the wild fish, further jeopardizing the future of the wild stocks.

Of course, if a state cop found them here, they'd all be arrested or at least fined well into the four digits. But, as Walter was fond of saying, "state laws are there to protect the State. Somebody's got to protect the fish." To Hank, driving a metal rod through a genetically modified steelhead seemed as ethically clear-cut as putting a sick dog out of its misery. Plus, they ate pretty fucking great.

"My turn to float," Andy said.

So Danny took his place at the end of the pool, Hank took his place at the top, and Andy floated its length. Almost immediately, Hank could hear the aquatic clank of their spears hitting rocks, and then in a sudden wave, the fish were darting toward him. From the fuzzy limits of perception, gray ghosts turning, dodging, disappearing. He held still against the ledge, not breathing, not moving, his gun aimed at the boulder in the center of the channel. Then, as always, a fish pulled up behind it, a fish missing its adipose fin. Hank focused on the red of its gill plate and fired, his spear severing the creature's spine and rendering it stiff as a thirty-inch two-by-eight.

*

BACK AT THE truck, Walter helped them load the eighteen fish into three coolers. Once filleted, there would be about ninety pounds of finished meat. "Andy," he called, "looks like you're low man again."

"Fuck that," Andy said. "I'm always low man."

"Be grateful you're man at all," Walter retorted. Which is exactly what he'd said to Hank thirty years back when Hank had complained about having to clean all the fish. What he meant, of course, was be glad you were invited in the first place.

Andy sighed. "Should I drop the fillets off at the shelter?"

Hank gilled a fish out of one of the coolers and slipped it into a plastic sack. Annie used to love steelhead. "One less to trouble you."

Walter handed Andy an opened beer. "No, bring whatever you don't want by my place. I know some folks who could use 'em."

Chapter Eight

HANK HADN'T SEEN Caroline since he left her spread in a huff the morning after Morell went missing. She hadn't called, which was her style—a show, he assumed, of how little he meant to her. Finally, he'd broken down and dialed her. He acted as if they'd left on good terms and asked if she wanted to go out for dinner. "Why don't you come up here?" she said.

So he came with an elk roast, which he'd patted with sea salt and cracked pepper and Bragg's and vacuum-sealed to speed the marination. It would take a good hour and half on her barbecue, which would give him plenty of time to lay out his proposition.

She didn't come out to greet him when he arrived, though Samson and Delilah did, barking at first, then licking. He gave them each a piece of jerky, which he'd brought especially for the purpose, and pushed through the back door.

Caroline was on the phone with a client, the standard night-before call: sunscreen, plenty of water, rain gear just in case. Though there was as much chance of it raining tomorrow as there was of it snowing, no guide who'd experienced the misery of being stuck in a sixteen-foot boat with a wet and cold and bitching sport would ever again leave it to chance. Precisely the reason Hank kept an emergency poncho in his first-aid kit.

"Sorry," she said when she hung up. Whether she meant for the phone call or for the other day, he didn't know. She wrapped him in a tight hug, and pressed her body against his in that way of hers, feet, thighs, hips, belly, chest, neck, all of it pressing, seducing. She smelled of homegrown tomatoes.

"You've been in the garden."

She kissed him. "You've been smoking a lot. What you nervous about?"

He showed her the roast. "Tenderloin. Thought I'd test my recipe."

"All that for us? I dragged down some manzanita from up on the ridge. Figured you could cut it. Jeez, Hank," looking again at the meat, "that'll take hours to cook. We'll never get a session in."

He left the meat on the counter and fished out the Stihl from the shed, gave it a dose of bar oil, and sectioned the manzanita into four-inch lengths. The wood was prime: It gave off that resonating ping when tapped. He dumped in just enough charcoal to get some heat going and just enough lighter fluid to bring it to flame. Then he was back inside and she was handing him a cup of tequila. Caroline had a thing for top-shelf tequila.

"Any word on the kid?" she asked.

He didn't want to talk about Morell.

Caroline was wearing her sandals and her peach skirt and a low-cut tank top, and summer sweat had dampened the hair on her temples, and when she turned, he saw it glistening between her shoulder blades.

Hank had long felt his life was missing something, some key ingredient, like salt maybe, and without it, the meal of his existence, though still flush with the right flavors, was lacking its foundation. If grilling could teach you anything, it was that salt didn't emphasize flavors so much as it highlighted underpinnings—salt revealed qualities you otherwise would have missed. He kissed Caroline now, right where she glistened.

It was how she made him feel: He wanted to brag about things, do a backflip, cast all the way across the pool and into the woods on the far side. She made him feel like he was twenty-five again, like life was an expansive plain of possibilities and passion and attainable wisdom. When things were good between them, he felt a wildfire within him casting light in all directions. When things were wrong, that wildfire reverted to arctic whiteout. He both hated and relished being so dependent on her.

But it was more than that too. Hank had lived with a half-dozen women in his life, and he'd felt close to all of them. But with each of those women, he had felt the divisions that separated them; they were two people sharing space, sharing bodies, sharing time. Two people, always, no matter how passionately they united. When things were right with Caroline, though, divisions vanished. Somehow, in his mind's eye, their two became one. They might be holding hands on a bridge or soaking in a hot spring or eating breakfast, but in those moments he felt a communal warmth he'd only known once before. With Riffle, in those first years.

He felt lucky to have Caroline at all. She kept to her established circle, mostly the valley's artisans, gourmands, and recovering hippies. Even after thirty-something years working the river, she didn't socialize much with the other guides. "They all think they know *the* way to do just about everything. Too much ego for too little ability." If it hadn't been for his flat tire at the ramp that winter dusk, and her feeling obligated to help, they might never have connected in the first place.

What she didn't have were intimate women friends, and he'd known her long enough to know why: Underlying her wit and smile and good graces was a thinly veiled competitive streak. She did her best to repress this element, but there is only so much a person can do to obscure their disposition. Her need to compete all but rendered her incapable of becoming close with other women, especially women her own age. After they caught on to her one-upmanship, they'd close up, take a step back, check their watch. She might reach out—ask if they needed a hand with this or that, or invite them out for coffee or wine—but her efforts were rarely reciprocated. He'd seen it happen time and time again. Women didn't accept, didn't authenticate or oth erwise reward, such confrontational behavior within their own ranks. Men, on the other hand, barely noticed.

On the river, she didn't have to obscure anything; in fact, it was this very competitive edge that made her such a competent angler and busy guide. It was one of the things Hank loved about her, that she never deferred.

But there were things that worried him too. He knew the precedent; she had a long history of selecting a partner from within her circle of male friends. There would be a one- to two-year coupling, during which he would occasionally spend the night but never move in. Dinners shared, rainy or starry nights observed, a few of life's tribulations weathered. And then, based on some contrived excuse, she'd end it. This winter, if they made it, would mark their third year together.

Hank had never left a woman; they'd always ended it with him. He'd gotten good at sensing "the talk" coming.

It was in part because of this feeling of imminent termination that he'd selected tonight to proposition her. That and recent events had once again revealed life's fragility, its whimsical turns and drops. This moment was as good as any other—and better, because it was now. But, if he was perfectly honest with himself, he'd have to admit he'd chosen tonight for another, less romantic and more utilitarian reason: Annie was coming in three days, and having a woman would go a long way toward demonstrating his worthiness.

"You should throw that meat on," she said.

"I'm about to." This was the moment. Now. Kiss her neck, she'll turn, take her in your arms, and explain it to her. Make her love you.

He grabbed the elk. "Be right back."

At the barbecue, he found the coals not yet ready. He stirred them, restacked them, blew a few streams of air, then lit a cigarette. And fingered the ring in his pocket.

He'd never been married before, a bachelor for almost sixty years—was now really the time to change things? He never felt lonely when he was with Danny or Walter. What would they say? *This better not affect your fishing.*

But yes, it was the right time, because he'd sensed a shift in Caroline in the last months. She was rising from the bed too quickly after they finished. She was waiting longer to call him back. They were seeing each other less frequently. Pretty soon, she would produce some bogus excuse, and that would be it. He'd lose her for good, the one woman who'd ever really known him.

Caroline left her men when she felt lonely in their presence, and she felt lonely with them, Hank suspected, when she felt stymied by their proximity. She liked to act tough and untouchable, but Caroline, like anyone, was precariously balanced between contentment and desperation. Someone's expectations, and her unwillingness or inability to meet them, could tip that balance and send her stumbling. In those moments, she would be overcome by the loneliness she otherwise kept at bay. It was the guy's gaze that did it. She would see behind his vision a judgment about her, and that would make her feel small and isolated and trapped, and it was in that moment that she would strike. End it. Hand the guy his remaining things and say, "It's been fun."

The ring, then, was a signal. She would see in it his total acceptance of her. That he would never judge her. That with him she would forever be free to be whoever and whatever she wanted. She would know that he appreciated her charities and her flaws equally.

Of course, he understood the risk. After her previous marriage, she told Hank early in their relationship, she had sworn off the institution as "an archaic social control" whose benefits were nil but whose risks were profound. That relationship had ended traumatically, and just before it was annulled, she found herself pregnant—a surprise she never revealed to the father. When the baby came, she had already made adoptive arrangements, and that was that. Her daughter was gone, to an established middle-class family, somewhere in the western half of the continent. That's all she knew. In the years that followed, she fought first on her own and then with an attorney to meet her daughter, but both she and the adoptive family, through their agent, had originally agreed upon a closed arrangement. All records were sealed, even from her.

Hank now saw Caroline's silhouette through the window, as she worked at something in the kitchen. That was something else they had in common, regrets.

The dogs, who'd been leaning their muzzles against his legs hoping for another stick of jerky, roared to life and raced around the edge of the house. Then Hank heard it too, the low rumble of a pickup in the distance. He started to walk around the corner of the house, to look toward the road, then realized that Caroline might prefer he stay back. This was her spread after all.

He watched while Caroline walked out to meet Sheriff Carter, who repositioned his cop belt as he swaggered toward her. Muffled by the distance, he heard, "Is Hank around?"

He couldn't hear what she said.

"Come on. Hank Hazelton."

Caroline turned and looked back, and Hank stepped into the evening sunlight. "Figured I might find you here," Carter called.

*

CARTER HAD COME to ask Hank about "this altercation" that had happened between him and Morell at Millican boat ramp, an event Hank recollected as completely and honestly as possible.

Carter admitted he'd found something in the boat that made him suspect foul play. He hated to "come knocking on doors like this" but felt "obligated by the facts." When Hank pressed, Carter explained that a pool of diluted human blood had been standing at the boat's lowest point. "Like someone had used the bailer to wash Morell's blood from the boat." But let the blood on the seat remain? Hank asked. It seemed like an overbaked deduction. "Maybe the person missed it. I don't know. We need that body to turn up to know anything."

Caroline locked the front door, which she never did, and watched out the window as Carter closed the gate behind his rig, some two hundred yards across the meadow. "Somebody killed that kid, didn't they?"

Hank picked up a knife now and halved a zucchini. "Had bad blood with just about everybody."

"Hardly the time for puns, Hank." Caroline checked the oven, the sweet potato fries sizzling inside. "Was he worth killing?"

Hank put the knife through the flesh of the zucchini and was overcome by the memory of a smell: the oily musk wafting up from O'Connell's body bag that afternoon when Carter unzipped it and asked for an identification. "People have died for less."

*

AFTER DINNER AND another sipper of añejo, they drove his truck down to the river and parked up an overgrown skid road. Guides had to be careful to hide their rigs when they fished lesser-known places. Joes would spot guide vehicles, remembering them from boat ramps or past trips, and venture down to see where and precisely how they were fishing. Precautions had to be taken if secrets were to remain secrets. Caroline sometimes joked that she would someday buy a second car, "a total joe rig like a Forester," to use on her free time.

They didn't bother wadering up, just grabbed their rods and followed the trail to the hourglass-shaped pool below, Time Traveler.

Hank had always believed that an astute observer could learn most everything about a person by watching that person fish. There were those who hurried between pools or swore after a botched cast, revealing a fundamental insecurity about their own abilities, their own worth. There were those who forced the forward strokes and rushed the backstrokes; these were the literal thinkers who had little use for intuition or any of its incarnations. There were those who always threw long casts even when the water was better matched to short casts; these were the self-involved people, the ones who failed to ask the right questions, always intent on their own answers. But Caroline's angling had for years stumped his best attempts at analysis.

Of course, there was the competitiveness. Normally, when two anglers reached a section of water they both wanted to fish, a ritualistic "no, you take it" occurred, during which both anglers secretly hoped the other would decline more potently and, hence, allow him to fish first without feeling shabby. But with Caroline, the ritual was condensed to non-existence: "You gonna take it?" already stripping out line.

"I'm happy watching."

But then came the mysteries. For one, there were the flawless casts, which, in their lack of glitch, revealed so little. No rushing, no lingering. She brought the line around, the rod continuously loading, and stopped: the fly and its line landing precisely where they should, every time. The casts were leisurely, effortless, efficient. Walter had said once, after watching Caroline fish Sawtooth, "If the contest was to expend the least amount of energy and still deliver the fly, that lady would win all day, every day." Was the fishing lazy? No, it was smart. Power applied only when and where it was needed. And there was her approach to fishing the run: Instead of fishing the entire length of Time Traveler, one cast for each two steps downstream, she fished four small places, a dozen casts to each. These four places weren't random; they were the bucket, the seam, and the two ledges that regularly held fish. Was this a form of hurrying? No, she spent as much time on the run as Hank or Walter or Danny.

She rose one on the first ledge, the steelhead taking in a silver swirl.

And then there was how she fought a fish: brute bullying, for the most part. She used heavy leaders and broke a rod or two a year. After the initial run, during which the fish might peel a hundred feet of line, she leaned from the hips into the rod so as to magnify her own mass. When the fish wanted to go upstream, she made it turn and go down. When it wanted to go down, she made it turn and go up. Hank might have been inclined to dub this a sign of her penchant to manhandle those in her control, but then she also knew just when to give the fish slack; she intuited the fish's next move and responded preemptively. When it jumped or wrapped around a boulder, her rod tip was down before Hank could think that it should be. It wasn't manhandling, it was pure empathy, pure persuasion.

"Shit this hen's heavy!" She laughed now as her reel squealed out bursts of line.

Did she treat the men in her life like she treated the fish? Would it be so bad if she did?

Because there was the tenderness once the fish was within her hands. The empathy becoming genuine intimacy. Whereas most anglers, even the experienced, would rush to tighten a fist around the fish's tail joint so that it could not flee before they were done admiring it, Caroline only touched the fish with the backs of her wet fingers, a glancing caress down the silver side. If it splashed away, that was its right. Her other hand held the fly, and when the fish seemed eager for release, she'd turn the hook and unpin it from the jaw. The fish wasn't a trophy, wasn't a show of her abilities or an object of her control. The fish was an equal partner in an intimate dance.

"Twelve pounds? Thirteen?" Hank offered her a hand up from the water's edge.

She climbed up herself. "Did you see her explode on it?" An ear-to-ear smile. "Fuck me, that never gets old."

He touched the back of his fingers to her cheek, and she slapped his ass.

"Your turn, cowboy."

*

During the afterglow of that fish would have been the perfect time for the ring. But Hank had stumbled, unsure of himself, of the moment, of how Caroline would react, and then they were back at the house, finishing the tequila and laughing, and Caroline insisted they go for a walk. So up the trail they went, through the hanging valley and the old pastures, past the leaning pole barn her grandfather had built, past the moonshine barrels her grandmother had kept, past the markers where they'd both been buried, and to the top of the ridge. The stars were hot and close against that Malbec sky, the horizon dimming by the second. Far, far below, a second sky was mirrored on the river. That was the way with the Ipsyniho, the heavens and the land refracted and contracted until the two became one.

"Do you ever wonder if you'll live anywhere else?" Caroline said suddenly.

The nagging loneliness that often kept him up at nights rose as suddenly as that fish. She was an arm's length out, but five miles away. He would've traded everything to understand her.

She turned her back to him, tucked her hands in her fleece coat. "I want to talk to you about something." So this was it, the moment she would break up with him.

"Listen," he said, but then faltered. What could he say to change her mind? Had he ever persuaded her of anything?

"What?" she said.

He reached for the ring in his pocket and raised it between them. He'd planned to be on one knee, he'd planned to do it right.

But in the darkness she didn't see it, and she said, "I hope you and Annie will come stay with me. Will you? I want to get to know her. I want to learn this part of you." She wrapped her arms around him and laid her head against his chest. "Will you?"

Hank took a breath, finally. "That part of me doesn't like me very much."

"She asked to fly out here and stay with you, didn't she?"

"I haven't gone to visit her in fourteen years," Hank heard himself say. Was it possible? Fourteen years? It felt like fourteen weeks, and forty years. "I haven't called her but once in the last year." He wrapped his arms around Caroline. "She's been busy," he said. "I didn't want to be in her way. I didn't want to be a burden." Excuses, and lame ones. "She doesn't need me."

"Not true."

"It is. I lost her years ago."

"No." Caroline pinched him. "You never lost your daughter."

The memory of a winter night a couple years back, the anniversary of her own daughter's birth: She'd wept then, "I'll never know her name."

"Whatever happened between you two," Caroline whispered now, "don't waste this chance because of some stupid grudge."

"I'm not holding any grudges."

Chapter Nine

ANNIE ARRIVED AT the cabin as scheduled, just after five on Wednesday evening. Hank heard her rental car pulling up the hill and quickly dried his hands on the kitchen towel, lit the two candles he'd placed on the dining room table, and switched the stereo from *Cornell '77* to some sophisticated Portuguese music he'd bought for this moment.

He'd also bought Dockers and a button-up shirt, paid forty bucks for a haircut, and all but rebuilt his home in the last few days. He'd stocked the refrigerator with stuffed olives, sparkling water, soft cheese, prosciutto—a hundred and fifty dollars' worth of what seemed to him posh, East Coast, Ivy League sustenance. He felt like a foreigner in his own home, like a fish who was one minute holding behind a rock and then next minute pressed by gravity against that rock, gasping for breath in a waterless world. *This is ridiculous*, he thought at the last second, *I should have bought the green Dockers*.

Annie stepped from the car, a wide smile under a pair of enormous sunglasses, sunglasses so big they made her face look, proportionately anyway, like a mayfly's. "Hank," she said. "Look at you!"

He wanted to lift her and spin her, feel how much she weighed, throw her in the air and hear her giggle like she used to, hear her say, "Daddy again, again Daddy." He wanted to kiss her cheek, her forehead, her nose. He wanted to tickle her soft sides, the back of her knees, the bottom of her feet. But there she was, a woman every bit as tall as he. A woman wearing expensive shoes and windy cotton pants and a tank top and a necklace that looked like it cost more than his best rod. So he extended his hand, swallowed.

Thank god she pushed it aside and wrapped her thin arms around his neck and said, "Oh, your beard! I missed it. My mountain man father. Tell me everything."

*

HE GAVE HER the penny tour and demonstrated how to flush the broken toilet and helped her move her luggage into what would be her room, and smiled inwardly when she said, "Oh, I love the music." Surely this was a comment for his benefit, one quite divorced from fact, but even so it gave him a sudden rush of confidence, and he showed her the refrigerator. She didn't say anything about the provisions.

"When did you get this place?" she asked.

It had been a year or two after she'd left the last time, during his great binge of self-improvements. He'd gathered his emergency money, a few thousand dollars he'd been tucking away in twenty- and forty-dollar increments, and put a down payment on the place. For a couple years, the monthly payments had nearly drowned him, but then he refinanced and found a cheaper supplier of his liability insurance, which gave him the couple hundred extra a month he needed.

They sat on either side of the small island that functioned as counter space and as a divide between the living room and the kitchen. She was picking at a bowl of filberts and sipping from the chardonnay he'd poured for her. He was so distracted by the woman that was his daughter that he only partially followed her stories.

Her hair was longer in front than in back and curved down to her chin and was shiny and clean, hair he'd only seen in photographs. He was stunned a bit, as if a celebrity was sitting in his kitchen. She was wearing mascara, her only makeup, or rather the only makeup he could detect, and it lent her eyes a compelling vivacity; it was hard to look elsewhere. And there was her perfume: vanilla and warm. And she slouched in a new way, in a manner refined but casual. Now both her elbows sat on the table, just a couple inches apart, her hands up and feeding her mouth, which chewed and spoke at once, her face suspended there, unflappable. That's what it was about her: Her whole aura was slender and majestic, a whitetail doe in summer—so unlike the puffy, clumsy pubescent who'd come to stay with him last. Whereas she used to remind him of an overdressed Wooly Bugger, now she was a low-water Lady Caroline.

She was waiting for him to answer.

"Sorry," he said. "I'm just so shocked that you're actually here."

"So am I."

He didn't know what to say, how to respond.

She broke the silence. "Can we sit outside? I love that there's no humidity here."

He nodded. Whatever she wanted. His daughter, with him again.

⁂

THEY SPENT THE late afternoon at the house, on the small porch that extended from his bedroom. From there, they could hear the highway below, and between cars, the rustle of the river. A woodpecker was deconstructing the dead oak just down the hill. And honeybees buzzed in and out of their woody cavern.

She worked sixty-hour weeks, she told him, and had been surprised by how fulfilled she could be in the "private sector." She spoke fast, and he listened intently; no one around here spoke like this. "In graduate school, they lead you to think an academic position is the only option. They're pushing you in that direction, helping you carve out a niche of your own, but not just any niche, you know; it's got to be a marketable niche. Doesn't matter if you're doing something innovative, say arguing to reframe the discussions of Heidegger, if your cutting edge isn't part of the new collective direction, you won't find a position. I was deep into

Buber, which was my problem. Or so my advisor said. Buber, all of existentialism really, is passé. There is so much that is passé now. You have to be doing something in environmental, feminist, or language to find an academic job these days. Even logic is dead. Imagine that: a philosophy department without a logician. Amazing!"

"I can't imagine."

"But the private jobs? They're booming. Especially these ethicist gigs. Everybody needs an ethicist now."

"So, what is it you do exactly?"

"Preempt disputes, prepare for disputes, advise disputers, construct policies that will avoid future disputes. Really, pay me now and I'll save you millions in attorney fees later. That's what it boils down to. That and everybody wants to lunch with a philosopher; nobody wants to lunch with a lawyer."

She frequently pulled a device from her purse, checked it, pushed some buttons, tucked it back in her purse. Only later would Hank learn she was actually communicating with her associates back at the hospital. She was working.

"Like right before I left. A surgeon did something he shouldn't have, and now I'm helping reconstruct the hospital's policy to cover its ass in the future—and ensure the policy remains ethical, of course, whatever that means. It's part politics, part law, part common sense. Mostly, what I do is find the best bad option."

"Do you like what you do?" He couldn't believe that anyone in the entire universe—especially his own progeny—would like to spend her days doing this.

"I do. I love it. I love how busy it keeps my mind. There's always something to think about, a problem to work out, a question to answer. It's its own universe, this job, and that's what I love about it. A whole system of thought and code and significance. I could spend my life wrapped up in it."

"Huh."

"Hey," she said suddenly. "I want to take you out for dinner. Someplace nice. My treat."

He nodded at the kitchen. "I've got something marinating."

"Can it wait until tomorrow? Let's have somebody else do our cooking. My treat."

*

So, HE RINSED the marinade off the meat while she freshened up in her room, and they drove the twenty-two minutes to the four-star Campwater Lodge, to the restaurant there, and asked the exquisitely tailored host for seats that overlooked the river. The Lodge, as it was known locally, had an international reputation among anglers, and drew legions of high rollers every summer. Most of Hank's clients stayed there. A few of the especially gracious would invite him for dinner after the trip, an invitation he usually accepted, so long as he didn't have plans with Caroline. "This is the only gourmet restaurant in the world that lets you wear studded boots inside."

"What's a studded boot?"

Their table overlooked some of the most storied steelhead water in the world, runs that Hank fished infrequently these days because of all the joes that swarmed there. He pointed out an osprey and they watched as it tucked its wings and dove into the green pool. "Wow," she said.

"This place is in your blood," he said. "I'm a transplant, but you're a native. Did I ever show you where you were conceived?"

"Jeez, Hank."

"No, it's a beautiful place. You'll appreciate it. You've got legacy here."

She checked the device in her purse, pushed a couple buttons. Sipped her water. Pushed more buttons. "Sorry," she said. "I'll shut this thing off." But then she didn't.

The server came with a napkin over her arm, and held a bottle of wine for them to see. Annie barely acknowledged the person, but nodded at the wine. After a test pour, Annie sipped it and said, "Leave the bottle." She didn't say thank you.

Hank said it for her. "What would you like to do while you're here?" Meaning: anything else besides looking at that device?

She tucked the thing back in her purse. "I'd love to hike and raft and do all those outdoorsy things that I never get to do back home. And I'd really like to fish with you one day, you know, a guided trip, like I am one of your clients."

"Nah. We can definitely fish if you want but—"

"No," she said. "I want to see you in action. I want to know who you are when you're at work. Thad, my . . . my friend, he's a pediatric surgeon, and he has no idea who I am at work. It just seems strange. How could we think we know our intimates if we never see them at work, where they spent most of their waking energy?"

The inclusion here of Thad had seemed forced to Hank, almost as if she had been awaiting a chance to mention him. Hank tossed her a bone and asked about this Thad fellow, how long they'd been together, what they did together, all questions disguised as being about Thad when really he was just trying to elicit more information about her. But she was categorically restrained on the subject, providing bland and factual information that did little to color in his impressions of their lives. Like she was keeping something from him.

"Do you live together?" he asked bluntly, his suspicion getting the better of him.

"We do."

"Good," he said, though he hadn't the foggiest idea whether it was good or not. "People rush into marriage too frequently these days."

She glanced down at her plate, hiding her eyes, and he should have guessed what she would say next. But he didn't, and it rocked him. "Actually Hank, we are married. We got married in May."

The river, the osprey, the breeze through the firs. "Oh, I see."

She put her hand on his. "It wasn't a big service or anything. We had it at this tiny bed-and-breakfast in Thad's hometown, in North Carolina." She was awaiting his reply.

"I'm so happy for you. Congratulations. Really. Was your mom there?"

She nodded.

He nodded too, looking down at the water but seeing nothing. "Wow. Married. My daughter. How wonderful."

"But it was a tiny service and it was on short notice. It was a weekend whim, really." Then, the killer: "I was thinking of you the whole time."

He leaned back in his chair, tried his best to smile naturally. She would feel shabby for not inviting him, so he said, "No way I could've made it anyway. May is a busy time." A lie. May was the slowest month of his guiding year.

"That's what I thought." She hid her mouth behind the wineglass.

He'd never felt more alone, more pathetic, more undeserving. She hadn't wanted him there, that was the only explanation. "So that's why you've come? To tell me you're married?"

"No. I mean, that's part of it. But it's been so long, hasn't it? Too long. That's why I'm here. I want to learn you."

He thought of what he'd been doing in May, of the lonely days he'd spent tying flies while Caroline was on that meditation retreat in California. "You could have brought Thad. I'd like to meet him."

"I'll bring Thad next time. I wanted some quality time with my pop."

He swallowed whatever this feeling was, and leaned forward and kissed her cheek. "Congratulations. My little girl, a married woman. How is it? He must make you laugh."

"I'm sorry, Hank. I should have called you. I should have invited you, even if it was on a whim. Even if we hadn't talked in like forever."

He brushed this aside. "Don't think twice. I'm just glad you found someone who makes you happy."

As their meals came, as he forced himself to eat, as they laughed about this and that, he saw and turned over each of his failings as a parent, as a man. If Caroline had been there, he would have grabbed her and begged her to start a family with him, to start fresh and do it right from the beginning. He would do it now, could do it now, because now he realized: there was nothing else.

When the bill came, the server placed it by Hank and he reached for his wallet.

"No, absolutely not." Annie snapped it away. "This is my treat."

"Bullshit," Hank said, surprising even himself with the sudden and too-loud profanity. People turned and looked. "My treat. A late wedding present."

"It was my idea and I won't allow it."

Hank opened his wallet, intent to pay the server, before Annie could extract her credit card from her purse. But he found only thirty-eight dollars, less than half of what was needed. And by then, thank god the server had taken Annie's card.

Annie smiled and said softly, "Let me do this for you."

Chapter Ten

IT WASN'T LIKE this great error of his life had occurred in the capsule of a single moment, some apex scene where the bright sun disappears over the dark horizon and that's it. His great error was in fact a million little errors that had assembled slowly and imperceptibly, accumulating like a glacier's ice pack and measured like one too: not in days or even years, but in decades. What was life but a disorienting progression of fragmented ambiguities that resisted any attempts at ordering—until viewed through the fictionalizing lens of hindsight? Then, and only then, could sense be made of it. And by then, what was the point? Nothing could be amended.

Life wasn't like a river, no matter how many stupid pop songs said it was. A river could be known, its channel could be learned, so that even on the foggiest *predawn* morning, a person could pick the right line, one move at a time. No metaphor could capture or illuminate life's chaotic unknowns, its swift determinism, its painful irrevocability. No, life was a precarious balancing act between enjoying the time you had left and surviving the mistakes you couldn't quite identify. Of this much, Hank was sure.

*

HE AND ROSEMARY had been struggling for years. They'd dovetailed well enough when they were both single, unattached riverfolk. Put them in a boat, give them a sunny afternoon, and they kept each other amused and giggling all the way past midnight. That was the thing: Being happy riverfolk was about keeping the stakes low. Once the stakes got high, the island of merriment that was the river vanished. Then the river either became a mechanism for procurement or was relegated to scenic backdrop status.

Rosemary had been all too ready to relegate the river, and their former selves, to backdrop status, the panorama behind their new, ultimate-stakes lives. It was time, in her words, "to grow up." For Rosemary, the river life had been little more than a fun stop on the otherwise calculated trajectory of her existence. A short-lived rebellion from a life that had been scripted long before, by whom Hank wasn't sure.

That was the difference between them. She was of money and so needed to procure more; he was of nothing and so was content with less. Her pangs of insufficiency would be resolved, she thought, by a prestigious career; his would be resolved by a better understanding of his role in this place.

Riffle came as the turning point, the moment that definitively ended the rebellion.

But for Hank, there wasn't a road that led away from the river. The river was the river, which was to say, it was everything. If she wanted to call this a rebellion, she clearly didn't understand rivers.

The sun was orbited by the planets, the planets encased by their oceans, and the oceans fed by their rivers. There was a straight line, as far as Hank was concerned, between the river under his feet and the universe over his head. Everything flowed into the river, and the river flowed all the way to the Center. You could turn outward toward the arbitrary hubbub of concrete and career, or you could turn inward toward the infinite connection of water and gravity. When he explained this, Rosemary called him an escapist, which was exactly what he would have called her had he thought of it. He also would have said that only in a private moment of connection with a river and its creatures could the outer world so fully diffuse into the rumble of the nearby currents that the nearby currents could fuse with the ecological systems encompassing all; only in this moment would the complete cosmic reality condense and expand at once and render a single infinity of timeless divine. For Hank, for Caroline, for Walter, for Danny, no single moment provided this reward in such sprawling proportions as when a steelhead rose to a dry fly. It was that simple, and it was that complex. Maybe his life was "petty," as she had said, but if so, then he had fundamental disagreements with her unit of measure.

In the years after, Hank came to reduce these fights to a single essential disparity: Both he and Rosemary had only the highest of expectations for themselves, but how they defined "highest" differed entirely.

She had wanted to leave the valley a little after Riffle's second birth-day, but he'd refused. "We need to raise her with all the advantages," she would say. And he would completely agree. "We need to offer her the best education," she would say. And he would point to the river and say "absolutely." "We need for her to live in the cultural cen-ter, where her intuitive and rational mind can be developed." And he would say, "That's why we're here." For Rosemary, the valley was a last colonial outpost on the fringe of the civilization. For Hank, it was the rarest thing in this world, an authentic community built around the divine rituals of harvest, a refuge of civility and culture amidst a world intent on *hara-kiri*-ing itself on the sharp blade of "efficiency."

Finally, when Riffle was five and about to start kindergarten, they found themselves in a fight so hot it would leave them burned. Riffle was asleep in her room and they were out back in the firs and ferns. Rosemary had stayed in Ipsyniho as long as she was willing, "longer than she should have." She was leaving, and she was taking Riffle, and Hank could either come or he could become a weekend dad. A joe of a father. She said, "I'll fight you for custody and I'll win, you know it." And with that, she had played her ace.

Riffle was still the bubbling little river girl then, a five-year-old who already knew how to ferry herself to the far bank with just a couple quartering backstrokes. She had raised two steelhead on her own, learned to herd crawdads into the shallows where they could be collected en masse, and taught herself to build windproof shelters from driftwood. She could debone a trout with her bare hands and spot the bulge of a prime chanterelle before it emerged from the duff. Her tan was deep, her feet calloused, and he hung on every word she spoke. She laughed as easily as she sang, and it killed him to imagine her sprightly self in a sweltering concrete shit hole, a place divorced from everything real and permanent and important. A place enraptured by its own whoop-de-do.

In the weeks, months, decades to come, he justified his decision to stay analytically: If he'd come with Riffle, her connection to the river would be severed. They'd become tourists, on the Ipsyniho for a few weekends a year, and Riffle would lose precisely what made her *her*. The river would become an escape from reality, rather than a conduit to reality itself. By staying, he was providing for her the best he could, he was keeping a home for her in the highest place. She would go to town, experience all that self-indulgent hoopla, and then retreat home where her real education could continue. Looking back on it now, he would've made the same decision again.

And that's what was killing him. Because it was that decision that cost him his daughter. Wasn't it?

When he was completely honest with himself, though, he had to admit that the decision to stay hadn't revolved entirely around Riffle. He had been as concerned for himself as he had for her. He couldn't stomach the thought of a life down there, a joe's nine to five, dreaming endlessly of the weekend—forty-eight piddly hours where his life would be his again. He imagined himself taking to drinking, to gambling, to—god forbid—watching sports on TV.

And so, he'd told Rosemary—in admittedly regrettable language—to go fuck herself. And a week later, Riffle left in Rosemary's green Chevy, waving despite tears out the back window at the father who'd chosen to be near the river instead of her.

Chapter Eleven

THEY AWOKE EARLY, just like she wanted, and towed the boat up to Hank's standard ramp. He'd picked up sandwiches, called in his regular shuttle, and brought three rods—the seventy-one thirty-three, the forty-one nineteen, and the seventy-nine six, the same three he always brought on a guided trip this time of year. They were the first people to the ramp, a clean thirty minutes before legal light.

"How will we retrieve the truck?" Annie asked.

"Somebody will drive it down for us."

"Who does that?"

"Julianna and Petra. Ten bucks. It's their living. Good folks."

From his closet of wading gear, he'd found a men's tall-small that fit her nicely and a pair of boots sized in men's sevens. She wore them now, as she staggered over the dark beach along the first run. He'd have to keep a careful eye on her to ensure she didn't go for an unintended swim.

Like so many of the underinitiated, she tried to walk over the river's cobbles as if they were flat and solid concrete: legs parallel, arms down, center of gravity somewhere just above the waist. Most every step, her footing slipped or shifted and she was falling out of balance.

"Try bowing your legs, sweetie." It was understandable she'd forgotten how to wade. "And keep your arms out, so they're ready to balance you."

Casting came more quickly. He started with the single-hander loaded with a weight-forward, medium-belly line, and knotted on his go-to dawn dry fly. She'd learned to cast all those years before and still retained a frayed mastery of the basics. Eleven and one, wait for the backcast to straighten before moving forward, don't cast more than you must, you won't catch fish with your fly in the air. She cast a stalling line across the current, and after the current straightened it, he reminded her to follow the swing with the rod tip.

It took a while, well into the dawn, but then the rhythm returned to her, and she sent a clean thirty-footer across the tailout. The fly landed and was in swing and Hank was just about to congratulate her when she lifted the fly into a new backcast. "I've forgotten how satisfying it is to feel the rod chuck the line."

"Sure, but the point is fishing." It was a stupid thing to say, and not even true, and he instantly wanted it back.

Her next cast landed in a pile.

But whatever. Annie was there with him again, tucked between the black ridges, the river reflecting the last stars as they faded into the crystalline dawn, and what more could he want? A father and a daughter in a moment disjointed from its history, in a moment between histories. She laid out a new cast and followed the skating dry fly, and it was as if she'd stayed with him all these years and still went by Riffle and allowed him to share all that had been shared with him. In that moment, her fly waking over the glassy surface, the legacy remained intact. He lit a cigarette and tucked his hands in his wader pocket and tried to memorize every detail. Perfection never lasted.

"When did you start smoking so much?"

"Cigarettes?" He'd first dabbled with them in adolescence because the girls he liked liked boys who smoked, and he'd continued to smoke the occasional stick into his forties. But the daily habit began later.

"I don't remember you ever smoking when I was a kid."

He'd started in earnest only twelve or fourteen years back, during a week of self-destruction. There had been the three boxes of Camels from the 7-Eleven, the binge at the tavern, and the dirty fight with that random trucker. And, of course, the crash on the way upriver and the broken leg. Funny, looking back on it, how the cigarettes had lasted longer than the limp. Rather than tell her this, he lied, though he wasn't quite sure why. "I started smoking cigs when I quit smoking grass, twenty-something years ago."

"I didn't know. I never knew."

"I kept it a secret."

"What other secrets did you keep?"

He snuffed the smoke on the sole of his wading boot and dropped the butt in the film canister he carried in his wader pocket specifically for this purpose. "That's it."

LATER THAT MORNING, just about the time the red sunlight appeared on the ridge tops, she said suddenly, "I wish you still smoked pot. I mean instead of smoking cigarettes." He had just finished explaining where she should cast, where the fish held, and where she'd want to stall the swing of the fly. She must have smelled his breath. "Thad smokes pot."

"The pediatrician?"

"He doesn't smoke all the time, just an occasional weekend. You won't get cancer from smoking every pot every now and then. You should quit those things."

"I think that ship has sailed."

"You can still quit. There are all sorts of gadgets and gums to help. Cigarettes are evil."

"But do I want to quit, is the question." He'd decided a few years back that smoking enhanced his daily life sufficiently to justify the possibility of an earlier demise. A more contemplative and satisfying middle age seemed a worthy trade for a shorter, more abrupt old age. Maybe even a smart play, given how horrendously aggravating those years after seventy-five looked, especially when you were on your own.

And the pot these days didn't resemble the stuff he'd enjoyed thirty years before, when he could smoke a whole twisty to himself and have a nice, fishable buzz. The last time he'd tried a toke of the new stuff, off one of Danny's joints, he'd ended up lying on shore for an hour trying to determine which voice in his head was his own.

"I just want you around, that's all." She made a new cast, but looked to him instead of following the swing.

"I've always been here, always will be."

She glared off down the shore, and he thought she might curse him for so rarely calling. He cursed himself for that lapse all the time, which made him feel more shabby and awkward, which in turn made him even less inclined to dial her number because then he'd had to face her rightful judgment for not calling. It was a lame and pitiful loop he'd been in now for years, and he hated himself for it.

But she surprised him: "Thad lost his father last year. It was real sudden."

A long-shelved memory appeared as vivid as the tailout before him: the lonely drive to his own father's deathbed, the rain splattering up from the log trucks, the manic beating of the windshield wipers. It had taken a week for the man to pass, the first week they spent together in twenty-something years. "Heart attack?"

"Stroke."

"Good way to go. Fast."

"Gosh, Hank. When did you become a masochist?"

*

HE TOLD HER all the standard stories, the little anecdotes that instilled the scenery with a sense of history and narrative, the stories that lent plot to this place. It was these stories that gave clients a feeling of possession, of mastery, and it was a sense of mastery over fish or place or both that drove them to dig deep into their tipping cash.

Over the years, the stories had morphed, becoming simpler and less concerned with the absolute facts of their parent events. Sometimes, when Hank was feeling inspired, he would fill in the gaps with florid details, maybe add a character and delete another, maybe twist the event for hyperbolic effect. What did it matter if they were true or not? These dudes would forget the story the moment they stepped off the plane back in LA or Houston or Duluth. It would fade like the fish, like the river, like Hank himself, into the scenery of their own tale in which they, of course, were the hero.

But this time, he was driven by a compulsion to be entirely truthful.

As they drifted past the cement pillars and barren foundation of what had once been the Thompson Cottage, he told her about the newlyweds from Eugene who had bought the place, arrived for their honeymoon, and had a hundred-year-old fir smash through it the first night. "The tree crushed the front half of the house and they had no exit. But that was the least of their problems. It also cracked open the woodstove and the fire swept through the debris. They had no choice but to jump off the balcony into the river. They were nude, of course." Only after he finished telling her about how they didn't make it to shore for a quarter mile and about how they'd sprinted through town like a rogue Adam and Eve did it occur to him that he couldn't quite recall if the fire in the house had started when the tree fell or sometime later. And maybe they hadn't jumped into the river nude. Maybe they hadn't jumped into the river at all. He'd told the exaggerated version so long, he couldn't determine where the exaggerations ended.

Nonetheless, Annie enjoyed the story, and recounted one of her own, about a German couple she'd helped while vacationing in Grand Cayman who had their clothing stolen as they skinny-dipped. "The whitest people I've ever seen."

"You were in the Caymans?"

"Oh yeah, regularly," Annie said. "It's Thad's favorite place."

Of course, Hank thought. The guy is a tourist in his favorite place.

Which only spurred Hank to tell more stories. At Barrier, he explained the unique pool's geologic history, how it had once been a lava tube that had been buried by subsequent volcanic eruptions.

"As the river ate down through the valley floor, it uncovered the tube, busted through the top, and now runs right down what remains of the cylinder." The geologic stories were much easier to keep straight.

As were the historical facts: at Boat, he pointed to where the tribal fishermen had kept their summer camps, to the place where they smoked the fish, to the runs from which they netted the chinook, the silvers, the eels, the smelt, the steelhead. "They had names for the runs on the river, names that had been passed down for generations. In the best runs, they even had names for the important boulders and ledges."

"Why do you all call this place Boat, then? Why don't you use the original names? It'd be a nice show of respect."

"We don't know the names. The legacy was broken after the Rogue River Wars, when the cavalry rounded up all the remaining natives in southern Oregon and marched them to a camp on the coast. The first European anglers didn't arrive for twenty years after."

Just after lunch, they stopped at Mossy Rock, at the pool of apparently stagnant water behind it, water that was separated from the main flows by a granite ledge. This hot spring was a place he never stopped with clients, a place the guides never shared with a tourist. They anchored and stripped to the bathing suits Hank had suggested they bring and tiptoed their way into the scalding water. To cool the pool down, Hank grabbed the boat's bailer and heaved in a few gallons of icy river water.

"Do you remember coming here with your mom and me? We used to come all the time."

"Maybe I remember, but only viscerally. No details, only this feeling against my skin. Holy shit," she sighed, her eyes shut, her head resting back on the rocks. "It's so womblike."

"Funny you say that." Hank pointed at the shady patch of sand beside the pool. "That's where you were conceived."

Annie glanced at the patch. "Looks uncomfortable."

Hank smiled. "That's not my recollection."

*

THEY HADN'T RAISED a fish all day, though Annie didn't seem too concerned. She wasn't that interested in the fishing, and repeatedly deferred a run to Hank, saying she liked watching him more than bumbling around at it herself.

But Hank made sure to have the boat at the top of Faux-Colman by 3:30. They waded onto the midstream ledge and into casting position and waited for that band of shade to fall over the bucket in the tailout. He knew fish would be holding there, and the sudden loss of the glaring sunlight would wake them from their midday stupor, and a correctly cast dry fly might entice a fish to come busting through the surface.

"That elk jerky," she nodded back at the boat. "You hunt too?"

"Not really. I mean, I carry a rifle in the boat during elk season and I usually get one, but I'm not of the hunting temperament. I just like meat, and cows kill salmon."

She thought about this. "What about chicken?"

"Rats with feathers. A ruffed grouse, now that's a bird worth eating."

A lock of hair had ended up in her mouth and she blew it to the side, just like Rosemary used to. She was so much her mother's daughter. "What else do you like to do?" she asked.

"Besides fish?" The shade was just now crawling up through the rapid. The steelhead would be ready to see a fly soon.

"Yeah, besides fish."

He shrugged. "I like boating. Swimming. Reading. Cooking. You know. But steelhead are enough."

"What is it about them?" She was looking downstream, into the sunlight, the baseball cap he'd lent her pulled low, and the river reflected in her sunglasses. "This is, like, what you do."

From the tone, he could tell she had meant, *all* you do. He tried not to be insulted. "What is it about steelhead?" It was a frequent question from the spouses of clients, who often accompanied their mates on the trip, forced to watch their partner flail obsessively at the river. Nonetheless, it was still an impossible question for Hank to answer.

Should he tell her of their awe-inspiring life cycle? How they were born in a small patch of gravel in the headwaters and lived in the vicinity for two years before descending the river to the ocean, where they would traverse the Pacific shelf all the way to the Aleutians and Russia's eastern shore gorging on baitfish and crustaceans before turning and swimming all the way back to their natal river and—impossibly—to the same gravel from which they were born, where they would spend one to ten months without actively feeding before spawning themselves. Their offspring, which would emerge a few weeks later, would do it all again.

Or should he speak of the mysteries, the questions yet to be answered, both biological and behavioral, like what allowed some rivers to have enormous fish and other rivers to have only smaller ones, and why were some populations more inclined to take dry flies than others, and how was it they were able to find the precise location of their birth after so long?

Or of the cunning and attractive features of their personalities? For instance, their curiosity; they frequently jumped vertically out of the water and looked straight at a person on shore who'd just spoken loudly. They sometimes tracked a swinging fly, nipping at it with their mouths or tickling it with their fins. And of course, they often ignored a real insect to strike a pinecone or leaf.

They were the underdogs of the fish world too. Once inhabiting every coastal trickle from the San Mateo north to the Skeena and around to the Kamchatka Peninsula, they had been vanishing at a steady pace for generations. In the fifties and sixties, the southern California populations vanished, in the seventies and eighties, the northern California populations, in the nineties and oughts, the Oregon and Washington populations, and in the coming twenty years, the Canadian populations, which were on a straight trajectory toward oblivion. Now, only a few American rivers still had wild runs, the Ipsyniho being the most notable, and even here the fish were a couple bad years away from extinction. Their populations were robust when their rivers were pure, delicate when their rivers were damaged.

But for him it really came down to the steelhead's rivers: wild, rugged, raw places, places forgotten and untouched, places with mysteries. Steelhead offered an opportunity to explore these places with purpose, and in intimate proximity.

He could go on for hours; in fact, he had and probably would again.

The appreciation of all things steelhead was one thing he never had to explain to Caroline, and one thing she never had to explain to him—the reason, maybe, she'd kept him around longer than his expected shelf life.

"They're individuals," he finally answered. "Each one is different, and each one is worth getting to know. And," he added a second later, "each one is worth fighting to save."

"But it's a fish, Hank." She was looking off downstream, and he wondered if he'd heard her straight.

He blurted, "They're the coal mine's canary," and then worried his tone had revealed too much.

She turned to him. "We need fights, don't we?"

"You and me?" He was about to charge on, to say, I never wanted to fight with you, but she continued before he could.

"All of us. We need something to fight for. We need a cause."

"We need love too."

"Maybe," she said. "We'd like to think so anyway, but really, we just fear loneliness."

The shade had fallen over the water and he didn't like where this was headed. He handed her the rod and said, "Here. Drop that fly on that seam. The one near the patch of yellow grass."

She cast the two-hander like he'd showed her, but her top hand overpowered the bottom, and the fly landed quite some distance from where he'd hoped. Nevertheless, the current brought it around, and a half-second later, it was gone in a bolt of silver brighter than the sun.

She did nothing—a reflex remembered from her youth?—and the fish leapt again, coming down broadside and leaving a divot the size of a car door in the surface. Annie's rod was bucking and the reel was screeching out line and the fish was leaping beside them, then turning and blurring downstream as fast as any fish Hank could remember.

He pulled the boat's anchor and helped Annie in, who was by now laughing obscenities, and they were off following the fish through the rapid and into the next pool, where Hank anchored again and Annie was able to regain all that backing and most of the fly line. Soon the fish was beside them, and Hank waded out and reached a hand for the leader and followed it down to the fish, gripping the fly in one hand and slipping the other under the pectoral fins. It was a female of ten or eleven pounds, gunmetal and cobalt.

"Can I touch it?" Annie asked.

He helped her find delicate purchase on the tail joint, and unpinned the fly and said, "She's yours to release."

Annie didn't waste any time. The fish kicked and was gone.

On shore, Hank was shaking from the excitement of it all, as if he hadn't been party to thousands of landings in his life, but this was his daughter and everything was different. She'd handled the fight, the landing, the release, all of it with innate competence. The early lessons must have remained in her somewhere.

Annie pinned the fly on the hook-keep.

"So?" Hank asked.

"It was fun," she said. "I'd forgotten how fun." She seemed about to say more.

"What is it?"

"Nothing."

When he probed, she finally came out with it: "It seems kind of wasteful, that's all.

To hurt the fish like that and then just let it go. To catch it for no reason."

"For no reason?"

"Yeah, I mean, if we were keeping it and eating it, that would be one thing, but to just let it go . . . it seems cruel." When she saw his face, she amended, "But it was fun. Don't get me wrong. I really enjoyed it."

For the next hour as they drifted toward the takeout, as she spoke about Thad and their courting, about the trips they'd taken to Europe and South America, about the life she had been living since he'd let her go so long before, as she spoke about all these things, one word she had said echoed back again and again like a rifle's report ricocheting between the ridges: *wasteful.*

*

ANNIE SAW THE body boat before Hank did, near a patch of heavy brush in the Wright Creek Run. As they neared, Hank saw three firefighters reaching long poles into the limbs. He oared down, hoping to get Annie below their boat and out of sight before they succeeded in retrieving whatever it was they were after.

As he passed, one of the firemen recognized him and shouted across the water. "Had to turn up eventually."

Chapter Twelve

IT **WAS A** good thing they fished when they did. The next day, the air temperatures climbed into the low hundreds, and the water temperatures followed suit, climbing into the midsixties, and the fishing shut down. Hank knew the steelhead would be crowding into a few holes, those fed by icy submerged springs or cool tributaries, and that they would likely refuse every presentation and every fly an angler offered. It hadn't been this hot since that week with Patrick O'Connell.

Annie slept in the next morning, and Hank left her a note with ideas for breakfast and drove down to the fly shop to find out what he could about Morell.

Danny had done great things for the store. The former owner had been a royal schmuck, dishing out trips only to guides willing to work for less than the going rate, underpaying the fly tyers, refusing to lift a finger to help on any conservation projects. In fact, the guy had sided with the State and lobbied for the new hatchery complex. The only reason he stayed afloat was because Danny worked there. Even at eighteen, Danny could talk Ipsyniho steelhead all day, every day. The customers loved him. He'd had this way back then of making a customer feel like the most interesting person in the galaxy, which usually prompted them to buy more than they intended. When Danny quit, the shop lasted only six months or so. No surprise. Danny bought the inventory for a steal, about the same time the twins were born.

Now the shop was booming, even in these less-than-easy times. For one thing, Danny knew precisely which rods, lines, and flies to carry. There were no bullshit products on the walls, gimmick rods or soulless lines that had all the right advertising and all the wrong heart. If you found it here, you knew it would work. For another, Danny had started a blog and contracted a pair of geeked fish junkies to write for it, how-to bits and fishing reports and videos of people landing big fish. Joes from all over the West tuned in daily, and when they needed something, they clicked on the shop catalog for discount rates. Because of the onslaught of orders, Danny had recently hired a full-time box packer.

Danny was there with the twins, who were watching cartoons in the back office while he helped customers. Hank went past the counter and into the office and took a seat between Miriam and Ruben, and lost himself in their world of high voices and flashing pinks and blues. Ruben whispered, "Do you have any jerky?"

"Not today, sorry bud."

But Ruben rested his head on Hank's shoulder anyway, and the minutes quickly became a half hour. When Danny came in, he said, "Sorry about that. It's been like a Saturday around here."

Back in the shop front, Danny poured them each a cup of coffee. "I take it you've heard?"

Monofilament was spread across the counter, and Hank went to work tying up the leaders Danny had started but not finished. "Heard what?"

Danny pulled shut the office door so the twins wouldn't hear and said, "Andy. Carter arrested him last night."

"Arrested?"

"It's gotten real ugly," Danny said, leaning on the counter now, close enough to whisper. "Carter isn't talking, won't return my calls, and Andy is locked up and can't be bailed out until Monday."

"What did they find?"

Danny shrugged. "Fuck if I know."

Hank looked out the shop windows, across river road, like he was expecting to see something there that would answer his question, and all the others. "Has Andy been charged with any—?"

"He was arrested for murder."

"Fuck off," Hank said too loudly. Both the twins turned his way, spotting him through the glass pane separating the office from the shop floor. Ruben smiled.

"At least that's the word." Danny shrugged. "But like I said, Carter's not returning my calls."

*

HANK CHECKED THE sheriff's office, Carter's home, and even the hospital, but didn't find the man. Finally, the morning heat already too much for his Bronco's air-conditioning, he turned upstream toward Annie.

Andy Trib might have been a transplant, but the guy was solidly Ipsyniho now. Just last spring, he'd laid spike strips across an access road being used by log trucks to reach a headwater clear-cut; two trucks, driving in tandem, rumbled over the strips that morning. Andy then laid another strip lower on the road, which ruptured all four tires of the service truck sent to repair the first blowouts. But vandalism wasn't the only trick up Andy's sleeve; he also had a way with words and had, three times now incited protests at the Board of Forestry's annual meetings. Maybe most impressively, though, he'd once organized a midnight incursion onto a cattle ranch that had for years allowed its livestock unfettered access to Feather Creek. The cattle had devoured the shoreside vegetation and trampled the soft clay banks, causing catastrophic erosion that had smothered the spawning redds downstream. Hank, Walter, even Trout Unlimited had failed to convince the rancher to amend the situation. So Trib quietly solicited donations from guides and clients and caring citizens and, by the cover of darkness, led a team of thirty-something volunteers down the waterway. In one night, they constructed a twenty-foot buffer all the way down the creek, restricting cattle access to a cobbled beach on the inside of a bend. But in the savviest move of all, Trib convinced a reporter to show up the next morning to document the improvements; the small-town headline read: "Local Rancher Repairs Damaged Stream." After that, the cowman left the fence standing.

When they'd first met, Hank asked Andy why he'd chosen to move all the way to the Ipsyniho. Andy said he'd been reading about the river since he was a boy and had always known this was where he'd "make his stand." "Got to live someplace, and figure the Ipsyniho needs all the friends it can get."

It was precisely this determination that had bound Andy and Danny all those years before, when they were both brimming with that omnipotent optimism native only to twenty-year-olds. They had been fast friends from the beginning, and in the years since, they'd been through drought and high water. To Danny, Andy was a brother, a confidant, and an advisor and an uncle to his children. Their bond was deep and immovable, and it was this bond, more than any battle on behalf of the watershed, that had endeared Andy to Hank. Say what you might about Andy's occasional elitism or his often banal sense of humor, the guy was Danny's closest friend.

But Andy had never gone out of his way to please those he didn't respect. Carter, for instance. Only a couple years back, Andy had called the state game trooper to report two people fishing hardware in the fly water. The trooper responded fast, as they usually do to reports of poaching, but decided not to issue a ticket. Probably because the anglers in question were Sheriff Carter and his grandson and the location was just one pool up from the legal boundary. No fine may have been levied, but that didn't stop Carter from showing up at Andy's house to give him hell. In the time since, Andy had taken to calling Carter a "lazy-ass fuckup," and Hank had once heard Carter refer to Andy as that "prissy know-it-all."

Surely, this arrest had more to do with spite than evidence.

The thermometer on the deck read ninety-two degrees and it was only 10:15. Annie was sitting on the couch fanning herself with a magazine and reading a book titled *The New Global Ethics: Contamination, Consumption, and Future Generations.* When he proposed they go for a hike someplace cool, she flung the book down and said, "Yes, that's exactly what I need. Anything but another bullshit rehashing of Kant."

They drove with the windows down upriver, parked at a wide spot, and followed the rocky trail that threaded Slide Creek Valley. Hank had packed them a lunch of cheese and crackers and fruit, and by the heat of the day, they were lounging at the base of Magic Falls, two thousand feet above the valley floor and the watershed's coolest spot. The falls fell from a windblown cliff into a cylinder-shaped ravine, where the water-chilled air remained trapped. Caroline called this place "air-conditioning alley," and in fact, Annie found it so cold she pulled on a fleece.

Stunted firs grew from the craggy rocks, none taller than four feet, their compressed frames sculpted by their environment. Some, Hank knew, were over a hundred years old. Tiny cutthroat trout rose in the pool below, eagerly attacking any flake of dirt he tossed their way.

"This is where the native Ipsynihians spent the hot days," he said. "People have been weathering heat here since King Tut."

They'd been lost in conversation more or less since leaving the truck, mostly Annie's excited answers to Hank's questions. Like her mother, walking fueled her talking. For which Hank was glad. On the river, she'd been pensive and aloof, but here she was almost giddy. And he was too. He was eager to learn everything he'd missed, to memorize all the stops in her life in the years since they'd last seen each other.

Since leaving the truck, he'd learned much about Thad, about Thad's childhood in an old-money North Carolina family, about how they'd met at a party in graduate school, about how he liked to paddle a sea kayak around Nantucket. Thad was "brilliant," she said, "capable of accomplishing anything he set his mind to." He'd been a star at Johns Hopkins, a star since; jobs had fallen at his feet. He was a master of every hobby he ever tried, and with half the effort of those failing around him. "People resent him," she said, out of breath, "because he makes everything look so easy."

He'd proposed under a full moon on a Caribbean beach, after insisting on a Thursday night that they fly there the next morning for a weekend in the sun. She called it either "impressively" or "oppressively romantic"; Hank wasn't sure which.

Something about Thad led her to transition to her dissertation, though only half the words she used to describe it made any sense to him. In fact, the only term from the title that he recognized was "imperative." He asked a couple times for clarification, but her attempts to elucidate did little to improve his understanding. He got the sense that graduate school was mostly about learning a new language with which only the graduates themselves could communicate, in effect creating their own little island community. What he wondered, what he couldn't be sure of, was whether what they were talking about was really any more complex, sophisticated, or illuminating than what everyone else talked about. But, nonetheless, he found listening to her easy navigation of the language its own kind of music. Here was his daughter, probably the smartest person he knew.

They sat together on a mossy slab of granite, the falls roaring nearby, and ate Gorgonzola on crackers. Out in the distance, they could see square clear-cuts on most of the ridges and the rusty smoke of a new forest fire. Late summer in Oregon.

What had the view been like from here a thousand years before? What would it be like a thousand years from now?

"Do you and Thad think you'll ever have kids?"

"Hank."

"Just asking."

Annie shrugged, and that was that. She changed the subject. "I have to ask. Thad asked me and I didn't know the answer and that got me curious and I called Mom but she said you were the one who picked my name."

It was thirty years ago, but he remembered as clearly as he did the fish she landed yesterday.

"I mean," Annie said, "'Riffle is not really a name other people have. There must be a story."

"No story really," Hank said. "Just the name I picked for you."

"I could understand Brooke or Finn or something like that."

He'd been standing in a riffle holding Rosemary's raft when she told him she was pregnant. The air had been cooling with evening, the sun in their eyes, the breeze picking up. But that wasn't why he chose the name. The name hadn't come to him until the night after she was born. The fire had died down in the cabin and he got up to add a new quarter round and there she was, her face compressed and wrinkled and wedged against Rosemary's breast. A smear of milky saliva ran along her cheek and he cleaned it with his pinky. This was his daughter. This was his family. In that moment, he felt more whole and satiated and essential than he had at any moment in the decades before or since. The name had come to him then, in the lee of this new life.

"Riffles have mysteries. They might be five feet deep or five inches, it doesn't matter: you'll never clearly see the contour of the bottom." She didn't seem to understand this. "A riffle is the river's point of balance."

"Sometimes I wonder," she said, looking up at the cliffs that surrounded, "what might have happened if I hadn't changed my name."

She was saying so much more than just those words. But did she mean, what might have happened if she'd stayed, or did she mean, what might have happened if he'd moved with her to Chicago?

He put his hand on hers, and his heart pounded with the risk—this was the first intimate gesture they'd shared since that embrace when she arrived.

She surprised him. She leaned and rested her head on his shoulder and said, "Tell me a story. Tell me a story from back then." And for a small moment at the base of those falls, it seemed everything might work out.

Chapter Thirteen

ON THE RIDE up to Caroline's, Annie asked, "Did you know the guy?" meaning Justin Morell. Hank had just finished explaining what Danny had told him at the fly shop, that one of the other guides had been arrested for murder. He hadn't said much about Morell before this moment; he didn't want her impressions of Ipsyniho to be tainted by violence and by death. Deep down, maybe, he had allowed the notion that she might, someday, return to Ipsyniho, might buy a little home along the water and be near him again.

"I did. He was a young guide. We weren't close. But I knew him." He fished around on the seat beside him and found the picture he'd taken from the corkboard at Morell's house, the one of him and Walter. "He took this picture."

Annie pointed at the image. "Who's the old guy? He looks familiar."

"Walter. A good friend. You spent plenty of time in his boat when you were little."

Annie set the photo on the dashboard. "How old was he?"

"Walter?"

"No, this dead guide."

"Twenty-something."

Annie put her arm out the window and let the wind lift it up and drive it down—just as she had when she was five years old. But now she shook her head like something wasn't right, and retracted her arm. "Twenty-something."

"Just a kid, really."

They arrived at Caroline's for dinner a little after seven, just as the evening's coastal winds began sweeping through the firs and rustling the alders. Annie held open the gate, her sundress waving in the breeze, those dusty sandals below. Her hair was held back by a bandana, and she was wearing the sleek polarized glasses Hank had given her. Except for the lack of a substantive tan, she looked like she'd lived her whole life in the watershed.

Though no local ever would have pulled a device from her purse and said, "Shit, no service."

Caroline and Annie hit it off from the get-go. They drank a glass of wine while Hank cut mushrooms and onions and squash and threaded them onto the kabobs and another while he massaged the elk tender-loin he'd put on marinade at 5.00 a.m. Like Annie, Caroline was a confident and articulate converser, just as capable in a conversation about politics as she was in one about stream ecology. And Caroline had, herself, spent half a decade living on the East Coast, in what she sometimes referred to as her "parallel life." But most impressive to Hank, Caroline was capable of asking Annie challenging questions about philosophy. Twice Annie said, "Oh, that's such the right question." When Hank left to put the meat on the grill, neither of them seemed to notice.

Out back, he smoked a cigarette and listened to the simple sizzling of food over heat.

There'd been a message on the answering machine at home, a message he'd listened to twice. It was from Danny, who'd finally gotten a hold of a deputy friend. Turned out Carter believed Justin Morell had been hit in the back of the head. "He says there's a divot in Morell's skull, like someone clocked him with a baseball bat." Danny was worried about Andy. "Maybe you best not go repeating what I told you, about Andy and Morell getting into it on the lower river. Maybe it's time we all went hush-hush on this one."

That seemed futile at this point. Stories of conflict traveled like wind in the Ipsyniho Valley. But Hank would do Danny any favor.

When Hank returned, Caroline gave him a kiss on the cheek and whispered, "She's terrific, so bright and hilarious! Are you sure she's yours?"

Annie was across the room, checking the device in her purse. "Got her mother's brains and my good looks."

Caroline refilled Hank's wine glass and said, "You know, Annie, your mom and I were good friends back when she used to run raft trips. We couldn't have been even your age. Twenty-five, maybe, something like that. Is she still living near water?"

The three of them carried chairs out to a wrought-iron table in the grass, and Annie recounted how her mom had quickly climbed the ranks at a Chicago architecture firm, how she'd settled down with a city planner, bought a place with a view of the lake. Now they were both retired and spending half the year sailing the world. They'd spent last winter in the Mediterranean. "I'm continually amazed by how together she is. I mean, she went to school while being a single mother. I can't even imagine that. Such an accomplishment."

But Hank had been there any time she needed him. It wasn't like she had been ditched, not like so many single mothers.

"Next time you see her," Caroline said, "ask her if she remembers the night we drove to the beach and swam in the moonlight. You should know, Rosie was"—laughing now—"wild back then."

"Aren't the beaches here freezing?"

"Not freezing. Forty-something probably," Caroline said.

"Talk about an accomplishment," Hank said. Then felt silly for saying anything at all. Both Caroline and Annie were looking at him. "She really was wild."

*

THE TENDERLOIN WAS overmarinated and so didn't grill at the speed Hank had anticipated. The outside remained tough from the excess salt and the inside was pink and stiff and he'd fucked it all up. He shouldn't have put it on marinade when he did since the cut had already been exposed to salt the day Annie arrived in town, the day they went to the Lodge for dinner. Or he should have diluted the marinade. Or he should have wrapped it in mashed potatoes to extract the salt from the original soaking and then started again. Or . . . whatever. He'd fucked it up and there was nothing he could do about it now.

"I don't know what you mean," Caroline said charitably. "It's delectable."

Annie nodded, gnawing at a bite. "It's very good."

"Thanks," Hank said. "It's meat, but that's all it has going for it."

Caroline had made the dessert, and it turned out exactly like she'd planned: a blackberry cobbler with hand-churned ice cream. She'd picked the berries that day while her client fished Heart of Darkness, a run on a lower drift that split a gauntlet of blackberry bushes. It was the first place the berries came ripe in the Ipsyniho Valley, and Hank was sure Caroline had selected that float for the berries, not the fishing. As a garnish, a pair of mint leaves topped each bowl, and their aroma lent the dessert a crisp chill. It was spectacular. Each bite sent you traversing strata of flavor: musky dawn, saccharine fog, dusty thundershower. Hank went back for a second helping. Then a third.

"You guys do it right," Annie said.

"Anything worth doing." Caroline's mouth was full of cobbler.

As the sun set, they walked Samson and Delilah up the old skid trail to the ridge top and looked east. The last rays were sending orange streaks through the smoky air, and the few clouds above them seemed to have been placed there with pink pastel.

Caroline sent the dogs into the meadow to run loops and tire themselves, and they went straight to the thicket in the far corner, their noses to the ground. "Must be a raccoon over there," Hank said.

Caroline called once, and when the dogs didn't return, she shrugged and said, "Old Mr. Raccoon has nothing to fear from those pacifists."

Pacifists they were, despite a combined weight of hundred and seventy pounds. Hank had once seen them chased up the shore by a mother duck, just sixteen ounces of waddling quack. He turned to tell Annie the story, but found her typing a message into that little device. "Now?" he said instead.

She didn't look up. "I know. Can't believe there's service here."

Caroline tossed him a glance: *Let it slide.* She put her arm around his waist and called again to the dogs, who were now obscured by the brush.

"I remember when we couldn't get a landline," Hank said. He and Rosemary had tried in vain for a year to convince the phone company to put a line up to their house on Rock Creek. He'd had to organize most bookings by mail then. Despite the inconvenience, he was sure the world was better off then, when a place equaled a headspace. Now cell phones and these newer gadgets meant you could transpose one place, one set of concerns, over another—a place could vanish even though you were standing on it.

Caroline sparked a joint and passed it to Annie. "Rosie and I smoked a few of these in our day."

Annie looked from the device to the weed. "Oh wow." She typed a couple last words, and tucked the thing in her purse. "Really? Mom?" She pinched the paper and brought the joint to her lips. As she exhaled, "Hank?"

He waved the joint away, but Caroline said, "Come on, stud. Everybody's doing it."

Caroline could handle her pot in a way Hank could not. She tried to tempt him every now and then, often while naked, but Caroline's dope, like Danny's, was too strong for an old bugger like him. This time, though, it was Annie handing him the joint. "Come on, it'll be fun." What it was, was a chance to bond with his daughter.

He inhaled shallowly, just a little, but when he exhaled, hardly anything came out, and so he took one more. That one tasted pretty good, so another couldn't hurt.

"Look at this!" Annie said, effervescing now with the stoke of it all. She spun and said, "I mean, it's fucking beautiful out here!"

Caroline laughed. "In love with the ground under her feet."

"But the sky!" Annie said. "And look, there's the first star! Holy shit," looking back toward Caroline now, "you can touch the stratosphere from here!"

Caroline took Hank by his beard and pulled him toward her and wrapped her arms around him and said, "You."

Annie smiled at them, and for a moment, Hank imagined what it might have been like if he was hugging Rosemary now, if this glowing soul dancing before them was the Riffle they'd raised together. He imagined it so clearly that he felt it.

They'd spent their lives together in the valley and she'd grown to value the place above any career, and that vacuous feeling that kept him up nights had never existed because his greatest accomplishment lived a short walk away, and Riffle said, "You two are so cute together. So adorable!"

The dogs erupted. Hank was slow to turn, slower than Caroline and Annie, but he turned in time to see Samson and Delilah sprinting across the meadow, howling in fear. Behind them, a fat old skunk lumbered up the shoulder of the meadow.

*

IT WAS SOME time before Hank felt comfortable to drive. The weed had affected him profoundly. He hadn't just felt high, he'd felt altered: He'd touched a parallel world, a place where things went like they should have. But what had spooked him, what had left him ataxic and dislocated, was that in this other world, things hadn't been any more right. There hadn't been the warm satiation, the soulful abundance. It was just as distressing, only differently so.

The hours it took to clean the dogs gave him a chance to get a grip. Caroline had a stash of V8 in the pantry, and they lathered a dozen cans into the dogs' fur and then, while the freshly washed mutts rolled in the dust, two more cans on their own arms. The smell of skunk would follow them for weeks, a surprising whiff here and there and a steady sourness under all their midnight dreams.

"That smell," Annie said, sniffing at her fingernails as they rumbled off Caroline's land back toward River Road, "I think it'll always bring me back to this moment."

Once at home, Hank went straight to the Internet, to the one place removed from all places. He was squinting through his reading glasses and pecking at the keys when Annie put her arms around him. "Slave2chrome" had posted a technical question on Speypages about matching lines to a specific rod. He owned the eighty-one thirty-four with the stiffer tip pattern and was looking for a Scandinavian line for throwing dry flies. "If this guy follows the line charts, he'll end up with a five-forty, which he won't even feel on that rod. He won't even feel it! A five-seventy, that's what he needs. This is important."

"Are you all right, Hank?" Annie's breath smelled of toothpaste and she was wearing her pajamas.

"Of course." She looked like she had something important to say, something on the tip of her tongue. He asked, "What is it?"

"Caroline's great. I like her. How long have you been together?"

He told her and explained how they met. But he didn't tell her that he'd wanted to marry her or that she wasn't inclined to share her life with a man. He wanted to say all this, he wanted a moment of perfect honesty, a moment without any of the filters he'd been maintaining since she arrived. He was exhausted by worrying all the time what she thought of him. And yet, he couldn't stop.

Annie said, "Do you remember the last summer I was here?"

The question caught him off guard. He looked to the computer screen, to the images of rivers on his screen saver. "Umm, boy, that was a long time ago."

"I think about it," she said.

And of course he thought about it too, so much so he didn't know where to begin talking about it, and the moment grew awkwardly silent. Finally he found words: "What do you think?"

"Oh . . . ," she said, like she was about to say more. But then she leaned in and kissed his cheek and said, "I'm glad you're happy."

He forced a smile, because he wanted her to believe he was happy. Then he said, "I'm glad you're happy too." And watched her walk down the hallway and into her bedroom and shut the door in her wake.

Chapter Fourteen

HANK LAY AWAKE most of the night. Any time he dozed off, the drowning rushed in and he shot upright gasping, the adrenaline coursing to his hands and feet, turning them to needles.

Annie's arrival had thrown him, his routine, out of whack. He felt dislodged, in a way, from himself. Here he was trying to impress her, trying to be someone or something that was remarkable. He had repeatedly caught himself shoehorning facts or details into casual conversations, looking for any chance to prove he hadn't wasted the last thirty years. There was the Guide of the Year Award from the Wild Steelhead Coalition, the River Steward Award from the Ipsyniho River Trust, the Lifetime Recognition Medal from the Native Fish Society. But what did any of these slips of paper mean to a doctor of philosophy? From that height, his accomplishments must look like specks of dust. But of course Hank didn't see these awards as accomplishments, he never had; they were the cairns marking his real accomplishments: successfully lobbying the Board of Forestry to protect the headwaters of Steamboat Basin; identifying a lingering population of winter steelhead in Feather Creek, a population assumed extinct for forty years; petitioning the state fish and wildlife board to abolish the catch-and-kill regulations for wild fish in the Ipsyniho Valley. These were the successes of his life, the things that made him a household name in the households of Ipsyniho steelheaders. But what could they mean to her, a cosmopolitan woman for whom the Ipsyniho and its polite residents were little more than an amusing stop on a backwoods vacation? To her, the Ipsyniho and its troubles would look insular, peripheral, obsolete. Maybe that's how she saw him too.

It wasn't that he felt any resentment toward her, that wasn't it. She had brushed aside his life's work: "wasteful." And there was that device, how she longed for it even when he was right there to keep her company. And there were the little things, like the phone at night, how she didn't brag to Thad about the river or the hikes but instead rushed to ask about the goings-on back home.

But there was his overflowing appreciation for her willingness to return, for her eagerness to explore his life and share her own, some of it anyway. That flood of loneliness, which had been undercutting his once-stable banks, had ebbed for the moment. And for that, he was infinitely grateful.

He did mean something to her, that's why she was here.

Poor thing. Imagine her own loneliness in that moment, in all the years of moments since he said he wouldn't move to Chicago. What could she have thought but that her father didn't fully appreciate her, didn't love her as a parent should, as all the other fathers loved their children? He remembered that feeling from his own childhood, and it killed him to think he'd passed that most isolating reality on to her. His greatest failure.

They had planned on collecting crawdads that day so many years before. Hank was to teach her the method he'd learned from Rosemary, a system she'd learned from her octogenarian landlord. Hank had borrowed a half-dozen traps and gathered chicken scraps and fish entrails, and was now busy packing their lunch. "With any luck, we'll have a feast tonight," he said. Teenage Annie had, in the week since her arrival, remained aloof and pensive. Hank had assumed such behavior was typical for any seventeen-year-old female left isolated from her gaggle of friends, and hence, he hadn't pressured her to divulge her feelings. In truth, he was worried she might have had her heart broken by some adolescent Romeo, or her virginity swiped by some Chicago Don Juan, or any number of personal traumas he wasn't the least bit qualified to understand. Though according to all those parenting books, her remote demeanor should have been seen for what it really was: an invitation for dialogue.

"Do you even care?" she had said as he smoothed mayo over the sandwich bread. He turned to find her scowling behind him. This was the first he'd seen her all that morning, and he had no idea what she was talking about. He asked her to clarify, but she stormed outside. He found her waiting in the truck, listening to her headphones. She'd stayed listening to her headphones as he placed the traps on the way upstream, as he dropped the boat into the river, as he oared them downstream. She refused to fish, she refused to pull the traps. She just listened to those headphones. He tried to parse the events of the prior days, but he could locate no fight or miscommunication that might have ignited this rage—he figured she must have brought it with her. Only when he handed her the sandwich for lunch did she roar, as if this sentiment had been building for years, the Clark's Fork turned into the Missoula Sea by a quarter mile of glacier: "You're just so into yourself that you can't even see the people around you!" It was exactly the kind of blindsiding comment that he'd come to expect from Rosemary. It was meant to lure him into an argument, and he refused on principle to bite. "I'm sorry, sweetie. I don't know what you mean. But I'm here, and I want to understand." Was that what he'd said, or what he should have said? "That's because," she continued, "you don't care about anyone except yourself, you know that? You love this river so that you don't have to love me." She was crying now, and he reached for her, but she pulled back. "Don't touch me." And then the clincher: "You left me." Annie had on her own reduced the situation to the simple but caustic equation: Dad chose the river over me. And what could he say? Caught off-balance and underprepared, he did his best to articulate the reasoning behind his decision to stay. "Ultimately it was about you. It has always been about you." But his articulation lacked something, confidence maybe, and Annie saw right through it. He pulled the anchor. "Would you like to oar?" he asked. She turned to him, calm now, and said, "You mean nothing to me. Do you know that? Do you care? Nothing."

If only that were true, she could have been free from the burden that was her father. Maybe his life had been more than worthless, more than wasteful, maybe it had been *harmful*. He'd certainly harmed her.

Because he was a selfish prick, so selfish it'd taken him fifty-something years to notice.

But back then, he'd still been the hero of his story. And that fight was the first that cut through all his bullshit, the moment when the truth rose through the currents of self-delusion and smacked him as he so deserved. It sent him staggering through middle age. Every time he picked up the phone to call her, he remembered her words. And more often than not, he simply put the phone back on the ringer; she was better off without him. *She'll call when she's ready.*

No wonder she hadn't invited him to the wedding. It was a miracle she was here now.

He couldn't waste this opportunity as he had so many others. If it killed him, he had to make things right with her—with the only part of him that would live past him. If only for her sake.

Chapter Fifteen

ANDY TRIB WOULD go before a grand jury, charged with murder. Danny called to deliver the news, and when Hank called Walter, Walter said, "I'll pick you up, and let's give that two-bit sheriff the love he deserves."

Hank left Annie a note on the counter, and forty minutes later he and Walter found Carter meeting a reporter at the Ipsyniho diner. They ordered coffee and sipped it silently as they listened to Carter answer the reporter's questions.

Carter had been born and raised in the valley, and was just a couple years older than Hank. He'd been elected sheriff for the first time in the seventies and, as far as Hank could recall, had run uncontested every cycle since. In a valley of libertarians, there isn't a lot of interest in being the long arm of the Man. But Carter had taken to the work and, in the eyes of most, did a decent job balancing the responsibilities of his position with the god-given liberties of his constituents. For instance, Carter let a lot of bad laws go unenforced, though he'd never admit as much publicly. Everyone knew that if you shot a deer or elk or bear out of season for the meat, Carter would look the other way. "A man has got a right to feed his family." If you were sipping a beer on the way home but keeping between the lines just fine, Carter would let you keep the bottle. "A man has got a right to cool himself down." And if you were growing a plant or two or fifteen on the hill behind your house, Carter would shrug. "A man has got a right to farm his soil as he sees fit, don't he?"

And so it came as a surprise, especially to Walter, that Carter had rushed to arrest a guide for a murder that wasn't even a murder yet for sure. "Nobody has even seen that autopsy paperwork. Carter is looking to make himself a star here. This is a chance to end up on the Eugene news, and he knows it." Walter sucked his tooth, called the server, asked for another coffee.

Finally Carter was shaking the reporter's hand, and Walter grabbed his arm as he came past the table.

"Hey guys. Didn't know you did breakfast down this way."

"Have a seat, Cart," Walter said. He nodded at the space beside Hank.

Carter checked his watch. "Love to but I'm swamped today. Don't know if you've heard, but there've been some developments on this Morell case."

"Now, Cart. Have a seat."

Hank smiled at Carter, trying to counterpoint Walter's barely bridled aggression. Walter always had a hard time holding his temper.

Carter sat, said, "Figure I got a minute or two to spare."

"I'll make it brief, then," Walter said. He finished his coffee and leaned forward. "This is bullshit. You know it, we know it, everybody knows it. Trib didn't do shit to that little punk. You've had it out for Trib for years, on account of his being a foreigner." To Walter and Carter and most other folks native to the valley, the word *foreigner* applied to anyone born outside of Oregon.

"Whoa, whoa, whoa." Carter waved at the allegations. "All due respect, Walt, but you don't know every angle on this one. I've got some information."

"Really? I know Morell's head was cracked like an old watermelon and I know that Andy and he were having a bit of a tussle, and I know you found a fish club in Andy's boat you think might be the 'murder weapon,' and I know you got your eye on running for the state senate. That ain't the whole story?"

"Well." Carter cleared his throat. "There's a bit more than just that. Who told you I was running for the senate?"

"What more do you got than that?" Walter slapped a hand to the table. He leaned back and looked to Hank for support.

Hank said, "You're picking on Trib. Just about everybody in the valley had a bone to pick with Morell. And half of us got a fish club, the rest a Pulaski."

Carter shook his head. "I can't be in the business of talking about ongoing thing-or-merathers. No offense, gentlemen. You know I got nothing but the utmost respect for both of yous, but this is an in-process matter. We're talking about a killing here."

"Or we're talking about a cocky kid who slipped and cracked his head on rock," Hank said.

"Here's the short and long of it," Walter said, his voice quivering with anger. "Trib ain't a foreigner no more. Sure, he ain't no native, but he's got rights all the same. We can't sit by while you or any Johnny comes along and fucks with his shit. He's losing clients every day you got him locked up. You know that. Now, if he was caught in the act, or you had some of that DNA gimmickry, that'd be a different story. But to everybody in the know, it looks like you're just getting even for that state trooper thing, and well, that ain't right, and you know better."

"He should have known better," Carter shouted, then glanced around to see if anyone had heard. Leaning closer, "I was fishing with my grandson for fuck's sake. You don't go calling enforcement on something like that. Talk about rights."

Hank and Walter shared a look.

Carter passed a hand through his hair and said, "I hear you, Walt. I do. But I've got a responsibility to solve this thing. Trib says he was home alone that whole day, but his truck was seen at the ramp, and that's not the all of it. According to Morell's girlfriend, Trib showed up at their house the night before Morell went missing, yelling and carrying on." Carter stood up from the table, suddenly thinking better, it seemed, of continuing this conversation. "Just give me few days on this one. I'm the sheriff for god's sake. You know I don't go messing in folks' business unless I got good reason."

He walked all the way to the door before turning around and coming back. In a whisper, he said, "And don't go telling nobody about the senate, all right? My mind ain't made up on that yet."

*

HANK AND WALTER drove straight to the fly shop, and found Danny at the casting pond with a customer. He was demonstrating a single-spey with a Scandi head. "The fly drags and provides the resistance. And you can pivot at that moment and send the cast anywhere." Danny rotated forty-five degrees in midcast and sent the fly across the parking lot and into the bed of Hank's truck.

"Dropped her in the bucket," Hank called.

Danny smiled and lifted the line in an oval that climbed twenty feet over his head and carried the fly all the way around and then out, across the casting pond to the circular target on the far end.

"Kid's good," Walter muttered.

"The best."

They waited by the coffee pot while Danny finished with the customer. The guy wanted the rod, but said he "needed to check with the wife" before he bought it. When the customer left, Danny said, "Now he goes straight to his laptop and buys the thing used online. Shit. This business, I'm telling you."

"We were just about to go see Andy, if they'll let us."

Danny nodded and pulled out his cell phone. A moment later he said into the device, "Hey, wondering if you can work the front for an hour."

*

THE COUNTY LOCKUP had been built in the early sixties using plans drawn up probably a half century prior, and the place still retained all the charm of an old-West jailhouse. There were two cells, each with bunk beds and a toilet, separated from each other and the larger room by heavily rusted iron bars. Outside the cells, there was a woodstove and a stack of split fir, and a few feet away, the jailor sat reading a hunting magazine. Andy was the only occupant. Not a lot of arrests were made in Ipsyniho.

Walter knew the jailor's father, and when Walter asked, the guy pointed his magazine toward the cells and said, "Have at it."

"I keep waiting to wake up," Andy said, slouched against his cage. There were no windows and no natural light. The place smelled of urine and mold, and Andy looked as if he hadn't slept since his arrest. "I'd much prefer the one where I go to class naked." Before settling in Ipsyniho, Andy had done a stint at college. He brought it up often.

"Fuck this." Danny torqued on the cage bars and dust shook free from the ceiling.

"Listen," Walter said. "We know you didn't do it. Carter has got his ambitious head up the ass of some cartoon elephant."

"What?"

"Don't matter. Point is, we won't sit by with you rotting in here."

Hank checked to be make sure the hunter was lost among his carcasses, then pulled a paperback copy of *The Habit of Rivers* from his back pocket. "A little something to keep your mind on the water." Hank and Andy had always had books in common.

Andy tucked the book down his pants, checking the guard as he did.

"You can keep that copy."

"Tell us," Danny said. "What do you need?"

"I didn't fucking do it," Andy said. "I didn't. Sure we had our shit, but I'm no killer. You know me, I feel bad as hell when I bonk a fish. You gotta help me. You got to make Carter know." Andy said this last part to Walter.

"I'm working on it," Walter said.

123

"I can't stomach the thought of everybody thinking I'm guilty. This is slander. I'm going to sue the piss out of him."

Sue was a dirty word in Ipsyniho. Sports sued. Locals worked things out like people. "You ain't gonna sue nobody," Walter said. "Now listen, somebody musta seen you that day."

"I was alone. I parked at the ramp and walked down to this spot I found, just a few casts. I was alone. That was it. Then I came back up. Didn't see anybody. Didn't see anything."

"This spot I found" was code for "a secret place that I've never shown you." So, Andy Trib had a few tricks up his sleeve after all. Who knew.

"You didn't see Morell?" Hank asked.

Andy glanced at Danny before answering, and Hank got the impression there was more going on here than he knew. Andy shrugged. "I didn't see anything."

"But you told Carter you were at home alone."

"It was simpler. I didn't think anybody saw me up there. And he came gunning for me, asking all these questions, and I got spooked. So I told him I was at home. It seemed easier."

"Do you have a lawyer?" Hank asked.

Andy nodded. "My father, he hired a guy from Portland. I'll see him tomorrow." Andy came from money, everybody knew that.

"That's a start," Walter said. "But a lawyer can't recognize his own dick unless he sees it on paper. We'll work the source, we'll work Carter."

As they left, Andy called out, "Hey, do me a favor."

"Anything."

"Bring me something worth eating. That guy"—Andy nodded toward the jailor—"is bringing me leftovers from his house and, I swear, the meat's rotten."

Chapter Sixteen

H ANK AND ANNIE spent the day in a raft on the fast and mean upper river, where *Class IVs* were stacked one atop the next; Caroline was at the oars. Annie seemed to love the ride. For a time, she sat on the bow, her feet dangling over, her hands gripping the oh-shit cord. When the raft punched into a standing wave, Annie would shriek, then laugh. She looked fifteen up there.

"Your mom had a reputation," Caroline said while feathering the sticks, "for not putting up with any bullshit from her clients."

"I'm not surprised," Annie said. "She's got a similar reputation now."

"Once when we were running a joint trip, I watched her broadside the boat through a rapid. This one guy took a wave in the face and fell inboard." Caroline laughed at the memory. "Later, when I asked your mom about it, she said the guy had been telling sexist jokes all morning."

They were passing Wolf Creek. Hank pointed at it. "We spent weeks last winter up there transplanting beavers."

Annie laughed. "Excuse me?"

"From other drainages, private ones, where the owners were going to shoot them for flooding out their fields. Beavers are listed as vermin in the Beaver State, go figure, right? But you put a few beaver families in a basin and water temps go down, rearing habitat goes up, and silt stays off the redds."

He had to stop this, stop trying too hard in all the wrong ways. Like a teenage boy, he was, compulsively showing off for the pretty girl.

This time Caroline bailed him out. "Your dad here has a reputation of his own. Bet you didn't know he's somewhat of a guru."

Annie smiled. Whether out of humor or surprise, Hank didn't know.

"He all but invented dry-fly-fishing for steelhead."

Hank corrected her, explaining that dry flies had been fished over Atlantic salmon for generations and that Lee Wulff and Roderick Haig Brown, two famous authors and anglers, both fished dry flies to steelhead before Hank was born. "I'm just a fisherman."

"But you can't deny you've advanced the technique. You've changed the way people think of it entirely. See," Caroline said to Annie, "people used to fish dry flies that mimicked natural insects, thinking steelhead were striking because of some latent reflex to attack buglike things. But your dad didn't buy it. He thought steelhead were striking because of curiosity."

"That's not *my* theory," Hank said. "Enos Bradner was arguing the curiosity theory sixty years ago. Lee Spencer argues it now. I got it from him."

"But you're the one who caused the radical shift in the flies people were fishing," Caroline said. "Because of your dad, people now fish big flies in unnatural ways, not like bugs. Just look at the people on the river; they're all fishing Hank's way."

Annie said, "Huh."

"And you can't deny," Caroline continued, "that you developed the lines for turning over those flies. That's all you."

"It's silly," Hank said. "Fly design. Presentation. Who cares?"

"I think it's pretty neat," Annie said.

"It's why we're together." Caroline laughed. "I always wanted to date a rock star."

They lunched in the shade beneath Eagle's Nest, and after, they sprawled out for a little siesta. Annie took a book up the bank and sat in the moss, and Caroline rested her head on Hank's shoulder. After a minute, he realized she was watching Annie.

Her own daughter was grown and out there somewhere. In the years they'd been together, he'd twice seen Caroline come unhinged, both times in the winter when she wasn't working much. The first time, he'd found her locked in the bathroom, shaking and speechless. The second time was just last December, when she'd become distraught after seeing a film about an orphan who escaped Auschwitz. When Caroline lost it, there was no bringing her back. She didn't even want solutions, he'd come to understand; she simply wanted him to take her in his arms and share the burden. Now, he passed his fingers through her hair and told her he loved her.

"What a blessing," she said.

He wanted to say, *Yours will come too*, or something else optimistic, but he knew better. Caroline would never meet her daughter. And even if she did, neither of them would know.

Caroline stood and pointed to the top of the cliff. "Come on, Annie. Forget that book and follow me."

Annie laughed. "You're kidding."

"Don't be a siss. It's a thrill." Caroline grabbed her hand and all but pulled her up.

Hank called out, "It's a big jump, Caroline."

"She can handle it."

Hank pulled himself from the ground and hurried to catch up.

Eagle's Nest was a massive slab of granite that teetered over the river. From the lip to the water was easily fifty feet, and downstream was a torrent of *white water*. According to Walter, the native Ipsynihians had once used the place for a coming-of-age ceremony that concluded with a headfirst dive. "It'll be fun," Caroline called.

Hank caught up with them near the top. Annie was laboring for breath and shaking her head. Beads of sweat were tracing down her back. "Really, I'm not sure."

"But you've climbed this far," Caroline said. She was smiling that smile of hers, the one that was meant to dare its receiver into being as carefree as she was.

"She's not interested," Hank said. "Carrie, stop it."

Caroline laughed. "Ah, Hanky-Jo. Always worried about your women." She stood higher on the hill than either of them, her hands on her hips as she caught her breath. Her muscular arms were ripe from the day's rowing. "Come have a look, Annie."

This is what Caroline did. She challenged people into contests of resolve—contests they probably wouldn't win. Caroline had leapt from Eagle's Nest a thousand times; to her it was known risk. To Annie, it was probably five times higher than anything she'd jumped before. And with that rapid downstream, this was for real. This wasn't just some lake jump.

Hank touched Annie's shoulder. "You don't have to do this."

"At least look," Caroline said.

Annie climbed another step. "I'll look, but I'm not much of a jumper."

As Riffle, she'd been a fanatical jumper. Hank had always stopped the boat by small cliffs and large boulders, places in still water where a person could jump in safety. And Riffle had charged off these places again and again, only quitting when Hank insisted they move on. As she grew, he actually became a little concerned, concerned that he might have created a person without a healthy dose of fear.

So he was pleased when Annie peeked over the lip at Eagle's Nest and shook her head. "Jesus. People jump from here?"

Caroline said, "You'll feel great after."

Annie backed away from the edge. "I'm not a big free-fall person, actually."

"You'll feel so alive." Caroline backed her heels to the edge. "Let's do it together."

"Leave her be," Hank said. "Caroline, enough already."

Caroline took off her baseball hat and her sunglasses and tossed them to Hank. "We're not your responsibility, Hank."

Annie walked one more time to the edge, her toes a little closer to the lip this time. "Really? You think I can do it?"

Caroline smiled. "I think you should do it. I think if you don't, you'll regret it rest the day. You'll regret it on the flight home. I'll wait for you below." And with that, Caroline backflipped out of sight. A moment later, the splash echoed off the far shore.

"Holy fuck," Annie said, looking down. "She went in headfirst."

She always did. In diving and elsewhere.

Hank nodded toward the trail. "After you." But Annie was still looking down. "Annie?"

"I'll do it if you do it."

"Jump?"

She nodded. She was scared, but she was smiling. "I want to do it."

Caroline's echo from below: "You'll love it!"

Annie tossed Hank her hat and sunglasses. "I'd rather *we* do it together."

And so, he pulled off his shirt and set the sunglasses and hats in the shade and joined her on the edge. The water was a mile below. "You're sure about this?"

"One, two"—she jumped and he followed a half second behind.

⁕

AFTER THEY SHUTTLED the truck and cinched tight the raft, Hank and Annie followed Caroline up to her house. Caroline had organized a barbecue that night in Annie's honor, and the guests would be arriving in another hour or two.

Annie said, "I really like Caroline. She's just so alive, you know? So fucking real. She just does what she wants, no bullshit, no conditions. I can see how she and Mom were friends. Mom is like that too, just in a different way." Then she said, "I'm glad you two have each other."

"Have" might have been a strong word. Caroline "had" him, surely, but he would never "have" her. "To have" implied a certain degree of permanence, and permanence wasn't something that interested Caroline.

129

He remembered something she had said one rainy winter day. They were lying on the futon in the loft, watching the water braid down the window, and she told him of a Chinese proverb she'd read and found especially illuminating. Caroline often read Asian philosophies. Did yoga too. "It's about this old twisting tree. It grew itself to have as many limbs and knots as it could, to be as ugly as possible. Why, right? Because only the ugly and useless are allowed to live the life they desire. The beautiful and straight are cut down to be somebody else's lumber."

"I'm lucky she keeps me around," Hank said.

"She's crazy about you," Annie smiled. "That much is obvious."

A minute or two passed as they climbed the gravel road up from Steamboat Creek. Annie was looking absently out the window. "It must be lonely around here if you don't have someone."

Before thinking better of it, Hank responded, "No. It's never lonely." Why say that, he wasn't sure. He also wasn't sure why he was still talking. "With a river like this one, there's always some sense of purpose."

"Purpose?"

"There's always something to do, a way to stay busy."

"Isn't 'staying busy' what people do when they're lonely?"

"No," Hank said. "People are only lonely when they have no purpose."

Annie thought about this for a moment. A pensive moment in which Hank imagined her deconstructing his logic, testing his assumptions, measuring his deductions. He was no match for her intellect.

Then Annie surprised him. "I get lonely sometimes." She was staring at the passing trees.

He wanted her to say more, he wanted to know all about her loneliness, wanted to confess his own loneliness, but he didn't know how to talk to this woman that was his daughter. That's what he had realized these last few days: When near her, he didn't know how to be himself, let alone how to father. "These trees are cedars. One of the last original stands in the valley."

*

THE GUESTS ARRIVED on Ipsyniho time, driving through the open gate a half hour, an hour, two hours after the time Caroline had told them on the phone. They parked out front of the house, and for several minutes after each truck came to a stop, dust hovered in the calm air, an ethereal mist backlit by the setting sun. Soon adults roared with stories and children chased the blissful dogs. Someone produced a football, someone else a bocce ball set. Yonder Mountain String Band was playing from a truck stereo. And there was IPA being pumped from a keg.

This wasn't the first time Hank had attended a party at Caroline's house, but it was the first time Caroline had hosted a party that should have been, according to the unwritten and unspoken rules that governed these things, hosted by Hank himself. He was considering a public proposal, right here in front of everyone, when a Frisbee came careening by and his hand snagged it out of midair.

"Over here, Hank!" He sent the disc long, and surveyed the crowd.

Caroline was crouched before a little girl of seven or eight, helping her fix a pigtail that had come undone. As he neared, the little girl said, "Thanks, Ms. Caroline," and bolted after the other kids, now out in the middle of the meadow. Caroline watched her go, before returning to her business with the food.

He busied himself with the meat, waiting for her to finish a conversation with Mildred Harrington, the ninety-eight-year-old widow who lived in a crumbling farmhouse just a mile down the road. After taking the elk roasts from their marinade—he'd get it right this time—and placing them on a rack to drip dry, he leaned too close to Caroline's ear and whispered, "Thank you for this."

She said without looking, "Your place is a shit hole, no offense."

Annie was laughing out back with Rita and Bridge, two of Hank's oldest friends. Rita was the valley's midwife, had been for as long as Hank had been a guide. She wore a pair of faded Carhartts, flip-flops, her gray hair in two easy braids. When they'd first met, Hank had been madly infatuated with her; this was before she and Bridge had made children of their own, before Hank had met Rosemary. Back then, she'd been exactly his type: sturdy but luscious, fierce but festive, a mountain momma through and through. He'd made his infatuation known to her in a less-than-sober moment one moonless night, and they'd found themselves kissing wetly and horizontally. There had been a falling out with Bridge, but in time, the transgression was forgiven, and life carried on as before. The river had a way of putting things in perspective.

In the years since, Rita had become, in a way, the valley's closest approximation to a spiritual leader. There wasn't a lot of organized religion between the headwaters and the ocean, but there was an almost universal respect for the power and sanctity of natural birth. In a place a full hour from the nearest hospital, in a place where the year was marked by the birth and death of seasons and species, a midwife was an essential guide between this realm and the former, this realm and the next. Her role was to shepherd the unborn into the dry light and, as the responsibility so frequently fell to her, the dying into the darkness. Few in Ipsyniho asked for a doctor when they were pregnant or a priest when they were dying; these were natural events, not medical or religious ones.

Besides, Ipsynihians had a fundamental distrust of doctors, of the silent control they tended to command over their patients. When at a medical crossroad, you never could be sure if a doctor was telling the whole story or just the simplest one.

Rita had assumed her most crucial role from her mentor, Eleanor Karr, when she passed away some three decades back. Now, there was a monument to Eleanor in downtown Ipsyniho; there were no monuments to presidents or congressmen.

Bridge called himself a contractor, and he had on numerous occasions helped Hank with the house. Just as recently as last week, he had come over with a bed full of tools and supplies, and helped patch a leak in the roof. That was the thing about Bridge; if you needed help, he was there, no questions, no hesitations. That was the covenant by which he lived, community first, a covenant conceived maybe as he hitchhiked away his twenties from Alaska to Argentina and back. It was Bridge who had, decades prior, taught Hank to quarter, cool, and butcher elk. He laughed now at something Annie had said, his long beard bouncing.

Hank arrived just in time to hear Annie ask Bridge, "So are you a fishing guide too?"

Bridge put his arm around Hank. "Nah. What would you say I do, Hanky-Ray?"

"He'll tell you he's in construction."

"I farm." Bridge smiled.

"Oh, of course," Annie said. "I've seen a lot of blueberry and hazelnut farms along River Road. Is one of those yours?"

Rita answered, "We live just down the road here."

"Lucky you," Annie said, turning to take in the view.

"You two actually have met before," Hank said. "Rita caught you."

"Caught me?" Annie canted her head to the side, a display of confusion—her mother's mannerism. Hank had always loved that one, in both Rosemary and his little daughter. She mastered the mannerism early, just about the time she started speaking complete, if abbreviated, sentences. He remembered how back then Annie would furrow her eyebrows, an exaggeration of Rosemary's expression, and raise her voice a full octave on the last syllable.

"I attended your birth." Rita smiled. "But I almost didn't make it. You were quick to get out here and see what all the fun was about."

"You were small," Hank said. "Five pounds, three ounces. When the contractions started, we took a walk on the river trail, and at first your mom was stopping and breathing through each contraction, but by the end she was bear-hugging trees and howling something fierce. We still thought you were a boy then. Were sure of it." It struck him then just how vivid these recollections were, more vivid in a way than his recollections of last week. That was the funny thing about hindsight: As if the whole expanse of a person's time lay in a straight line behind him so that at any given moment if he turned, all he saw was a tiny speck that made him think, *Is that all?* but if prompted just so, part of that distant trail would suddenly climb up and loom larger and closer than all the rest. There was Annie as an infant, here was Annie now, and somehow there was nothing in between.

Annie pointed at the distant river. "Tell me I was born in some back-eddy."

"At the cabin we were renting off Rock Creek, actually."

Annie asked Rita some question about sterilization, and as Rita began to answer, Bridge touched Hank's arm and nodded toward the woods. "Got a minute?"

They strolled off a few steps and Bridge pointed his beer back toward town, which was there shimmering in the distance. "What do you think about this Andy Trib business? You know the kid better than me."

Hank lit a cigarette, still remembering the pasty texture of Annie's vernix on his fingertips. How Rosemary's sweat-glazed skin reflected the candlelight. "What's that?"

Bridge repeated the question.

"There's no way he's guilty. The kid's as tender as a daffodil."

Bridge nodded. "Exactly. A rosebud with testicles."

"What does your man the sheriff have to say?" Sheriff Carter and Bridge went back to primary school, and if anybody had an inside line to Carter, it was Bridge.

But Bridge swatted at the question. "Cart has gone all tight-lipped on this shit. You know he's running for some office or another? Suddenly rotten with ambition, that one. Some jerks get a sports car, some a younger lady-friend, others do a two-for and declare their candidacy."

"Either way, you go tits-up in the end."

"Thank god." Bridge and Hank clanked beers.

A moment passed as they took in the view. Then Bridge laughed. "Heard about his diaries?"

"Carter's?" Hank couldn't imagine Carter reading, let alone writing.

"Trib's. Supposedly, there's like a hundred of them. The kid's been scribbling faster than a prepube."

"Are they fishing journals?" Hank asked. "Most of us write shit down. It's a lot to keep balanced."

"Maybe. Probably. Don't know what else that brie-for-brains would be writing. I love the image, though. Trib sitting on his porcelain throne writing in his diary. It's too much." He was laughing. "Wonder if that's what he learned in college."

But if Trib was too tender, who then?

Danny's truck rumbled through the gate, and the twins leapt out the passenger door—two redheads bailing before the truck even stopped. Danny hollered after them, but they were already sprinting toward Samson and Delilah and the other mutts.

Bridge gripped Hank's arm, leaned in close. "So what's up with Caroline throwing your party? You two getting serious?"

"Who's Caroline?" Hank smiled.

Bridge slapped him on the back. "You filthy hound."

Hank swigged from his beer. Mostly to keep himself from beaming.

"It's natural, it's right," Bridge said, "if you want my three cents. 'Cept of course you're getting uglier every day and she's just coming into her prime. But besides that."

Hank fingered the ring in his pocket, which he'd carried with him continually for weeks now. Tonight was the night.

Later that evening, the sun that much closer to the ridgeline, Hank found Annie and said, "There's somebody I want you to meet."

The twins were grabbing at Delilah's tail and laughing uncontrollably and she was whipping around and around and licking at their faces, and Danny was chuckling at the scene with Trey Something-or-other, a recent transplant to the valley Hank had met a few times in the last couple years, but could never quite remember. There were more and more people like this every year, retirees and yuppie dropouts who moved up the Ipsyniho, but hardly looked twice at the river. He didn't have much in common with these folks; they spoke of falling stock indexes and rising bond rates and seemed to think of him as some novelty character in the movie of their lives. The bearded fishing guide.

"Annie, this is Danny and . . ."

"Trey," Trey said, extending his hand. To Hank he said, "We've met a few times, actually."

"Have we?"

Annie turned to the twins and dogs. "Your kids, I haven't seen them stop laughing in like ten minutes."

"Good. Once they stop, it usually goes to hell." Danny clanked Annie's beer with his own. "Tough to believe you're related to this ol' bear."

"Careful," Hank said. "This ol' bear still knows a thing or two."

It wasn't that he wanted Annie and Danny to connect—how impossible with Annie being recently married—though he'd be lying if he said he hadn't fancied the idea, if only momentarily. "You two used to play together." He pointed his beer at Trey. "Not you. These two."

"I remember," Danny said.

"Yep. I've got pictures of you both splashing naked in a mud bog at Carnival. And another series of crawdadding. You're naked there too."

"Lots of nudity," Annie said. "Doesn't anybody believe in diapers around here?"

It was time to impress her. "Danny here owns the fly shop in town and is somewhat of a celebrity. This guy's mug is in all the catalogues and advertisements."

"Really," Annie said, maybe impressed, maybe not.

"I don't know anybody," Hank continued, "who is as good with a pair of oars or can throw a fly as far."

Danny scoffed. "You're forgetting yourself, old man." Then to Annie, "This guy, he's humble to a fault."

"I'm just realistic." Hank swigged his beer, about to tell of Annie's philosophy training. But Annie jumped in, still watching the kids. "Were your twins born here in the valley? With Rita?"

Hank put his arm around Trey's neck. "Come on, Trey. Let's go snag us another round."

*

THERE WERE THE elk roasts that Hank had made, the cougar backstraps and venison burgers that Bridge had brought, the pot of crawdad tails Caroline had boiled, the two full-length fillets Danny had contributed, a mess of homegrown veggies tossed in salads and churned in salsas, and a whole table of salads and pastas and halved melons. There was a second grill too, this one filled with chicken quarters and veggie burgers and other proteins of deficient genre. Hank stayed upwind.

Folks ate on paper plates and sat in lawn chairs and on tailgates and coolers, everybody within earshot of the grills, everybody with a drop-dead view of the valley. The sunset was crimson and violet, and its warm rays turned the dusty air to sepia. The conversations occurred in patches, three people here, six there, but every once in a while, larger groups would coalesce around a particularly riveting story or good-natured jab. There was a banjo and a fiddle and a pair of guitars, and later folks would be up dancing, and after that, Caroline would lead a group down to the creek for a midnight skinny-dip. They were awash in brandy and good humor.

And at some point, it occurred to Hank that he hadn't seen Annie or Danny in some time, though he did find the twins snuggled up in Caroline's bed, the quilt pulled tight to their chins. Miriam wore her horse PJs. Ruben his bulldozers. They both had Danny's lava red hair and their mother's delicate face, and Hank took a seat on the end of the bed just to watch them sleep for a time, watch but also to listen to the soft rhythm of their synchronized breathing. It occurred to him then that he might, someday, make a better grandfather than he had a father. If only life was charitable enough to offer such chances.

When he finally wandered back outside, a few trucks were rumbling across the moonlit meadow, headed back toward the valley, their taillights illuminating the dust in their wake. He watched as Bridge's rig stopped at the gate and as Rita cinched tight the gate. Funny how folks treated these gates; though there hadn't been roaming cattle here in a generation, still nobody dared leave one open.

He wandered up the meadow, a wide swath that seemed to lead into the star-freckled sky. Above him, the universe glowed maroon in the west and indigo to the east, and around him, the land quivered with crickets. He would die in this watershed someday, maybe in twenty years, maybe in twenty days, but in the moments before it happened, would he ever think, *Yes, I was enough?*

From somewhere below, a song wafted with the breeze. It was the Hunter and Garcia song, "Brokedown Palace," Caroline's favorite, and the words came in shifting echoes that seemed to be growing from the land itself.

Fare you well, fare you well. I love you more than words can tell.

When the time came, would he die alone in some dark room, or would he be looking into Annie's eyes?

Listen to the river sing sweet songs, to rock my soul.

He had arrived at his own father's deathbed seven long days before the man passed. Long enough for his perennial resentments to wither, then sprout anew.

His sisters had both been there and were doing a better job than he, so he kept mostly to the periphery, only occasionally holding the man's hand during swells of pain or telling him stories as he slept, but mostly he remained with the paperwork and the telephone in the corner.

His father was dying, Hank had done his best to remember. He was just a man and he'd done the best he could and what else could a child ask? It was then that the resentments had faded to sympathy.

But in the last days, Hank had realized he still needed something from this stranger, though he couldn't quite name what that something was. One afternoon when the sisters were eating in the cafeteria, he leaned over his father as he slept, trying to find the face of the man he'd known so long before. It had to be there somewhere. He put a hand over the sagging neck, trying to make the chin look as it had all those years before. He concentrated to remember the nose when it was narrower, less red. The eyebrows too, thinner and brown. But the father from his memories was nowhere in that face. Until the eyelids opened and there were those same storm-washed eyes, and Hank sat back in his chair, struck anew by a too-familiar pain.

"Betsy, come back," his father had begged then. Again and again, he called that name.

But who the fuck was Betsy? Not an aunt or sister, and certainly not his mother. He left that afternoon and took a walk by the creek behind the hospital. There were chubs rising against the oily film of the surface, beer cans waiting in the eddies. When he returned a couple hours later, still without whatever it was he went searching for, the nurse touched his shoulder before he could reach the room and told him his father had passed.

*

BACK AT CAROLINE's, he pushed through the front door and heard Annie's laughter. She and Caroline were in the kitchen picking at leftovers, Danny and the twins already gone. Everything the two women did or said seemed to them impossibly funny, and Hank watched for a while trying to let the mood take him too, and when it didn't, he swiped the brandy and pulled hard to see if that would help.

It did.

And soon they were all standing before Caroline's bathroom mirror brushing their teeth and trying not to crack. But it was no use. The more they tried, the more they had to try, and then a little toothpaste shot from Annie's pinched lips and she sank to the floor with the hilarity of it all. Caroline buckled right after her, because of her, and they rolled against Hank's knee and he went down too. Toothpaste foam was everywhere and no one could stand, and the laughing turned to gasping and the gasping to crying.

Chapter Seventeen

THAT'S THE RUB of being a fishing guide, Hank thought come 4:15 the next morning: Even on a day off, you can't sleep past dawn. Even on a day when your head pounds like a salmon thrown too soon in a cooler. He sipped the glass of water he'd left on Caroline's bedside table, took some deep breaths, focused on a distant spot.

"I hate brandy," Caroline muttered in the dark.

"Agh, don't say it."

He lay back, having no other choice given he was too dizzy to stand and too uncomfortable to sit. Caroline backed her naked body against him, and said, "Are you up?"

"I'm done sleeping, if that's what you mean."

She rolled and the silky warmth of her inner thigh was across him. "You know what I mean."

Afterward, they lay together and watched the warming sky out Caroline's bedside window. It would be casting-light in another fifteen minutes.

"Do you think Annie is having a good time?" he whispered.

For a long moment Caroline said nothing, and just when he thought she might have slipped back into sleep, she whispered, "She wants you in her life." To Caroline, that meant everything.

"I don't want to blow it." He thought of Annie sleeping in the other room, her mouth wide open, her hand folded under her chin—just like when she was five. "I don't know how to talk to her."

"Complete sentences, Hank."

"You know what I mean."

"She's here," Caroline said, plucking a pill of lint from his belly button. "Stop worrying what she thinks."

He imagined their next conversation, tried to picture himself letting go of all those expectations he'd kept kegged up, those expectations that turned his tongue to lead.

"Let your guard down. You're so uptight around her. Really, Hank. You're a different person when she's nearby. Tell her a secret. Put yourself out there. Be real, be intuitive." Caroline shrugged. "Be Hank Hazelton. She's here to forgive you."

*

When Hank came in from cleaning the party shrapnel strewn around Caroline's house—the beer bottles and paper plates and corncobs—Annie was stretching herself awake. "Morning."

Guided by Caroline's advice, he'd thought of a couple points of conversation while outside, that poem he'd published years ago in *Gray's Sporting Journal*, that philosophical French novel he'd found at a used bookshop about the stranger who shoots a guy on the beach because the day was hot and the sun was in his eyes, but the hangover had disrupted the usually well-traveled bridge between mental idea and verbal articulation, and now he just smiled at her. It was all he could muster.

"You guys really throw down," Annie said, trying to stand up but then collapsing back into the couch. "Shit. Still buzzing."

The shower started in Caroline's bedroom, the water coursing through the house's vascular system, a rumble and trickle in the walls, then beneath their feet.

Hank poured his daughter a glass of water, found a straw in a drawer, and delivered it to her on the couch. He'd planned on making coffee, but now he couldn't overcome the compulsion to sit back into the soft couch. The Tylenol had helped with the pounding but done nothing to rejuvenate the depleted muscles. He felt like he'd been oaring twenty-four hours straight.

Annie set her feet across his lap and covered her eyes with her arm. "Why does it have to be so bright in the morning?"

Hank couldn't get past those feet, laid so casually before him, touching him. He did the only thing he could think to do: began rubbing at the soles. Caroline often joked that she kept him around because he gave the valley's best foot rubs. And now Annie was squirming. "Too hard?"

"No," she sighed. "Just. Right."

Maybe his hands could articulate what his words could not.

*

ANNIE INSISTED THEY needed a fried breakfast, something with potatoes and eggs and equal parts butter and salsa. "It was my magic cure in graduate school." She found all the ingredients in Caroline's refrigerator and set to work, still in her pajamas, her hair tangled with sleep.

Caroline and Hank were cuddled on the couch, watching the fish tank. Each nursed a mason jar of water. From the recessed speakers, Dylan sang "Desolation Row." Caroline pushed at his pocket. "Your keys, they're cutting into me."

Without a thought, he reached in and pulled them free and tossed them to the floor—but the ring came out too and bounced, then rolled across wood floor. Caroline watched it until it came to rest against the far wall.

He hadn't bought a diamond or even a ring with a setting, just a band of white gold with the wavy contours of a riffle. He'd designed it himself and paid three trips' worth of profit to have it crafted, and now it was sitting there in obvious view.

"What's that?" Caroline hadn't taken her eyes from it.

"What?"

"That."

A stick of butter sizzled in the frying pan. Dylan wailed. Samson barked out front. And Caroline pushed off the couch. She was at the ring before Hank could stand. "It's—"

"It's beautiful," Caroline held it to the light. She wasn't much for jewelry, owning only a couple necklaces and a few pairs of earrings, none of which she wore more than once a year. But this ring, it was exactly her style.

Besides the wavy riffles cut into the band, he'd also had an inscription engraved. She was holding it to the light when he plucked it from her hand.

"It's custom," Caroline said. "You had it made?"

His brain was still hog-tied by the hangover, and he said the first thing that came to him, in a whisper. "It's for Annie."

"For me?" Annie said, leaving the kitchen. "You got me a present?" It made sense: She was a jewelry person, she was wearing three rings now and a pair of small earrings. He took her hand and slipped the ring onto two fingers before finding it fit on her thumb. "I was saving it as a surprise."

"Holy shit." Annie held it to the light. "I love the design. What are those? Waves?"

"Riffles," Caroline said. "It looks great on you. Hank, you've got an eye."

And Annie smiled and kissed his cheek and lifted the ring again to the light and kissed him one more time. "I love it. And it fits too. How did you know?"

"Luck."

When the meal was ready, they carried their heavy plates outside into the cool morning. From the height of the sun, Hank knew it was between 9:30 and 10 o'clock, midday for a fishing guide.

They sat in lawn chairs and ate slowly at first, the pace increasing as the churning seas of their bellies settled and became placid and trustworthy again.

"You know your cures," Hank said.

"Trial and error," Annie said, while extending her arm to get a look at the ring from afar.

Caroline said, "My remedy is the hot springs."

Annie jumped at the idea. Sometimes she was the same little girl he remembered.

Caroline poked him in the shoulder. "You two should get a quick soak. Before the day gets too hot."

He argued they all should go, but Caroline insisted on staying and spending some time with the dogs. "I've been neglectful." But really, Hank knew, she was trying to give them some space, trying to give Hank a chance.

And so Hank and Annie drove up the Forest Service road to the top of the ridge, and followed a spur down the other side to the grove of ponderosa pine in a hanging basin. At the dead end, they parked and followed the rarely walked trail down to the oval hole in the earth, a black pool of steaming water. Echo Basin Spring it was called, by the few dozen locals who knew it existed.

Hank turned his back while Annie stripped to a bathing suit and tiptoed in. "This is perfect!" Her voice ricocheted from the cliffs. "It's boiling!"

Annie told a story of a hot springs she and Thad visited in Costa Rica, how they'd been soaking, just the two of them, in this large stone pool when a lone man appeared from the woods. He was tall and tattooed and spoke perfect English. He waded into the pool, strangely close to Annie given all the room, and began explaining the ins and outs of critiquing coffee, which he claimed was his career. "International publications," he bragged. It wasn't long before he was talking exclusively to Annie. "Thad was so anxious all he could do was chuckle. That's how you can tell Thad is nervous." Thad kept chuckling as the man slipped his hand onto Annie's knee and she smacked him in the nose. "Blood was just pouring out, and the guy was thrashing around, shouting something about never being able to taste coffee again, and Thad just kept chuckling. The whole scene was so Woody Allen."

This was half of what a father wanted to hear: his daughter defending herself. The other half left him queasy. "Why didn't Thad step up?"

"He's not like that," she said. "He'll talk circles around just about anybody, but physically he's as aggressive as a kitty."

Hank thought of Danny, how he would've ground that coffee prick to Turkish grade dust. He asked her where they'd gone together last night, if she remembered him as a boy.

She evaded the questions. "His kids are so sweet." And then she was asking about the pictographs on the cliffs surrounding the pool. Stick figures of people with bows, of elk, of fish. "Are they telling a story? Is that the point?"

"Sure." Hank turned and studied them for the first time in years. That's when he noticed the slab of unweathered rock, the chisel marks at its top and bottom, where someone had cracked free one of the images. Stolen it. Given how few people knew about this place, he had a pretty good idea who was to blame. Walter had a thing for Ipsynihian artifacts. He had a vast collection of obsidian arrowheads, crumbling reed baskets, and leather bags that left a powder on your fingers if you touched them, not to mention the darkest and most distressing item of all: a human skull.

"Why would someone take it?" Annie said.

To Walter, this collection was a show of admiration for the valley's first people. No one spoke with more fervor about their accomplishments. He spent his winter months reading pioneer journals and studying anthropological records, and he could give a full account of the linguistic history of the Ipsynihians, all the way back to their ancestors in what would become British Columbia. "Just think," Walter often said, "if somebody had cared back in 1880, if somebody had even tried to record their stories, imagine all we'd know about this place."

"Did you and Mom ever come here?"

"Once," Hank said. He remembered the day vividly, though he wished he didn't. "I was trying to impress her."

"Did it work?"

"I don't think I ever impressed your mother."

"Of course you did," Annie said. "Tell me about that day."

Hank tried to change the subject, but Annie insisted. So he told her how he'd come up the day before and stashed candles and wine and a bouquet of foxglove. How he'd written her a silly love poem and tied it with monofilament to the bouquet. The mono had actually been two sections bound together by what he considered the purest of bonds, the blood knot. "Ten-pound test, because it perfectly balances strength and suppleness." He remembered every detail; pain had a way of extending a memory's half-life.

"Sounds like a lot of effort."

Hank smoothed the water with his hand, and thought about what Caroline had advised that morning. He took a chance. "I asked her to marry me. Right here. About where you're sitting." It was just days after they discovered she was pregnant.

"Seriously?" Annie asked. "But you guys never married."

He had stashed the ring in the pool and come up with it after a dive. She was reading the poem he'd written, and when she turned around, he was holding the ring in his fingers. He said her full name, said he wanted to be with her for as long as the pictographs had watched this pool. "She said no."

Annie was watching him, and he smiled at her to show that it meant nothing, that this rejection hadn't been that big of a deal. "It wasn't that we didn't love each other. It was the time. We were raised when marriage was about subordination, about ownership. None of our friends were getting married. It was an act of rebellion. We were a generation of rebellion. Your mother especially. It made sense why she said no."

But at the time, it hadn't made any sense, and the rejection devastated him. To him, marriage was the logical and ethical precursor to children. When she said no, he took it as a sign of their bond's frailty, of its temporality. A square knot in two-pound test. To him, it meant Rosemary was thinking of the little baby as hers, not theirs. That she was already leaving him.

Rosemary's refusal had been as gentle as such a rejection could be. It was compassionate and thoroughly reasoned. And yet its mere fact caused Hank to begin severing his emotional ties and to start retreating within himself, extricating himself really from what they had been creating. The authenticity of their intimacy, the very sincerity that so fueled his love for her, began to wither: He was hedging his bet.

Already a prominent figure in his life, the river became his most intimate partner, maybe the only one. Only on the river could he fully detach from the protective mechanisms he now spent so much energy maintaining with Rosemary. Only on the river could he let his guard down and revel in the pleasures of unbridled connection.

"It hurt you though, didn't it?" Annie was watching him.

"Sure," he said. "But she was right, I guess. A divorce would have been ugly, and expensive."

Annie laughed, though without a shred of humor. She turned away, as if she were looking carefully at the surrounding trees. "I think I've had too much hot water."

They climbed from the pool and dried and dressed, and Annie asked, "Do you ever feel like you're repeating somebody else's life?"

Her eyes were wet and she was biting the inside of her cheek, a nervous habit of her mother's. He thought about hugging her, but instead pulled on his shoes. "What is it?"

She found a rock and sat. "I shouldn't have married Thad. I didn't want to marry Thad. I loved him and didn't want to hurt him. But I don't want to be married to him."

"Oh." A surprise that left him unsure of what to say, or what to do with his hands. He tucked them in his pockets.

"He's generous, and caring and kind, but I don't want to be coupled right now. I don't want to be tied down by somebody else's expectations. I don't want to be responsible for someone else's happiness. It's too much. It's not healthy. It doesn't make any sense, practically or philosophically. I should have said no."

He understood. He understood as he'd come to understand Rosemary. The coupled life would interfere with all she imagined for herself. She'd be forced to make concessions, and in the end, she'd be less the person she had intended for herself—she'd live less of her own life. But he also understood as he'd come to understand himself. He knew just how thin and fragile these youthful visions of the life to come were. He knew how quickly the life-to-come became the life-back-then, how suddenly ambition became acquiescence. And he understood how lonely the free life truly was. "You might want a person later. Life becomes heavier."

And strangely, he suddenly felt something for Thad, something new, something opposite of the resentment he'd been feeling since he learned of their marriage. He saw Thad as a boy eager to grasp the life he'd imagined for himself, even if that life wasn't ready to be lived, even if he wasn't ready to live it. The term *son-in law* now fit even though Hank had never met the man and had only seen two pictures; Thad felt sonlike.

Annie smiled despite the tear sliding down her cheek. "I feel most lonely when I'm with him."

She folded up against Hank's chest like she had when she was young, and he remembered what his hands were for; they wrapped around her shoulders and rubbed at her goose bumps. "You came here to see if you can live without him?"

"No," she said, "this trip isn't about him. I came to learn you, Daddy."

Daddy. It was the first time she'd called him that in decades, and it fractured him wide open. Daddy: he'd been one once and maybe he could be one again. He kissed her forehead, and blinked through his own tears, and said, "You feel lonely with him?"

"Do you think I'm a bad person?" she asked. "Do you think I've done a bad thing?"

He didn't know shit about good and bad, but he knew she had done no wrong. "As long as you listen to yourself, Riffle, as long as you don't compromise yourself."

She didn't say another word, and only because of that silence did he realize he had called her by the wrong name.

She took a step away and looked up the trail and wiped at her eye as if coming awake. Finally she said, "But what about other people? Sure, listen to yourself, but sometimes that means compromising some else's future. Right? Have you never thought of it that way?"

He didn't know what she was getting at, but he had the distinct feeling that he'd done wrong. "Sorry, it's an old habit." He'd meant using the name Riffle.

But she turned from him. She cleared her throat. She pointed the way they'd come. "I wonder what Caroline is up to."

Chapter Eighteen

ANNIE WAS NEEDED at work. "Telecommuting," she called it. A lawsuit had been filed and she needed to prepare for a series of conference calls. Hank made her a pot of coffee, a sandwich, and left to drive upriver and chat with Walter. As he left, she thanked him while holding the phone to her ear.

He'd decided long ago that he wouldn't tell her everything, he just couldn't. But he'd told her parts that he'd never told anyone else—even Caroline didn't know that he'd once proposed to Rosemary—and in that telling, he'd found a surprising release, like a tree leaning in him had finally fallen to rest.

The ring wouldn't be a problem. He would just order another one for Caroline, and when he admitted what had happened that morning, Caroline would laugh, and that would help relax any awkwardness. He didn't have much cash left, he'd spent most of his reserve on updating the house for Annie's arrival, so he would pay on credit. But no big deal, this expense was worth a little debt.

He started the truck and pulled left on River Road.

The missing pictograph had gotten under his skin. The skull was one thing; it was spooky for sure, but it was still just a material object, something long on its way to decomposition. The pictograph on the other hand was alive; it contained the fragment of a living story, and without that image, the tale told on those cliffs was incomplete. Caroline would see it just like Hank did, and so he hadn't told her about it, worrying that she might hold it against Walter.

But there was more to talk about than just that pictograph. Cherry Creek Timber was again lobbying to cut, or "salvage" as they called it, the forest burned during last summer's Williams Creek fire. The drainage was home to a small but lingering population of winter steelhead, and cutting the fragile hillsides would require some long-closed roads be reopened and regraveled. Even if every precaution was taken, the cutting operation would further destabilize the hillsides and dump sediment over the spawning grounds. The only benefit to the logging, as far as Hank could deduce, was to Cherry Creek's bottom line, and the handful of men paid a dirt-low wage to do the actual work.

Business had long been doing all it could to fuck up the watershed. Long-term damage for short-term profit. And Hank was, unfortunately, used to the stomachache the steady barrage of logging and mining caused. But this plan was different. It was more sweeping, more potentially harmful, and something about its premise, something about that word *salvage*. Such bullshit. After learning of the proposal, he'd lost his cool and thrown a glass across the house. It shattered, and Annie had called from the other room, "Everything all right?"

Salvage. All lies and misdirections. On one level, the word assumed that trees left dead and standing in the forest were wasted. They needed to be rescued, otherwise they would be worthless. Which, of course, was simply crap. Dead and standing trees were an essential component of a healthy forest, home to all manner of bird and insect life. And once they fell, many would find their way into the creek bottom, providing refuge for all species of fish. But more generally, the dead trees acted as reservoirs of nutrients for future generations of flora and fauna, nutrients that would be stolen if the trees were to be cut and trucked to a mill.

The word *salvaged*. It encapsulated all that was wrong with how people had come to think of the natural world. As if the trees, the minerals, the animals were there for our benefit, for our immediate gain. But weren't we just another player in this system? Might we be here for their benefit too?

Walter had long argued that the old division between nature as resource and humans as resource extractors was hogwash. But so was the new division between nature as beauty and humans as corruptor. The answer, Walter figured, was in the destruction of silly divisions in general, starting with the most flawed and dangerous of them all, the lie of "natural" versus "artificial." People were too quick to term human actions and human products as "artificial" and any action or product of an ecosystem, planet, or galaxy as "natural." But "ain't a human a natural critter too? Just as natural as an ape or deer or steelhead anyway. Anything that natural critter does is 'natural,' am I right? So stop thinking of us as outside of the 'natural' and start thinking of us as part of the 'natural,' and well that'd just about change everything, now wouldn't it? Good luck finding a fool dim enough to 'salvage' his own toes."

But how would Walter justify "salvaging" that pictograph?

WALTER WASN'T HOME, but his door wasn't locked either, and so Hank let himself in, as Walter would surely do if waiting at Hank's house. He poured himself a cup of orange juice—Walter always kept several jugs of the stuff in the refrigerator, believing vitamin C could cure or prevent any ailment if taken in sufficient quantities—and took a seat at the kitchen table. He started flipping through a fishing magazine there, but quickly grew bored of the grip-and-grins and the empty promises and was about to toss the rag aside when he saw an article called "Ipsyniho Chrome." He didn't even have to read the byline to see who'd written it. Someone—Walter surely—had taken a black Sharpie to a page-sized photo of Morell cradling a fish half in the water, half out. He had Satan horns and a tail, and a dialogue bubble read, "Notice the impressive girth of my wanker."

Hank left the magazine and began checking the obvious places first, the cabinets and the shelves, then found himself on hands and knees looking under and behind the furniture. Soon he was checking the bedroom, the gear room, the bathrooms. He looked especially closely at the bedroom closet that contained the other artifacts. He knew the skull was in the shoe box on the bottom, though he couldn't bring himself to open it.

He poured himself a second glass of juice and considered leaving, but then decided to walk around back and check the boat port.

The driftboat was gone. Walter was probably running a trip. He moved some spare oars out of the way and found a green tarp. When he tried to lift it, he discovered the tarp contained something small, heavy, flat. A minute later, he was looking at the stick figures and salmon. Fucking Walter. Some things were inexcusable.

Walter arrived an hour later, his boat rattling against its trailer as the truck climbed the gravel driveway. "One for two," he called as he gently let himself down from the cab. "Farmed the first one gloriously, you should have seen it. A real blowhard, couldn't cast thirty feet if God himself had given him three weeks of lessons."

"Where'd you get the rises?"

"Guess."

"Faux-Colman."

"Close. Tinsel Town." Walter pointed his wading staff at the orange juice. "Pour me one, kid."

They sat on the tailgate eating filberts Walter had roasted in his solar oven, and discussing how they'd handle the new Cherry Creek offensive. "What pisses me off," Walter said, "is if we win, they just try again. If they win, it's over, we're done."

Hank bit a filbert in half. "We got to win every fucking time. They just got to win once."

Walter tossed a nut in the air and caught it in his mouth. Sometimes he was agile for an old bastard.

"With the Morell death and all," Hank said, "we probably shouldn't use spikes or strips or boom-booms on this one. Better to stay small, go through legitimate routes."

"Agreed. Wouldn't want any office cop up in Salem thinking they've got a problem down here in Ipsyniho. God forbid they replace Carter with somebody worth a shit."

They agreed they'd work this the regular route, the phone tree, the e-mail alerts, the blog postings, see if they couldn't drum up enough anglers to flood the state office with complaints. "And I'll get on the horn with the old faithful," Hank said.

"Make sure you get Cynthia at the Sierra Club, and remind her she still owes us one. A long shot, but if you appeal puppy dog–style, you might get her. The yuppie guilt runs strong in that one."

The nuts were gone, and Walter clapped his hands like a coach announcing the huddle was over. "Let's get a motion in. Still got time to get upriver."

Hank checked the sky. "There's something else, Walt."

"Stop your pussyfootin'."

Hank cleared his throat. "I was up at Pine Basin Springs, and saw one of the pictographs was missing."

Walter smiled. "Knew you'd give me shit about that." He spat on the ground between them. "This valley ain't some museum, you realize. There ain't some curator that comes around and keeps things safe in their climate-controlled boxes."

"No offense, Walt, you know I have nothing but the utmost respect and all, but really. You can't just take these things. They're part of the valley."

"And they're still part of the valley. Don't go getting your waders in a bunch. That pictio-graph was already loose. One more freeze and the sheet would have fallen free. Likely would have busted. I did it a favor, that's all."

"But still."

"Still what?" Walter pointed his wading staff at the sky. "If we're going make it to Red Gate, we best get on."

Hank didn't move. He had dinner plans with Annie, and there was no way he was giving in that easy. "You're a selfish old prick, you know that? Let me take it back up to the spring."

Walter climbed into his truck. "Fuck you and your high horse." As the Chevy rumbled to a start, he called, "Rather fish alone anyhow."

*

BUT WHEN HANK arrived back home, he found a note on the table that read, "Danny stopped by and offered to take me out for dinner. Couldn't remember what your plans were for tonight. Hope I didn't leave you in the lurch. See you before too long."

So he extracted some prepackaged burritos from the freezer and set the toaster oven to three-seventy-five and started making the calls. First the Sierra Club, then Trout Unlimited, then the Native Fish Society, then the ten leads on the angler phone tree. By the time the burritos were done, he was already drafting up the action alert.

The phone rang a little after eight, and it was in his hand before the end of the first ring. Steve Burke, his client the day Morell went missing. "Sorry to call so late, but I knew you'd want to hear." Carter had just called him and asked for a full description of the events of that day. "He asked three times if you had left me alone at any point during the trip. Three times, Hank. Like he thinks you might be the one who killed that guide. But haven't they already arrested someone?"

It was probably Carter just tying up some loose ends. Hank told Steve as much, thanked him for the call, and put on a movie.

*

COME MIDNIGHT, ANNIE still wasn't home. His movie had ended and he couldn't keep himself awake any longer. He crawled into bed, but left the door open so he could hear her return.

156

Chapter Nineteen

HANK FIRED UP the Bronco at dawn, loaded the rods, and headed upstream.

It was Annie who woke him, though only from a thin veil of sleep. She'd come creeping by his door a half hour before fishing light, like a teenager returned from some illicit rendezvous. He'd risen in hopes of catching her, but her door shut just as he reached the hallway. In the kitchen a few moments later, he'd found himself tossing a coffee cup into the sink and letting a drawer slam shut.

He parked on the Wright Creek Bridge, the blue green water swirling below, and lit a cigarette. It was Danny he was thinking about now. Danny with his arm around Annie. He pulled hard on the smoke—too hard—and gagged on it.

Below, off Lee's Lip, he could see a fish holding. Fish were always holding at Lee's Lip.

He'd named the spot after Lee Spencer, this generation's greatest mind. An archeologist by training, Lee now lived most of the year in a trailer at the refuge pool upstream, a pool as long as a semitruck but never as deep. At times, three hundred fish would hold there, awaiting higher water and better spawning conditions. In the days before Lee, the fish were often shot by drunk assholes, and at least twice, they'd been dynamited. Since Lee, they were hardly harassed even by bears.

Lee's days were spent recording what he saw. He kept a journal beside him and made notes whenever he saw a fish stir. If a fish rose to the surface, he recorded the time, the air temperature, the water temperature, and the item for which the fish rose. If the pod of steelhead became nervous, Lee examined the sky for eagles, the shores for coyotes, the water for otters. Anything and everything those fish did, he recorded. And from more than a decade of such notes, Lee had amassed an exhaustive understanding of steelhead behavior. For instance, he understood the fish possessed an acute sense of smell. If a deer crossed the riffle upstream, they would smell it in the water and begin jumping to get a better look. If a person touched the water upstream, they would begin a nervous daisy chain around the pool, their collective shape forming the mathematical notation for infinity.

But more than recording simple observations, Lee had been recording the ecology of a place, how the land affected its creatures. His was true nature writing. Lee wasn't a tourist in a place, he wasn't inspired by some fleeting moment of natural majesty, he was a character in the story of an ecosystem. His notes didn't turn the place into a portrait to be admired; they documented the thin tendrils of connection between him and the fish, the fish and the water, the water and the sky.

The last time Hank fished with Lee was right here at the lip, a year back. Lee used a fifteen-foot rod and a hookless fly and would often raise a fish where others had failed. He knew how to position himself to make short, perfect presentations. On that day though, the fish had been especially dour. Neither Hank nor Lee had raised a fish by midmorning, when they ran into Danny here on the bridge. Hank had said, "Impossible day, with this warm water." Lee pointed to the fish on the lip below. "That's a big buck." Danny had snuffed his joint and said, "Well, I'll go waste a few casts." Of course Danny made one cast, twitched his fly just right, and that big buck somersaulted over the fly. Lee had turned to Hank and repositioned his hat. "That kid knows his fish."

Hank lit a second cigarette now, though not because he needed it, and looked across the empty bridge.

What Lee understood was the ecology of place, how patterns super-seded their players. And what worried Hank, what had his stomach twisting, was that the ecology of harm might be no different.

But the rumors about Danny and his ex had been bullshit. Anybody who *really* knew Danny, who fished with him, had known the truth. Besides, one look at those happy twins and any fool could see Danny wasn't a violent man. Having a temper was one thing, being violent was another. Ask anybody who knew Danny, they'd all say the same thing: He couldn't have meant to cut her.

The official report six years ago, Carter's report, stated that it had been an accident, that Danny had tripped with the knife in his hand. Hank never asked why he'd had a knife in the first place, why he needed one when he and his pregnant wife, Shoshana, were arguing along the side of the road. There were plenty of good reasons—they'd been trailering boats at the time and occasionally a tie-down would stick or an anchor line would wrap around an axle—which folks who knew boats would understand. Whatever the reason for that knife, she'd spent the night in the hospital. The divorce came through before the birth, though people said it'd been a long time coming.

Danny wasn't afraid of pissing people off. If the wild fish were in need, he stepped up and did what was right. So he wasn't exactly loved by the bait guides downriver, the ones who argued adamantly to maintain the hatchery program and the catch-and-kill policy on natives. And the folks at the chamber of commerce didn't much like him either, on account of his rallying to stop the upriver golf course that had been proposed a couple years back. Danny was quick to be the point man on any controversial issue. It was the very feature of his personality that had made him so popular among fly anglers—though it had done little to make him the most beloved guy in Ipsyniho. And so, after the newspaper article, a lot of people had rushed to call him a danger, a criminal, a threat. Which was ridiculous.

And that's where Hank had left it for the past six years. Hank, Caroline, Walter, Danny's devoted customers and fans, anybody who knew Danny had left it there too. "Nothing more than flung dung," Walter had quipped the one time they talked of it.

But here Hank was staring at the water, thinking again of that knife. Thinking of it now not as Danny's friend but as Annie's father.

Chapter Twenty

JUSTIN MORELL'S MOTHER would be taking his body back to the family plot near their home in Grand Rapids, Michigan, but before leaving, she wanted to host a "celebration of life" in her son's honor. The girlfriend helped organize the event at his house, and word quickly spread up the valley. Despite any hard feelings that might have existed when the kid was alive, all of the riverfolk put on long pants and shoes and tucked in their shirts and came armed with flowers or fruit or smoked fish and generous stories starring Morell, stories that his mother could carry home and cherish like the boyhood pictures she'd brought and placed around the house in lieu of the Marley and Floyd posters. She would tell these stories to her neighbors and the family friends who'd known Justin as a boy, and she'd feel warmed each time by the knowledge that her son and his magical gifts had been loved and appreciated by the larger community, despite the tragic and violent and still-mysterious circumstances of his death. That death would become a story of its own, one she'd imagine and reimagine until it felt as real as if she'd been there herself—but ultimately, it would be reduced to a random black moment in a life lived in light and love. It had to be this way, Hank thought; otherwise, how could she go on?

"Your son," Hank began, not knowing where he'd end up, "learned this river faster than anyone I've ever met." There it was, something truthful and warm he could give her. He took her hand in his. "He had a gift for understanding water."

Her grown daughter was there with her and she stared unflinchingly at Hank. Like she was thinking, *Is this the one who did it?* Clearly, she didn't need these stories, or didn't yet know she needed them. Hank did his best to offer a pursed, sympathetic smile.

Carter had called that morning, though Hank had let the answering machine pick up. He'd said, "Give me a call at your earliest convenience. There seems to be some contradictory info we'd like to pull straight. Hank, call me." The call made him feel guilty. Like this sister's glare.

The mother nodded now. "He spoke of you guides so highly. He was writing an essay, you know, we found it on his computer, and it was all about fishing and the mentoring between the older and younger guides. The essay was called 'Uncles.'" She smiled. "There's a line, 'uncles and keepers of the tradition.' Beautiful, huh?"

Hank now remembered the warmth of Morell's neck against the side of his forearm, the gasping sound he'd made when Hank slammed him against that truck. Some uncle. "He'll be missed," Hank said, turning and moving away now.

It occurred to Hank now that the last time he'd done this was at Patrick O'Connell's funeral. He'd flown to Arizona on a Friday and returned on Sunday and didn't feel a lick better for going. He'd been one of fourteen attendees.

Annie laced her fingers around his arm. "That was kind of you," she said. She'd been at the house making breakfast when he returned from the bridge that morning. He didn't ask about her failure to come home the night before, and she didn't offer an explanation.

The party was spilling into the backyard, where someone was barbecuing and someone else was opening beers. Here, thank god, no one was crying.

Annie, Caroline, and Danny stood in a crescent looking back at the house from across the lawn, sipping their beers and watching Morell's mother through the kitchen window. There was a table set up on the small porch. On it sat a guest book, photocopies of a Grand Rapids newspaper article featuring Morell as "State's Youngest Fly-fishing Guide," copies of the articles Morell had written, and a large framed picture of the kid, a senior portrait probably, his naive eyes smiling over them.

Someone laughed nearby, a raft guide. He was telling a story about a client that afternoon. Hank felt like telling a story of his own, some random event, something funny, but there was nothing but Morell and darkness anywhere inside him.

"What a waste," Danny said. Whether he meant the death or this event itself wasn't clear. What was clear was that he'd been looking at Annie when he said it.

She responded a moment later with, "I prefer the Jewish arguments about death, personally. In the Hasidic tradition, there's no separation between the finite and the infinite. It's all one realm. So when you die, your body reenters the world, through the soil, through the grass, through the deer. It's all God."

"Yeah," Caroline said. "I like that. It's all God. We live forever that way."

Walter brushed this talk aside. "New Age nonsense, all of it. You die, you're dead, that's it. There's nothing more to it. No God. No living forever. You're tits-up, you're lights-out, you're done."

"Come on, Walt," Hank said. This was his daughter Walter was affronting.

"You know it's true." Walter brought his beer to his lips, but paused before sipping to say, "Anything else is delusion."

Annie was speaking before Hank could muster a reply. "It's all delusion. Nobody's arguing that. The point is we're free to pick the delusion we find most helpful."

Walter scoffed and left them and disappeared back inside.

"What's gotten up his ass?" Danny asked.

Later, there was a toast and Morell's sister told a story about her little brother as a three-year-old fishing in mud puddles in the family driveway. "He sat there for hours, sure some giant fish lurked in those four inches of water." People were laughing and crying as if this image somehow encapsulated the Justin they knew. There were other stories like this told by the mother, who downed a whole glass of white wine before standing. She touched the framed picture of her son and said, "If only your father could have seen the man you became."

And that's when Hank found himself overcome. He'd so far managed to keep this whole event at arm's length, but in that moment, with the mother touching that high school portrait, he swallowed hard at the tears welling within him. He looked for Caroline, and she wrapped her arms around him and dried her cheeks on his shirt. Even Walter was leaning against the fence, his head down, his hand covering his eyes, his shoulders shaking with sobs.

Hank hadn't been the uncle this boy needed, hadn't even tried. He put an arm around Annie and decided the next patch of water he found on the river, a hidden place that held fish, he'd name it after Morell.

Chapter Twenty-One

"I WANT TO see where I was born," Annie said as they drove upstream. "Can you take me to where I was born?"

And so Hank turned up Rock Creek and followed the winding road through the oaks and their neon leaves, then through the golden savanna with rusty patches of poison oak, along the one-lane pinch beneath the sheer cliff, and to the saddle and the dozen homes there. A whitetail deer bounded across the meadow and sailed over a fence, its erect tail visible over the horizon even after the creature itself had disappeared. On the other side, a blacktail deer and her spotted fawn turned broadside and never stopped chewing as the truck rolled by.

Only two of the houses were occupied now, pickups parked beside forsaken stoves and overturned refrigerators and sun-faded mattresses. A shirtless boy threw a rock at them as they passed. His shorter sidekick pointed a toy rifle and yelled, "You're dead!"

"You lived here?" Annie said. "I lived here?"

"It didn't look like this then," Hank said. "These weren't our neighbors." He explained that the houses had been built in the late sixties by a group of hippies from Eugene. They'd pooled their money and come to grow soybeans and live the highest life, one focused on equal quantities of art, farming, and community. They'd never thought to check how soybeans did in the Ipsyniho's rocky loam.

"Your mom and I moved up here after the hippies left. This was where a bunch of our friends lived, raft guides mostly. That one was ours." Hank pointed to the slanted box beside a cluster of feral apple trees, the one with broken windows and weathered gray planks for siding. The grass out front was waist high and flashing in the breeze, and the open doorway glared back at them, black as deep space. Hank stopped and shut down the truck. "Your mom kept a garden over there and our latrine was down where those blackberries are growing now."

"Latrine?"

"There was no plumbing in the houses. We passed the communal well on the way in. That metal sea horse thing."

"Was there electricity?"

"A diesel generator. We dreamed of solar."

Annie waded through the grass, her arms outstretched and sweeping through the tops. She spun once, like she'd done so often as a two-year-old. And Hank was taken with a sparkling recollection of her, leaning over a purple iris, struggling to touch her nose to the fragrant petals—then falling forward into the flower and coming up laughing. "You don't remember this place?"

She shook her head no.

They walked to the house and peeked through the window frames. It was too dark to see much at first, until their eyes adjusted. Hank was the first to step inside, testing the floor to ensure it would hold their weight.

"You're going inside?" Annie seemed surprised.

He gestured for her to follow. "It's solid."

Annie felt the width of the doorway as she entered. She seemed so enormous there, a silhouette against the blinding day. He remembered her sitting there as a toddler, against the shut door. Nighttime or evening maybe. She'd been drawing, and Rosemary looked and asked what it was. A girl, Riffle had said. A happy girl. Why is she happy? Because her daddy is home.

Annie now fingered a hole in the wall at her waist. "I remember this. I put this here with a hammer. Why did Mom let me play with

166

a hammer?" She walked a few paces, pointing at the room's corner. "There was a stove somewhere here, right? You used to boil water on it. Once I spilled it and burned myself. I remember that."

Now only the chimney's ceiling hole remained. He'd stacked each day's wood along that wall, where it could dry before being put to use. Heating this place had been a lesson in futility. During windstorms, gusts flowed across the room, little breaths against your cheek, lifting loose papers from the kitchen table. During heavy rains, an occasional splatter would find its way to your brow. He might as well have been heating the open sky. How young he'd been then. How sure of himself. Sure of his family—and of his place within it.

"This place is making me dizzy," Annie kept a hand on the wall for balance. Years of autumn leaves lay piled in the corners, and mouse turds littered the floor. But it was the tilt that was most disconcerting. Like the whole house might at any moment slide off the ridge and into the Ipsyniho.

Hank gestured toward the back. "Do you remember the bedroom?" He guided her over a black hole in the floor, and they stepped through the narrow doorframe.

"There was no door here," Annie said. "It was a red sheet or something."

"A tapestry. Good memory."

"And the three of us would sleep on a bed right there." She pointed to the corner. "It was on the ground, right?"

"It was." As a little girl, she'd been the world's finest cuddler, like she'd known some secret about snuggling only taught in the womb. Those had been the best nights of his life, her curled into him, burrowing her little face against his neck. A oneness with another being he'd never achieved before or since. A oneness, he now realized, he would forever be chasing.

"You used to read by candlelight," she said. "I remember climbing on your chest and making you read to me. It's all coming back."

He didn't remember that, but he did remember so much. "You were born right there. Your mom hung from my neck in a squatting position and she was working so hard. She was a thousand miles away in her own body. She kept shaking her head and saying, 'Come on little baby, come to your momma.' And you were coming, coming fast, but then you just stopped. You stopped with your head out and nothing else. Mom was pushing and Rita was working down there but you weren't coming. It was like you had decided the outside world wasn't what you'd been promised and you wanted back into that watery place."

Annie looked horrified. "Poor Mom."

"Things got kind of scary for couple minutes. The pain was getting to your mom, and Rita whispered for her to get on her hands and knees. Finally, Rita held your head and neck and did this kind of motion"—Hank demonstrated with his hands—"and you slipped right out and into her arms."

Annie was looking at the spot on the floor. "You remember it so well."

"How could I forget?" That moment, the Big Bang of his adulthood. "You went right to the boob. We were so sure you were a boy, your mom just had this feeling—she'd had dozens of dreams about you as a boy—that nobody even looked to see. There was a warm blanket fresh from the oven and it was covering you. I think we all thought that someone else had looked, but nobody had. The placenta was born, the cord cut, and still we were saying, 'Our little boy. Look at our little boy.' Finally, it was like five minutes later, your mom passed you to me and I saw you were a girl. And that's when you opened your eyes for the first time. Little celestial blueberries." Even now, thirty years later, he got a little misty thinking about it. Those eyes had leveled on him the weight of a thousand generations; fuck this up and it's all been for naught.

Every other moment in this life was but a coarse photocopy compared to that one night of glistening clarity.

"Were you disappointed? Be honest. Maybe just a little?"

"Disappointed by what?"

"Me being a girl."

He laughed. "Are you kidding? I've never felt so lucky in my entire life. I always wanted a little girl. Some guys are naturally boy-daddies, others naturally girl-daddies. I've always been sure."

"But didn't you want a little boy you could teach to fish and row and, you know, be you?"

"No."

"Dads, you know, are always so interested in teaching their boys that stuff." She looked away, and he realized this was about something bigger.

"I taught you everything. Teaching you . . . those are my most cherished memories, you and me and the river. Do you remember the time you hooked that steelhead and dropped the rod? I had to swim for it?"

She nodded. "Sure."

He smiled to himself. The pinnacle of all his angling memories. "You didn't want me to land your fish. So you jumped in too."

"I can't believe you let me do that."

. "I didn't. You just did it. But we landed that fish. Out on a rock in the middle of the river."

"It was an island, wasn't it?"

"No, darling. Center Punch Rock in the tailout of Governor." If she wanted proof, he would have shown her the journal entry detailing that day. It sprawled onto three pages in the blue composition book on the top right shelf in his living room. "About five feet across, but maybe it felt like an island to your little feet."

For a moment they were quiet, holding their breath in the sacred space of that room. He wanted to embrace her, to feel her forehead against his neck, but she reached a hand to the wall for balance—she was looking for the door.

And that's when he realized what she had really been asking when she asked if he wanted a boy.

"Just so you know," he said, "just so there's no confusion, I wanted you back every second of every day after your mom moved you away. I fought for you."

"Oh," Annie said and walked the two steps out of the room.

Chapter Twenty-Two

WHEN THEY ARRIVED back home that night, a note hung from the door. Carter. He'd stopped by and repeated his request that Hank contact him immediately. "There's a few contradictions I'd like to hash out."

They hadn't been home long when the phone rang. Annie answered, and said, "Hey, sweetie." It was Thad and she was taking the phone to her bedroom.

Her voice carried through the thin walls, so he turned up *Cornell '77* and tried to focus on the book he was reading—she deserved privacy. But then she walked into the kitchen, the phone to her ear, and searched for something to eat in the refrigerator.

"Really?" she said. "And what did he say?"

"_____"

"Who's his attorney?"

"_____"

"Well, they only have sixty days to file that."

"_____"

"I know, babe, but you'll do fine. You don't need me there for that."

"_____"

"Just be confident. Keep thinking to yourself, 'I own this room.' You're gonna be fine. Trust me. These deps are standard procedure. Billy's right."

"_____"

"Yeah, I'll keep the phone nearby. Call whenever."

After hanging up, she cracked a beer and called to Hank, "You want one?"

"Sure."

She came over to the couch where he was lying on his back and he made room for her. The beer was sweating in his hand. "Again with this show?" she asked.

He shrugged. "It's *Cornell '77*."

"Were you there?"

He'd already been guiding for years by then. "This one is just, well, it's damn good."

"They all sound the same to me."

He hadn't rediscovered *Cornell* until about a year before, when a friend passed on an archival website, and he was able to replace the tape version he'd worn through in the eighties. He'd listened to this show often enough then that it became, in a way, the sound track of that period in his life, of Annie's childhood. Now he kept a copy in the truck and another in the home stereo. "How's Thad?"

"But it's repetitive, isn't it, listening to the same show?"

Maybe, but what was wrong with a little repetition in life? And in truth, he wasn't listening to the same recording. He'd found three different bootlegs, each recorded from a different place within the audience. The music might have been the same, but the sound was different. He liked to think that by listening to these three, he was triangulating some truth of that show. "Does it sound familiar to you?" he asked. "There's a picture of you dancing to it."

She shook her head. "Where's the picture?"

It was with twenty-one others in the top drawer of his dresser, the pictures he took with him to sleep on the loneliest nights. "Around somewhere." She didn't need to know how much time he'd spent with them, how much time he'd spent thinking of the past.

Annie seemed lost in a memory of her own. "No, the only music I remember from kidhood is that bearded guy."

"Everybody had beards then."

"The guy you and Mom took me to see when he came to Eugene. I was like four, maybe."

"Oh. Raffi. Jesus. You were always begging to listen to Raffi."

She hummed a riff. From "Baby Beluga."

"Don't remind me." He glugged some beer, took a chance. "Thad is a little clingy, huh?"

"Clingy? Maybe. He's a great doctor," she said. "He has a glowing reputation. And he's smart and he's articulate and he's capable. But yeah, maybe he has some dependency issues. I mean, he needs constant support. A housekeeper for his ego. But don't we all?"

She sipped her beer, and Hank knew enough to wait.

"I should've known what I was getting into. He's a serial monogamist. And you should see his relationship with his mother. They talk for hours on the phone. For the two years he lived alone, he dabbled in Catholicism. I mean, to each his own, but the pope?" She shook her head. "I should have seen what was coming." Then a moment later, "I shouldn't talk about him like this. He's my husband."

"I'm your dad."

"So says my birth certificate."

He didn't want to know what she meant by that. "Why stay with him if this is how you feel?" *So says my birth certificate.* If only she knew how hard he'd tried.

"I guess I haven't always felt this way. It didn't used to be so suffocating. I used to like the attention. He needed me, and I liked being needed."

He remembered that feeling, the clarity of purpose that came with being a necessary component of another's life. In hindsight, he'd relished that part of parenting—the help in the bathtub, the help overcoming a nightmare—even if at the time it had been overwhelming. In fact, that had been the most difficult adjustment after Annie and Rosemary left: transitioning from being needed to simply being. Maybe he was still transitioning. "Thad wants children, I bet."

Annie turned. "Good guess."

"And you don't?"

She sipped her beer. "I don't think I do. I mean, I'm pretty sure I don't. At least not now."

Rosemary hadn't wanted children either. A memory resurfaced: Rosemary in the passenger seat of his truck, the window down and her hair tossing wildly. They'd just learned that she was pregnant. She said, "Maybe I should make an appointment." She'd never mentioned the idea again, thank god. What would he have said to convince her otherwise?

"But there's a lot of pressure. From Thad. From Thad's mother. You'd be amazed how forward she is about the whole thing. Like I have some public responsibility to the family, so public that they can talk about my reproduction at the dinner table."

He imagined a wealthy Southern family's dinner: crystal, silver, china, and well-dressed but never acknowledged servers pouring drinks and removing dirty dishes. It was these worldly experiences that left him slightly awestruck of the person little Riffle had become. She would never have had these experiences if she'd stayed in Ipsyniho, if she'd become the person he'd imagined.

"What does your mom say about all this?" he asked.

Annie shrugged. "Mom's kind of in her own world right now."

He pressed her to explain.

"I think she's having a little midlife thing. She's postmenopausal now, you know. She tells me, 'Just leave him already,' as if Thad is an apartment or something."

And then the resentment—no, the hatred—he'd felt the moment Rosemary climbed in her car and drove five-year-old Riffle away from him forever was fresh and new and bloody again. *Just leave him already.* As if Thad was trivial, as if his desires and hopes and passions took a distant second to her own.

Annie must have noticed Hank's spike in blood pressure. "It's not that she's indifferent. It's just that to her, these problems have simple and unavoidable solutions. Might as well hurry them along and get on with life." Annie sipped her beer, then barely contained a belch. "Mom always kept men pretty peripheral. At least since you. She's still like that with her new beau, but he's too dense to notice."

"Since me what?" His tone surprised even him.

Annie shrugged. "I don't know, it's just, your leaving left some scars I think."

Hank sat up, and his beer spilled onto the carpet. He righted the bottle, but it tipped again, and he left it. "I didn't leave."

"Whatever." Annie waved a hand. "I don't mean to bring that up. I just mean that to her, a relationship is just a relationship. She forgets that they develop their own inertia. Commitment, legacy, you know what I mean."

Hank caught himself. This was Annie's conversation, one about her relationship with Thad, not about his relationship with Rosemary. But then he said it anyway: "I didn't leave anybody, just for the record."

Annie looked at a spot on the floor. "I misspoke." A moment passed as he searched for something better to say. She stood. "I should get some sleep. Thad is going to call first th—"

"Wait," he grabbed her hand. "I didn't leave anybody. I didn't. You have to know that. I fought for you, Annie."

She turned her arm free of his grip. "As you said." She righted the now-empty bottle, and disappeared down the hallway and into her room.

There on the carpet, in the room's half-light, was a sopping, dark oval.

175

Chapter Twenty-Three

HANK HAD A trip the next day, one he'd scheduled long before Annie called and asked to come out. The client was a regular from Denver, a suit in some major insurance firm there. He could cast and he understood that steelhead weren't always willing, and so the day should have gone smoothly. Hank often found himself on a bluff supposedly looking for fish but instead thinking about Annie, about "his leaving."

Clearly, the facts of how Hank came to stay in Ipsyniho had not been presented in his favor. She'd be leaving again in three days, which pinned him in a corner: Should he dare to set the history straight, or should he focus on building the present? Could he do one without the other?

If he broached the subject and the discussion swirled out of control as it had before, he might lose her forever. He'd been lucky to have her return as it was, a second chance, and an undeserved one. He couldn't risk making the same error again; he might lose her for good. But if he didn't broach the subject, she would forever see him as something he wasn't, a quitter. She couldn't respect a quitter.

But there was also something else. Last night, hours after she'd supposedly gone to bed, he stepped outside for a smoke. He couldn't not hear her voice through her open bedroom window. She was on the phone in the darkness, and he just barely made out the word *Shoshana*. She'd been on the phone with Danny at 2:00 a.m., talking about his ex-wife.

"Did you know this guy who was murdered?" his client asked just as they entered a churning mess of *white water*.

"Say again?"

Clang. The boat hit a rock, and Hank fell from the oarsman's seat, smashing his knee into the anchor release. He'd just kept his grip on the sticks, but it was enough, and he pulled hard now to straighten their course. His mouth was filling with a metallic fluid, and he spit a stream of blood onto the floor of the boat—he'd bitten his tongue. "Sorry." That was the first time he'd thumped a rock in years. He'd been distracted like this all day. "You okay?"

The client rose and sat back in his chair, already tightening his life vest. "That was a doozy."

Hank guided the boat into the pool and spit some more blood. His knee was stiffening, but it'd be fine. They'd been lucky. If an oar had gone, they would've taken the suck-hole broadside, and there wouldn't have been any recovering from that.

The dude didn't seem any the wiser. "Do you think this Trib fellow did it?"

Hank was certain the answer was no. But someone had. And it was probably someone he knew. It wasn't that Hank necessarily thought Danny had done it. Danny was a father and had too much to lose, and plenty of people hated Morell more. But still.

"Trib's innocent. I'd wager anything." He pushed on downstream. "I got a spot down here. Real consistent."

"I've heard of fistfights over low-holing," the client said, "but murder? It just seems a little extreme."

*

He found Carter behind his desk at the sheriff's station. The same wild steelhead was on the wall, the twenty-two-pounder Carter had caught and killed and had mounted in '74, the same steelhead that had prompted a young Hank to pour sugar in a young Carter's gas tank. The then deputy had never learned who sabotaged his rig. Or who did it a second time when the new engine arrived.

Carter had called the house two more times and, according to Bridge, sent a deputy knocking on doors looking for him. "The dweeb wouldn't answer," Bridge said, "when I asked why."

"Where's Cindy?" Hank asked, waiting in Carter's doorway to be invited in. Cindy had been the receptionist at the sheriff's station for as long as Hank had been a guide. They'd spent a winter holed up together in the mideighties, back when she was still fond of swimming nude in the upper river. Since then, she'd married, become head of the PTA, and later sent her three boys to the community college over in Bend.

"Budget cuts," Carter said. "We're down to two deputies now, no secretary, four rolls of toilet paper a month." Carter pointed at the chair across his desk. "Can I get you something? Ice water or, well, hot water? That's about the extent of it these days."

Hank sat, tried not to look at the steelhead, asked Carter how his family was doing. They bullshitted awhile, not because either of them was interested but because custom required it.

Finally, Carter got down to the heart of it. "I'm glad you stopped by, Hank. I've been trying to reach you. There are some contradictions."

"Like?"

"Like you say you were with your client," Carter put a finger to the sheet of paper before him, "Steve Burke is his name, all that day, but he says you might have been gone for as much as an hour of the trip."

"Yeah, if you add up all the minutes I spent pissing in the woods."

"So you admit you weren't with him for the entirety of the trip." Carter leaned back in his chair, studying Hank now in his best impression of a cunning detective.

"No, I was with him the whole time. Except when I was behind a tree with my dick in my hands."

179

"But he can't confirm that."

"No, I guess he can't." Hank found himself pulling at his beard. "What the fuck, Carter?"

Carter smiled that bullshit mocking smile of his, the one Hank had seen at Carter's Texas Hold 'Em tournaments, which he hosted once a month. He saved that smile for the moment before he laid a winning hand. "Look at it from my point of view," Carter said now. "You're the first man on the scene. And you had an altercation with Morell not that far back. And the last time a guy went missing on the river, it was your client." Again Carter checked that sheet of paper before him. "Says here that Patrick A. O'Connell died of blunt trauma to the head."

"He fell from a cliff, Carter." A cliff Hank shouldn't have brought him to.

"That's what your statement says. But you got to admit, it's all a little suspicious. There's precedent here."

Hank laughed because he didn't know what else to do. "You're joking." But clearly Carter wasn't. Hank stood and looked to the steelhead on the wall and at the view out the windows and at the fire tower on a distant ridge.

"Sit down, Hank."

Hank did. "We've known each other a long time, Cart, and so I say this as a friend." He let that linger. "I think you've gotten a little trigger-happy on this one."

Carter sucked through his teeth, leaned back in his chair, nodded his head. "Well, Hank, why don't you come straight with me. If not Andy, if not you, then who do you think did it?"

"Nobody."

"Come on."

Hank pulled off his hat and leaned across the desk. "See that?" He fingered a long scar just behind his ear. "That's where an oar clocked me. It caught a rock and wrenched free of my hand and hit me square. Knocked me for a loop. Pure luck I didn't swamp in the suck-hole. The truth is if you're on a river enough, bizarre shit happens."

Carter watched him, and Hank couldn't tell north or south what the man was thinking. Maybe he had a future as a politician after all. Carter spit a stream of tobacco into his coffee mug. "Maybe you're right. Maybe it was just an oar. But somebody swung that oar, Hank. And I think you know who."

He couldn't help but glance behind him and check: He had this keen sense that Danny was there in the room with them. "This was an accident, Carter. Plain and simple."

"Nah." Carter was shaking his head. "You're tapped deep into the river circle, and the way I figure it, you got a straight line on whoever did this. You're protecting him, or her. And if you don't come out and tell me, well then, I might just have to go looking into this precedent. I might just have to put you where Andy is."

"Fuck you."

Carter nodded at the steelhead on the wall. "That was a big fish, wasn't it? You know where I got that one? At that pool below the jumping cliff."

Feather Creek met the Ipsyniho just upstream. That pool was the staging area for the Feather Creek population, when it still existed in any numbers. A combination of bank erosion, overharvest, and chronic herbicide application on the farms in the floodplain.

"I used to fish the river all the time," Carter said as if Hank didn't already know. "My daddy fished it. My momma fished it. My daddy's daddy fished it. That's what we did during school, after work, on Sundays after church. We were a fishing family then. We were. Until you all went and got the laws rewritten."

"We didn't rewrite the laws."

Carter scoffed. "You fly guides got your own industry, and that's what the game commission pays attention to. The State's just one big corporation. You and I both know it. And they're a mismanaged one at that, one that makes mistakes."

In a way, Carter wasn't that far-off. The fly guides had argued that the upper river should be deemed fly-fishing only because the inefficiency of the technique, so went their logic, rendered it less likely to stress the lingering populations, but the Game Commission had glazed past those arguments and asked question after question about the number of trips run, the number of dollars brought into the economy, the lure of a "fly-fishing only" classification to out-of-state anglers. The approach had gone right for them that time, but less than a decade later, the bait guides made similar arguments about increasing the number of hatchery smolts released into the lower river, and the State had created the new hatchery complex—an action that undermined so many previous gains.

"You can still fish. Nobody took that away."

"Can't keep the big wild ones, can't fish bait in the runs near town, what's the point? Just a bummer, that's all, my grandson won't have these same opportunities. You know what he does for fun? He plays video games in his room." Carter punched some numbers on the phone, held the receiver to his ear, and said to Hank, "Y'all have been above the law a long time." Then into the phone, "Yeah, hello, Sheriff Carter here." He pointed at the door. "Give it some thought."

*

HANK SWUNG BY the fly shop on his way home. Danny's truck was parked out front as always, boat in tow. He pushed through the front door, the bells announcing his entrance.

"How'd you make out?" Danny asked. "Saw your rig at the ramp."

"Skunked."

"Tough day? Saw that the temps were down finally last night. Thought it'd be good."

"Everything looked right," Hank said. "The dude couldn't throw twenty feet." A lie.

Danny poured him a cup of coffee, added two creams as usual, and kicked out a stool.

Hank said, "You fished this morning, no doubt."

"Nope. Should have, the twins are with Shosh. But I was up late."

Hank held the coffee to his lips. "Up late doing what?"

Danny shrugged off the question. "Did you hear? Trib's out on bail."

A wave of customers arrived, and while Danny worked, Hank occupied himself at a vise. In the time it took Danny to sell a new Burkheimer, he spun up three Muddlers, each with a wide face for chugging through the meniscus. A customer wandered his way, though he didn't notice the guy until he heard, "You look familiar."

It was a well-groomed twenty-something, flip-flops, khaki shorts, shirt that read "fish fear me": a future blowhard. "So do you."

The kid reached across the vise and snatched up one of the finished patterns, holding it to the light. "You're that guide, right? The one with that twenty-pounder. You know, the picture on the blog."

It was true. Danny had taken the image last summer. That fish had risen through eight feet of water to smash a fly just like the one he was tying now. He'd agreed to let Danny post the picture because he assumed the sunglasses and hat adequately obscured his likeness. He wasn't interested in being recognized.

"I'm a guide too," the kid said, tossing the fly back. "Got my own boat and everything."

Hank looked up over his reading glasses. Those hands were baby-soft, the forearms veinless, the face evenly tanned. Obviously, a sticker from the marine board didn't mean as much as it used to. "The ratio is just about one to one these days."

"What?"

"Forget it. Good for you. Guiding . . ." What could he say about it? "It's a splendid way to stay poor."

The kid said, "I know it's hard work. It's not as romantic as it seems. Everybody says that you shouldn't get into it just because you love fishing."

"True enough."

"But you got it made, Hank." The kid surprised him. "Sorry, Mr. Hazelton."

"I'm no mister."

"You get to live a river life, Hank, and you get to live it on your own terms. And that's something."

Was it? There were costs this kid couldn't fathom. "But it's also about the fish."

"I know. I've been working on Canton Creek this summer, placing wood and restabilizing banks. And this winter, I've already signed up to lead a redd count up in the headwaters. Danny is showing me the way."

Danny was now pointing to a spot on a map of the river and explaining something to a customer. If this kid had earned Danny's respect, that said something. "Get out of guiding while you still can. Trust me on that."

He laughed. He thought Hank was joking. "I'm here for the long haul. I want to do something with my life that I can look back on and feel good about. We're going to save these fish. We're going to bring them back."

Hank handed the kid one of the finished flies. "Don't say you weren't warned."

When the shop was finally empty again, Danny flipped the "back in two shakes" sign. "Smoke?"

They stepped out the back door and into the alley, each taking a stool with them. Hank lit a cigarette and offered one to Danny. There was news about Cherry Creek, about the plan to log the Williams Creek fire. The California conservation groups weren't in; they couldn't spare the manpower. "They say they need to pick their battles," Danny said. "This isn't a battle they want, not now."

That was about the long and short of it these days. Pick your battles, and pick the ones you were likely to win.

"Do you think it will always be like this?" Danny was staring absently down the narrow canyon of the alley. "Or will these shortsighted extractive types eventually kill themselves off? I don't know if I have the energy to go a lifetime fighting these fucks."

"Tell me about it." Hank had come here for a specific reason, and yet he couldn't quite bring himself to ask. "These extractive types won't die alone, that's the thing. They'll take us all down with them."

"I worry about Miriam and Ruben, about what kind of world will be left for them in forty years."

"The whole galaxy will be digital then," Hank said. "Don't worry. They won't even need watersheds."

Danny was pondering the dumpster beside him. "It's a fucked-up world to be leaving to kids."

"Hey," Hank heard himself say, "not that it matters, but you never mentioned where you were that afternoon."

"What afternoon?"

"The one Morell went missing." It was a stupid question to ask, a senseless question, a question that could bring about nothing good. He knew all this, and yet he asked it anyway. "Just curious."

Danny frowned.

"I ask because everybody else has been real clear and straight up."

"I haven't been straight up?" Danny was coming off his stool.

Well, he hadn't been. He'd been up late last night talking with Annie, and he'd kept her out all night the night before, and he hadn't said a word about it. Neither of them had.

"What the fuck, Hank?"

An overwhelming bitterness rose up within him, like Danny himself had driven Riffle away that afternoon. "There's precedent, that's all." He heard the echo of Carter's voice and hated himself.

Danny's eyes narrowed, then flickered. He looked at his feet, and muttered, "Wow."

Danny wasn't reacting like he'd expected. He'd expected Danny to defend himself; he'd expected a chance to put Danny in his place. But Danny seemed weakened by the provocation, almost shaken by it. "What's this about?"

"You know what it's about."

A moment passed, and Danny's shoulders settled into a hunch.

"Have you always thought . . ." Danny looked him square in the eyes, a tender look that matched the frailty of his voice. "Do you think I meant to . . . that it was intentional I cut her? That's what you mean, Andy can't bleed a person but I can."

It was that voice that threw Hank *offguard*. A son's voice, confused and betrayed. He heard himself in it—then he saw himself from Danny's eyes. "No," Hank said. "That's not what I meant. I mean, it was, but I didn't mean to imply—"

"Does everybody think that? I mean I knew her friends did, and those fucks at the paper, but you? Walt too? Does Caroline think it?"

"No. It's not like that. Forget I said anything. Danny, I know you didn't have anything to do with Morell. Forgive me. I'm not myself."

Danny looked up and down the alley, like he thought someone might be watching.

"My client today, he was an excellent caster. I lied to you. I just fucked up the trip. Look," Hank pointed to the red rise on his knee. "I thumped a rock and we almost lost the boat, that's how not me I've been." Hank reached for him. "Danny."

"Y'all have talked about this, haven't you? Behind my back."

"No, we haven't. Danny . . ." He searched for whatever words might make this right.

Danny pulled open the shop door.

"It's not like that," Hank called after him.

Danny turned and looked back at Hank, at his feet and then his eyes, like he was seeing him for the first—or last—time. And then he was gone, the metal door clanking shut behind him.

Chapter Twenty-Four

ANNIE'S CAR WASN'T at the house. Hank found a note taped to the front door. "Went for a hike."

A padded envelope sat on the step. He tore it open and found the new ring he'd ordered.

Inside the house, there wasn't the message from Caroline he'd expected on the answering machine. He'd called her three times now and not heard a thing, though he'd seen her rig parked on the river that morning.

There was one message, though, from Walter. He asked if Hank could come on up to the house "pronto." He had some news, and he wanted "to get some things in order." Ominous language from a guy who'd survived chemo only two years before.

Hank arrived at Walter's to find the front door wide open. He called out, but there was no response. He knocked on the open door, called inside, but again heard nothing. It was like in those movies, when a friend arrives only to discover a corpse inside. Had Walter ended it and first called Hank so that his body wouldn't rot?

But then the bathroom door swung open and Walter stepped out and, upon seeing Hank's terrified face lurking in his living room, shouted, "What the fuck, sneaking up on an old bugger like that!"

"Sorry, I . . ."

"You trying to kill me? Good god, Hankle."

Walter went to the refrigerator and found two beers and nodded outside. They sat on the lawn chairs Walter had placed under the alder grove, looking back at the house and boat port. Hank lit a cigarette, and Walter asked for one too.

"What's with the hitch?" Walter was pointing at Hank's knee, which had been giving him a little grief since clanking the boat on that rock.

"Not worth explaining. What's with you smoking?"

Walter took a drag. "Told myself, if I got word the world was about to end, my first stop would be the River Market for a pack of Luckies."

"Walt, what the fuck's going on?"

A new cancer, Walter explained, pancreatic this time, and he couldn't afford treatment and he wasn't sure he wanted the treatment if he could. "That prostate surgery left me limp as a bonked fish."

"Jesus, Walter."

"They tell me I only got a few weeks while I can still be up and around. It hurts something ruthless already. You don't know pain until you got cancer in your gut."

"But you told me the doc gave you a clean bill, and that was only like two weeks back."

Walter shrugged. "Did I say that? Probably figuring I'd save you the headache. I've known since May. I tell you now only because last night, well, I can feel it coming."

"You should've told me."

"What would you do about it?"

Whatever he could. Bring Walter water and food, sort his medication, drive him into Eugene for treatment, whatever. He'd done all this the last time around, he'd do it again. He owed Walter that much. He owed Walter a son's gratitude.

Walter spit. "Save your pity for somebody who needs it."

A long stillness settled over them. Hank was imagining, or failing to imagine, the valley without Walter in it. Walter was as intricate a piece of this place as the Douglas firs, the river, the fish. "I'm so sorry."

"Agh." Walter swatted at the air. "I'm over it. We all gotta drift downstream at some point. It's simple, and I'm done being sorry about it. I'm glad, in fact. Glad I made it this far." He chuckled. "Fuck, I won. I'm seventy-nine and was a goddamn steelheader the whole way. I didn't die in somebody else's war, I didn't rot my ass in no office cube, and I sure as shit didn't sit by while evil little pricks fucked up my homewater. You should be so lucky."

Hank forced a smile. "True."

Walter tapped his beer against Hank's. "Anyway, thanks for being such a loyal fuck, Hankle. I love you for it, in a way."

Hank stumbled for words, stumbled to articulate something he didn't yet understand.

"Shush for once, and let a dying man talk. There's something I got to say." Walter swigged from his bottle. "That funeral couple days back, it brought things into focus. Got me thinking about all the shit I've done wrong in this life. Letting Mindy go. Damn. I was selfish and mean and I'd take it all back if I could." He pulled a sealed letter from his shirt pocket. "I don't have her address, she wouldn't want me to know it, but I'm hoping you can pass this along once I'm . . . once I'm tits-up."

"Course."

"There are other things too, things I'll spare you. But I wanted to say, 'cause I'm feeling powerful wrong about this, well, I reckon you were right about that pictio-graph. I probably shouldn't have taken it. I'm just another pile of cells in this watershed, and who am I to keep that thing? I told myself I was doing the valley a favor by taking it, told myself I was safeguarding it, keeping the legacy alive, you know, helping it jump this ravine we're sitting on these days. But now I see, I wasn't doing no such thing. I was hoarding it for myself. I've always been a selfish prick. Mindy was right about that. I probably could've listened better."

Walter finished his beer, and let out a careful belch, his hand against his abdomen like it was keeping him from rattling apart. "I want to return that pictio-graph. And I want to return the other things I took too. It needs to be done. Better out there than getting sold off at some estate auction. But the thing is, well, I'm not the man I was a year ago. Shit, I'm not the man I was a week ago. I'm an old buck, Hank, can't barely hold my lie no more. There's one thing I'm learning: Death is a bitch of a current."

"If you're looking for help," Hank said.

Walter nodded. "Thanks for that." He tightened, clenching his teeth and rising up in his chair an inch or two.

"What is it? What can I do? Here."

When the pain finally passed, he said the waves were becoming more frequent. He was only sleeping now thanks to a cocktail of drugs he couldn't afford. "Buying them all on credit. Never bought nothing on credit, 'cept that house. Now I'm deep in it."

"I got some money." He didn't really, but he knew he could put some together in a pinch.

"Fuck that. But there's something else."

"Anything."

"You got to let me borrow that twelve-gauge of yours. I've only got my rifles and their barrels are too long."

"Too long?" But of course. "Walt. No. There's got to be something else, there's got to be some chance."

"Keep your pleading tender-heart bullshit to yourself. It's not you who's gonna suffer through this. 'Through' ain't even the right word. There's no 'through' involved. It's just suffering, plain and simple. Give me your scattergun."

"I can't."

Walter swiped the beer from Hank's hand and chucked it over the edge of the bluff. "Give me your goddamn scattergun or I swear . . ."

Hank knew that when it came down to it, he'd give Walter the gun. It was the least he could do—the gift that would allow the man his final freedom.

"I figure sometime around the solstice, I'll drive up to Red Gate for one more session, and then end it, right there on the casting rock. Carter can pull this sack of bones from the river. I'm hoping to make it all the way to tidewater, but I'll let Lady Ipsyniho decide that."

"Sorry I threw your beer," he said a moment later. "Could you fish up that bottle? Don't want to leave it littering down there."

*

HANK DROVE THE Bronco, the first time he could remember Walter letting him do the driving. They started on a bluff above the Campwater, where Walter reburied a dozen obsidian arrow points. Walter rose from the dirt and wiped the sweat from his forehead and said, "The Ipsynihians gathered here to net and smoke salmon," as if Hank didn't already know. "They used to sleep up there, and work down here, and you see those ledges below the falls? That's where they netted the fish."

Hank remembered the shards of black obsidian that used to cover the ground here, probably where people had chipped points while the fishing was slow. When the sun was high, the ground used to reflect shards of light, enough to blind a person. But in the years since, the obsidian had slowly vanished, probably buried under dirt that blew or washed down the bluff.

Walter followed the old trail, which was now barely perceptible, a slight trough in the slope leading into the firs. There he found the rotten remnants of an old tree, its roots still clinging to the soil. He opened his bag and removed a crumbling reed basket. "This was my first find. I was maybe fifteen, and this tree was hollowed out, and inside there was this basket and a doll made of reeds about yay big. Gave that to Mindy as a wedding present."

Then Walter told Hank a story he didn't know. "The cavalry ambushed them here." He pointed to the high cliffs across the river and the open slope above. "They got the jump on them and shot dead the ones that didn't surrender. They were running up the slope, trying to get into the next ravine. Easy pickings for a rifleman on the bluff. Fourteen killed, only four men."

"Why?"

Walter tapped his wading staff against a fallen log, as if he was about to explain the importance of decomposing wood to a forest.

"The army thought they were part of the Rogue rebellion. Didn't even realize they spoke a totally different language."

The afternoon turned to evening as they continued up the valley, visiting five other once-sacred places that were now forgotten and overgrown. Some of the places Hank had been, but a couple were new to him, meadows and cliffs along unnamed tributaries. Hank listened to Walter's histories with a newfound intensity, trying now to memorize each detail so that he could share them, maybe with Annie, certainly with Danny, if Danny could forgive him.

With the sun nearing the horizon, they crested a hidden skid road and emerged on the ridge that towered over Feather Creek's headwaters. "Keep going," Walter said.

But they were at the turnaround. The wind streaming through the cab was cooler at this elevation, maybe two thousand feet above the river.

"Across the grass." Walter pointed. "You don't expect me to walk all that'a way?"

So Hank weaved the truck through the rocks and brush and then rolled along the grassy slope, descending to a pass he'd never before seen, not even from a distance.

"This'll do."

He parked beside two massive boulders, each as big as his truck. Boulders like these were rare in the valley, and Hank couldn't quite figure how they had arrived at a point so high on the ridge. Walter explained. "This used to be a craggy mountaintop, probably like the Hash Points over that way. These boulders were part of the top that froze and cracked free, they got hung up here on their roll down." Walter walked the path between them. "This was a special place for the Ipsynihian hunters. They'd send folks through the thickets below, and see how the slope funnels up here? The deer and elk would run straight up to this point, and come right between these rocks. Do it in the afternoon, and the wind is always right. Still works. My daddy put me right behind that boulder when I was eight and spooked a buck up from below. My first deer died right where you're standing, wasn't a ten-yard shot."

But it wasn't the boulders that had brought them this high.

They limped their way farther up the ridge, toward a rock outcropping there. Between Hank's knee and Walter's waves of pain, it took them almost an hour to walk what couldn't have been a mile, and by the time they arrived, the sun was setting over the distant ocean. Long columns of light traversed the valley, orange in the dusty air.

"The cave is this way," Walter said, paying the view no attention.

Sure enough, a cave as tall and long as Hank's living room extended into the rocks. The ground here was a powder of dirt and fibers, and the air smelled of musk and urine. Stick figures lined the walls, and a dozen rocks on the cave floor were charred black from ancient fire. Walter had never said a word about this cave, not in thirty-something years. From the pristine appearance of the place, maybe Walter was the only person who knew it existed.

He shrugged his day pack to the rocks, and began going at the cave floor with his wading staff. Hank tried to help, but Walter waved him back. "This is my doing." The man was more delicate than he'd been just a week before, that much was clear. He was panting hard and cringing against the pain. He'd loosened in a way, these last few weeks, the skin under his jaw hanging lower now, the muscles in his forearms less pronounced—like he was decomposing from the inside out. But he wasn't feeble, not hardly. When he encountered a pumpkin-sized rock in the cave floor, he used that wading staff to dig under and then lever it from the hole. A seventy-nine-year-old man displacing a rock that must have weighted fifty pounds. He wiped the sweat from his brow.

Soon he was looking into a substantial pit in the cave floor, maybe two feet deep, and he kneeled over his backpack and extracted the shoe box. The skull was there, in the packing peanuts that had encased it for so many decades. The whole skull fit in Walter's open hand; it must have been a child's. Walter placed it in the bottom without ceremony, then stood, looking down into its empty eyes.

"I found a lot of things here, Hank. More than I could ever put back." He reached an arm to the cave wall for support. "I sold most of it. Rich fucks in new cars and khaki hats used to come around to buy bones and other things, but bones mostly. I don't know what they did with them, sold them to museums or something, but they'd pay good money. I found three skulls here, sold two of them. Thought I'd keep the third as an investment."

His jaw quivered, and he squinted against tears. "That's how I thought of it. As an investment."

"You were just a kid. You didn't know any better."

"I knew well enough. I've known."

Walter pulled dirt over the hole, and sat, his hands balled into tight fists. "You don't know everything I'm sorry for."

Hank sat too and put his arm around this man who'd shunned affection his whole life. "You're a good man, Walt. I know you, and I know that."

Walter was shaking now, and Hank felt microscopic under these paintings of people and elk and fish. Walter had always been the resolute force in this wobbly world, the only person Hank knew who didn't have a private doubt. He was more than Hank's mentor, he was proof. And now the cave walls expanded outward and upward and Hank said what he could only hope was true: "You've made a difference."

Chapter Twenty-Five

HANK ARRIVED AFTER dark at Caroline's place, pushed open the gate, and drove too fast across the field. He didn't know what to expect, another man's truck maybe, but instead, there was nothing, not even a light on in the place. Samson and Delilah were tied to their posts, which was how Caroline left them when she was working or running errands in town.

He left the truck running and walked to the door, the dogs jumping tight to their chains. "Shut it," he hollered. They were barking like he was a common stranger, for fuck's sake.

The new ring was in his pocket, and he held it to the moonlight. Just a shiny reminder of something that didn't need remembering. It balanced nicely on the doorknob, and he made it halfway back to the truck before turning back. He'd pawn the ring and use the money to help Walter.

This was a fucked-up world for sure, but what he didn't know was whether it had always been like this or whether something had happened, something that sent everything spiraling into discordance. He had always thought—no, he'd always hoped—that there were seasons in a person's life like there were seasons on the river, a time of ease and plenty and a time of doubt and hardship. And since no calendar could help identify these seasons, a person could never really be sure where they were in the cycle. But now, now it seemed more likely there weren't any seasons at all, just a wheel of pain, circular and pummeling, and try as you might, you'd never clear it, you'd never move on.

He climbed back into the truck and turned off *Cornell '77*. There was just the barking and growling of the dogs, and that huge and vacuous night sky.

The pictograph was still wrapped in its tarp in the bed of his truck—it was the one item he and Walter hadn't had time to replace—and he considered running it up to the hot springs now, just to be done with it. But it was dark and the thing was heavy, and he wasn't in the mood any longer for setting things right.

*

CAROLINE'S TRUCK WAS parked beside Annie's rental in his driveway, and through the window, he could see them laughing as they worked at the stove. And just like that, wholeness and direction seemed once again attainable; maybe spring was on its way.

They had a glass of Grenache waiting for him when he pushed through the door. "Thought you'd gone lost on us," said Caroline.

Annie kissed his cheek. "Ever heard of a cell phone? Caroline told me not to worry, but jeez."

They were making spaghetti with the last packages of bear meat Caroline had in her freezer. "Did you know," Annie exclaimed, "Caroline shot this bear herself?"

Sure he did; he'd helped her butcher it. The bruin had three times busted into her trash cans, despite Samson and Delilah barking up a storm, and the fourth time she met him with the .270. That was a year back, and since, they'd been enjoying bear bratwursts, bear burgers, and bear burritos once or twice a week. "Pork of the woods," Caroline was fond of calling it.

"Pork of the woods," Annie said now. "Got to try it once at least."

Caroline kissed him as she handed him a head of lettuce and a knife. "Get chopping, that garlic bread will be ready soon."

It wasn't long, though, before Annie got a phone call, someone from work. She pulled on a fleece and took her glass of wine outside.

Caroline was telling him about her day. She'd taken new clients out, two women from a fly-fishing club in Seattle. They'd really hit it off, invited Caroline to come speak at their next club meeting, do a little fishing in the Sound. Hank was doing his best to listen, but it was Walter that he was thinking of now: at home alone, and with all that pain. Caroline kicked him in the bum. "Are you even listening?"

Hank pulled the knife across the leaves. "Walter. A new cancer. He probably won't make it until fall."

She didn't say a word; she stopped stirring the sauce and wrapped her arms around Hank's waist and pressed her head against his back. For a long moment, she stayed there.

"You okay?" she whispered.

"You know," he said, turning and letting her take him in her arms.

"I'm so sorry." She laid a kiss on each of his eyes, and pressed her forehead against his.

*

THEY WAITED FOR Annie to finish, the food going cold on the stove. Finally, Annie poked her head back inside and said, "Sorry, why don't you go ahead without me. It's an emergency. I don't know how long I'll be."

So they ate just the two of them, listening to the rises and falls of Annie's voice through the screen door.

"I think they call it a BlackBerry," Caroline said. "Everyone has one now, I hear."

"Poetic," Hank said, gulping some wine. "Blackberries invade and take over so thick nothing else can grow."

"Oh, you."

Caroline had moved her chair around to his side of the table, and they ate with their arms touching. He could smell the oaring sweat on her skin and the faint remnants of sunscreen. She refilled his wine glass, then her own. Something about her proximity now reminded him of her empty house, the dogs barking at him, the loneliness of that vast night sky. And then the bitterness was all he could feel. Walter was going to die.

She kissed his neck and slipped her hand into his lap. "How's this for a little distraction?"

She didn't return his calls. She went cold on him sometimes for no reason. And he lived knowing that she might leave at any moment. He lifted her hand from his lap and said, "I don't need distraction."

She frowned, and went back to her meal. "Okay."

What he needed was permanence and warmth and the knowledge that she at least would always be there. He was too old to go on like this. Too tired.

He took her hand and kicked free his chair and got down on his knees, and Caroline said, "Right here? Hank, how naughty—" But she fell silent when she saw the ring.

"Caroline, I want to share the rest of this life with you. I love you, and I want springtime forever."

All she said was, "Isn't that Annie's ring?"

He explained how life was so confusing but that love like theirs could order things and that he didn't want to lose her and that he'd been waiting to propose all summer and that he loved her and would do right by her and she'd never regret this. "You won't, I promise."

She got down on her knees with him. "Hank, I can't."

"Why not?"

"We just can't."

"Why the fuck not? That's not an answer."

"I've been married before, Hank. I'm not interested in being married again. I like what we have. It's perfect. Why mess with it?"

"'Been married before,' that's just an excuse. You married a prick. Please. Take this ring. Say yes. Make us family."

"Hank." Caroline held his hand in hers. "We both know you."

"What does that mean?"

"Have you ever been single? How many total months have you been alone since you moved to Ipsyniho?"

"Plenty. What's your point?"

"My point, Hank," Caroline said, rising to her feet now, "is that I know your pattern. We both know it. You latch on to whichever woman is giving you the most affection in that moment."

"Is that right." He rose to his feet. "You got a pattern too. Ditch whichever man you're with for no reason, just because things have become intimate and serious, because if you leave, then there's no chance he can leave you. You're afraid of love."

"I'm not sure you know what love is, Hank."

"This ring," he held it up for her to see again. "This ring says that I'll never leave you. That I'll be with you through heat and freeze. That I love you."

"That's what you want it to say."

"What's the problem with marriage?" he roared.

"I don't have a problem with marriage," she said, while gathering her things. She stopped at the doorway. "Trust, Hank, that's what I'm unsure about."

*

By the time Annie came back inside, Hank had the kitchen cleaned, minus one plate. He was scrubbing the specks of brown between the sink and the splash tile. Not even baking soda and vinegar was working.

Annie apologized for missing dinner.

He threw the sponge in the sink. "Oh, you're done?"

Annie took a tentative bite of the meat. "It's 2.00 a.m. back there. Even attorneys need sleep. Thanks for saving this. I'm so hungry I could eat . . . a bear." She laughed, and Hank took deep measured breaths. It was pinching in again, the drowning, and he knew there'd be no sleep tonight.

None of this was Annie's fault. He was pissed about Caroline and about Walter and about it all, and the last thing he wanted was to trouble Annie. Especially since they only had two days left.

199

She poured a glass of wine, and said, "So I have some bad news. I've got all day tomorrow, but I have to leave by eight thirty to catch a red-eye home. I've already switched my reservation."

He pulled hard on the last of the wine, and set the empty glass on the counter.

"I'm sorry I have to leave early," she said. "I could stay a month and still feel like I was leaving too soon. Like I was just getting my feet wet."

Hank whispered all he could muster: "What do you want to do tomorrow?"

She shrugged while chewing an oversized bite of bread. "What do you want to do?"

He headed for the door. "I need a cigarette." Like a fish needs water.

The flash of the lighter, the clarity of the first draw. The drowning ebbed, if only for a moment.

And so this was it, how he would spend his life. Alone and clinging to women who were perfectly content without him. The smoke filling his lungs, this world's truest companionship.

Annie slid open the door and joined him on the porch. "Can I?"

He handed her the pack and the lighter. "Don't start this. You don't need it."

"I want you to take me fishing," she said. "Not like I'm your client. I don't want a tour of the river. But like I'm you." She inhaled and broke into a hacking cough. "I'll never understand the attraction," she said, handing him back the cigarette.

"You don't want to fish."

"I do. But I don't want to learn *how* you fish. I want to learn *why* you fish." She laced her arm around his, leaned her head against his shoulder. "Will you take me?"

"Four too early?"

She shrugged. "I haven't been sleeping much anyway. To be honest."

Chapter Twenty-Six

THE RIVER RUSHED in at 2:33 a.m., smashing through the sliding door and knocking him to the floor, his nose and mouth filling, his hearing reduced to an aqua roar. He hit the ceiling but found no air. He clawed at the wood until his fingernails pulled back. So this was it: the way it would go. Deep space and comets, blackness and a sonic rumble.

He came to on the floor, still reeling from the pain of choking. He'd torn free a fingernail and the blood was smeared in trails on the floor. He had to stand and touch the chill of the sliding door to believe it had all been a dream.

He dressed for the day because he'd never sleep again and went to the computer to check the levels, the water temperatures, the run counts. He pulled the spinach tortillas from the fridge, the salami from the pantry, the secret sauce from the cabinet, and rolled up his signature boat wraps. He'd bring these and some homemade lox, some red onions, some flatbread. Of course some pistachios for between meals. He probably wouldn't be able to eat any of it; the flood's nausea had yet to recede. He looked now to discover his bloody finger had leaked through its bandage.

It was while he stuffed the flatbread's cardboard box into the recycle bin that he remembered something from the day before, an object that at the time hadn't even registered. It was a file sitting on Carter's desk, an old brown cardboard file, the kind of cardboard that had been replaced by clerical manila decades ago. Even from across the desk, Hank had gleaned the title printed in large letters along the rim: Homicide, E. Jackson. In those moments he'd been too distracted by the mounted steelhead, by Carter's bullying tone, by Walter's news. But now, in the half thought of sleeplessness, that file was there bigger and brighter than anything.

He chased this distraction back to the computer, and—using the Ipsyniho library's database—pulled up newspaper accounts of the murder dating back to the days immediately following. It seemed the sheriff at the time, Bridge's father, had suspected a random killing, a Manson-style execution job; Jackson had been alone in an obscure pull-off on a remote stretch of rural highway, and why would some-one want to kill a harmless fishing guide? There was a total lack of evidence, and the investigation went nowhere. As far as he could tell, no suspect had ever been named, no warrants issued.

Despite an hour spent peering through his glasses at the headache-bright screen, he didn't learn anything that would explain why Carter had that ancient file on his desk. The nausea returned and with it the shortness of breath.

So he rose and followed this desire for answers to Annie's bed-room door. He leaned an ear to the wood and heard nothing, not her voice, not her breathing, nothing. A moment passed and he remembered waiting by the tapestry that sufficed as a door as Riffle cried in those early days of falling asleep alone. He would read her two stories, sing her two songs, then say, "Mommy and I will be back just as soon as we finish cleaning the house." "Don't go, Daddy!" she'd yell. He'd wait just outside, bearing the heartbreaking wails and the desperate calls for his return. He'd hum to her through the tapestry, wanting all the while to tear it aside and lift her into his arms. She had cried for an hour the first night, a little less the next night, until she was finally, after days or weeks, falling asleep on her own, without a tear shed.

He regretted that, leaving her in a dark room alone. Sure all the parenting books of the era said it was the right thing, and Rosemary claimed it was necessary. But it went against his every instinct. He'd come to think of parenting as a fundamentally intuitive enterprise; if something seemed wrong, then it probably was. If millions of years of evolutionary pressure had instilled anything within humans, it was the proper way to raise our offspring. Letting our theories trump our innate impulses was simple hubris.

Danny was doing things differently. He lay in bed with the twins, one on each shoulder, humming songs until they were both out. "Sure, it takes awhile sometimes," Danny had said once, "but with them bouncing back and forth between homes, every moment counts." Danny was doing it better, and Hank found some comfort in that.

He turned the handle to Annie's room now and crept open the door. There she was, curled and asleep, her mouth open and a book beside her. She didn't stir as he crossed the room, as he leaned down beside her. Her breaths were slow and sour, an intake and a long pause, then a long sliding exhale. He was close enough to feel them on his cheek, close enough for Annie to blur into Riffle.

It was an exceptionally dry season, that summer fourteen years before. Wildfires burned in most of the watersheds in the Cascades, the Ipsyniho included. Thick smoke hovered over them and around them, red at dawn and corrosive gray at noon. It followed them indoors. It tickled their throats as they slept. It left them restless and spooked and up at all hours. And they weren't alone. A herd of cow elk wandered into city limits and ran up and down Main Street for an afternoon before finally lunging down the bank and across the river. A bear walked down the highway with no regard for the line of pickups and log trucks inching along behind him. Even the steelhead, Hank remembered, were uneasy. One afternoon, he counted sixty-two jumps in the span of a single hour. The fish were leaping straight into the air, a missile leaving its silo, rising three or four feet above the water before stalling and turning and crashing back to the surface: They wanted to see what was turning the sky colors.

Seventeen-year-old Annie didn't seem to notice the smoke, just like she didn't seem to notice any of Hank's efforts to ensure she enjoyed her month with him. He'd organized hikes and parties, and he'd spent two hundred dollars on front-row seats at the theater in Eugene simply because Rosemary told him Annie had a budding interest in the stage. But despite these best efforts, she remained reclusive, and he began to wonder if Rosemary had forced her to come, if Rosemary had lied to him on the phone when she said, "Annie couldn't sleep last night, she was so eager to get on the plane and see you." Probably, she couldn't sleep because she so dreaded the trip. Probably she felt pushed away by him, by her own father, and he knew exactly what that was like. But whenever he reached for her, she recoiled. She pretended not to notice his efforts, pretended to be bored by them. He understood that too.

The morning of her departure she wanted to be dropped off at the terminal, but he insisted on parking and walking her to her gate. She was a teenager for god's sake, anything could happen. But she insisted on carrying her own bags and on walking too fast, her hood up and her earphones in. He followed her gray shape through the darkness of the terminal tunnel and then through the noise of the congested gates. There were too many people in this world, and here she was trying to lose herself among them.

He was the one who forced the conversation, as she stood in line to board. "Did you even want to come?"

She didn't really answer, not at first, and he felt his face reddening and then felt foolish for being so angry with his teenage daughter, his flesh and blood, who had already suffered such a confusing childhood. He surveyed the other faces in line: an old lady scowling at him like she suspected him of some impropriety.

"What do you care?" Annie almost shouted, her earphones still in.

He tried to remove them so they could have a private conversation, but she pulled away from his hand. Glaring at him: "You don't care about anything that isn't wet."

Anyone who wasn't already looking turned to study him. A middle-aged, bearded man pleading with a striking young woman.

The line began moving.

"I care about you," he said, "more than—" Anything, was what he meant to say. But somehow, in that moment, the word felt hollow. He could feel a looming permanence under this goodbye, and he had to do better. "You're the most important—"

"You can't even say it." Tears broke down her cheeks, pulling dark mascara with them. "Look at you. You can't even say it."

The line moved forward.

"Annie, my sun rises and sets on you. It has since the moment you were born."

She pushed the pause button on her Discman and handed her ticket to the agent.

"Sorry, sir," the agent said to him. "I can't let you by without a . . ." He didn't hear the rest, because Annie was asking him a question.

"Then why did you do it? Why did you do that to Mom and me?"

The old lady was waiting by the concourse door, as if Annie might need her protection. The agent, too, was watching him as she tore someone else's ticket.

Annie was on the far side of the divider, just out of reach. "Your mom took you. Annie, you know that."

Annie pushed play on her Discman, the tears coming hard now. "That's what I thought." She turned from him and to the old lady and together they vanished down the concourse and into a future that Hank wouldn't see.

*

WHEN HE RETURNED from the porch and his fourth piss in as many hours, he found Annie awake too, drinking a glass of water in the kitchen. She was fully dressed, and it wasn't yet 4:00 a.m. When she saw him coming, she said, "Oh, you're up."

"I'm old, I'm always up."

He made them coffee, and while packing the snacks he'd prepared earlier in the cooler, they sipped the mud and talked of random things: weather, floods, Caroline's family. Annie was the one asking questions, eager maybe to learn all she could before she left. Or to fill the airspace with safe chatter.

He'd decided to take her to a new section of river, a section rarely floated. In fact, to his knowledge, only he and Walter had ever run it in hard boats. It was a canyon on the upper river, high above the highest boat ramp; they'd have to drop the boat from the road down a steep incline. There the river would curve away from the highway and go around Wolf Mountain before coming back and ducking under Fifth Bridge. They would bounce through some big rapids for sure, though nothing he couldn't handle, and hopefully be rewarded with a few unpressured fish. This was the only section of river where he was sure they wouldn't encounter other guides and anglers, the only section of river they hadn't drifted together at some point in their history.

Because of the heavy rapids, he tossed into the boat the floatation bags, which would keep water from filling the craft and, in the unlikely but conceivable event of a flip, keep the boat afloat. He also grabbed the river helmets and the bowline buoy, and the medical and survival kits he kept packed and ready in a dry bag.

"Where are we going?" she asked.

"A great section. Nobody fishes it. We'll be exploring new water. Your BlackBerry probably won't work up there."

She looked at the thing sitting on the counter. "Maybe we could do a different section?"

"You've seen all the others."

*

COME THE EARLIEST fuzz of dawn, they were standing at the wide point in the road, staring at the drift boat anchored in the eddy below. Hank had backed the rig up to the lip and lowered the boat over with the crank, doing all the work himself rather than put Annie in the awkward position of jimmying a craft down that rocky slope.

He hid the keys under the bumper for the shuttle driver, and touched Annie on the shoulder. She was studying the river now, which was half the width here, a frothing blur of white.

Above them, the dark mountains towered against the gray sky, lines of snow still tucked in their shaded recesses. A couple stars remained, and a sliver of the old moon. Not even the ravens were up yet.

"Wow," she shouted over the water's roar. "This is nuts."

He handed her the helmet. "Don't worry. It's the same river here as it is below." He helped her tighten the helmet's chinstrap.

She was looking at him squarely. "Are you sure about this?"

"I've been around too long to be sure of anything."

"That doesn't make sense. That doesn't make me any more comfortable."

"I oar better than I think." He wasn't concerned. He'd run this section twice before. Though not enough times to have the rapids memorized—they'd have to scout a couple—enough to feel comfortable. Besides, in a way, not knowing a section made running it safer; an oarsman always paid fuller attention when he was unsure.

He helped her take a seat and positioned the cooler and rods and bags in the center of the boat; it was best not to have too much weight in the rear of a drift boat when running big water like this. Though it was the same river, the rapids here were different. The *white water* downstream, even those Class IVs burdened with treacherous rocks and troubling reputations, were really small rapids. They might be long and they might contain a deafening suck-hole or two, but ultimately the *white water* along the boater's line remained below the forward gunwale. Pick the right line, stick to it, and you'd be fine. Here, the channel was often too narrow for the quantity of flow and the gradient too steep for eddies, which produced *white water* that often towered above the forward gunwale. Rapids like these provided a ride punctuated by blurring speed and breathless stalls. As the boat slipped down the face of one wave, it accelerated so precipitously the oarsman could fall backward off his seat. As the boat leveled in the trough and climbed the leading face, it slowed, slowed, slowed, until it just barely crested the next summit. If the boat lost momentum anywhere in the climb—say it skimmed a submerged rock or collided with the face of the leading wave or quartered slightly into the climb—it could stall out before cresting the next summit. At which point, the oarsman had failed, and no manner of panicked digging could save the boat from its sure fate: a slow slide back into the river's open mouth, a broadsiding turn, and a swallowing flip.

A few simple precautions would help keep the boat tracking straight and climbing strong. He moved the oarsman's seat up three inches, then removed the anchor and secured it up front. "Lean into the waves as we climb," he now told Annie. "And if for some reason we end up broadside, crouch against the upstream gunwale."

She repeated these advisories.

"Standard advice," he said.

He pushed into the flow and the river swung the stern downstream, and they were off at a speed that surprised even Hank. His finger throbbed beneath its bandage but there wasn't time for that now. The moves came quickly, long digs to ferry, short ones to straighten, then a drop and a quartering maneuver to surf the wall of the leading wave and circumvent a massive can opener of a ledge. It was fast, but it was as Hank remembered, and soon they splashed into their first pool.

Annie shouted, "Holy shit, that was wild!"

"Just wait," he said. "The rapids get better toward the bottom."

This canyon had been considered unnavigable for as long as people had been running boats on the Ipsyniho. The canyon's reputation kept all but the most aggressive kayakers from attempting it. It had been Walter's idea to run it, about ten years back. The summer crowds had become impossible, and Walter was annoyed enough to consider drastic options. He and Hank had hiked the six miles around Wolf Mountain to the canyon rim, hoping they might find a way down to the bottom. They'd brought rods and high hopes. "Only these impossible places will have fishing as it's supposed to be." But in a full day of trying, they didn't find a single entrance into the canyon that looked like it might also serve as an exit. But neither of them were ready to give up. Hank suggested they talk to Halis, the owner of Ipsyniho Mountaineering; maybe they could learn to rappel and ascend ropes. "Fuck that California shit," Walter had said. "We'll do this place Oregon-style." It took a year and another scouting trip, but Walter eventually convinced Hank to give the canyon a go. They took two boats just in case, and weighted them for big water. The run had been hairy for sure, but they were surprised with how readily the canyon accepted a hard boat. In a way, the canyon's narrow pinches seemed a better fit for a drift boat than the typically wider raft. They scouted every rapid and quickly came to see the patterns. A high bank on the outside usually meant a treacherous inside. A boulder slide along river-left usually meant a suck-hole in river-center. Soon they could predict the shape of the rapids from a quick analysis of the surrounding terrain. It was the final rapid that gave them the most grief, a serpentine chute bordered on either side by cliffs. It could be seen from Fifth Bridge, and had become known simply as the Falls, a Class V tourist eater. They didn't fish much that first trip, but when they did, they rose chromers. The second trip came the next season, a three-day expedition during which Walter and Hank each landed a dozen fish. They'd sworn then never to mention the canyon to anyone; if they were to keep the place as pristine as it was, they needed to ensure its killer reputation remained intact. They hadn't been back only because that winter Walter received his first diagnosis.

Hank might have told Caroline about the place, or Danny, but then they'd want to see the canyon and its fishing for themselves, and he'd be obligated to guide them through it, a prospect he dreaded, for reasons he only partially understood. More than fishing the canyon, he cherished the secret knowledge that a place like this still remained in this overly trodden world, and taking people here, even his closest friends, would make the place feel public somehow. So why was it that he felt so compelled to bring Annie here?

He was considering this question half an hour into the float as he oared the boat to shore where the river began a long westward turn. Annie was quick to jump onto land. The next quarter mile housed five prime fishing runs. None particularly long or wide but each three or four feet deep with knee-high boulders and a greasy surface—perfect dry-fly water.

Annie was laughing as she took off her helmet. "This place is primal!" she said.

"There's definitely something about it."

Above them, the slopes were dressed in reds and yellows and chartreuses. The foxglove, which was long gone downstream, grew copiously along the water, and higher, Hank pointed to clusters of Indian paintbrush and columbine. A pika, which had been lounging on a ledge watching them, squeaked and dodged.

In some places, bands of shale climbed a thousand feet upslope, winter's avalanche chutes. There weren't many trees here; the land was so fresh and new that soil hadn't had time to accumulate. In this part of the watershed, the process of biological succession was a few million years behind. The river itself looked prehistoric, the rocks fifteen to thirty feet across and bone white, like the spinal column of some ancient creature.

He handed her the six-weight switch. She shook her head. "I wanted to watch you fish."

"You wanted to learn why I fish," he reminded her. "This is part of it."

"Well, you should fish first at least."

"River etiquette says you fish the first run. I'll come down behind you."

"I go first because I'm a girl?"

"No. Because we used my boat, so you're my guest, so you fish it first." He heard how definitive his voice might sound, and realized she might be misinterpreting his meaning. "No pressure, though. Sit and enjoy the view if you'd rather."

She swiped the rod. "I'll fish."

He smoked a cigarette while she fished the first run, and then he stepped in above, throwing short casts into the pockets at the run's head. The fly bounced and skated and he used the long rod to stall it over the pillows of slack water, but then he reeled in and hurried downstream to Annie's side.

"Will I throw you off if I walk down with you?" he called, as she was just about to make a cast.

She nodded toward the bank behind her. "You'll be taking your life in your hands. My casting sucks."

So he walked with her down the next two runs, because he wanted to be near his daughter. He explained not the technique of fishing, but what fishing teaches a person to see. "Each run has its own fingerprint of currents, there are no two just alike. Skating a fly like this maps it out. See how your fly just turned broadside there? That's because of a microswirl in the flow, something you never would have seen other-wise. It's a meditation really, skating flies, not on the fish but on the hydrology of the river."

He couldn't tell if he was boring her or humoring her or what; he couldn't tell if she was even hearing him. And her silence made him self-conscious. He shouldn't have taken her fishing on her last day.

She'd come here today on another charity mission, not because she wanted to fish but because she wanted to give her old man a few hours in which he could feel like he was teaching his daughter something important. This day was about him, he realized now, and that felt pitiful and empty.

He started downstream to give her some space, but she stopped him with a question. "What did that movie say? Under the river is the language of God?"

A River Runs Through It. "Maclean wrote that under the cobbles and boulders are the words of God."

"Is he right?"

"Is he right. I don't know. There's ledge rock under there."

"So, no God?"

That wasn't a question that ever concerned him. God or not, what did it matter? It was the same world. "The ledge rock positions the boulders, which carve the flow into its currents. So it's the ledge rock that creates the splashes and gurgles and roars. All a river's words are formed by what's beneath the perceptible." Her fly was skating over a bulge in the meniscus, the swelling of a submerged boulder, submerged there because *of* the particular contour of the ledge rock. "The river really has no control over itself. It does what it always does and is what's underneath it."

She seemed to be considering this. And he felt a tiny rush; maybe he'd engaged her philosophical side. She turned to him after her cast landed. "An argument against free will?"

"Free will?"

"Nevermind," she said, turning back to the swing. "Old habits."

Old habits. Was that it? "Maybe it's an argument for entwined wills. Or no wills at all, just forces."

"That sounds like a dodge of responsibility."

"Which might be another force."

She fell quiet and seemed to be focusing on fishing, and he felt some need to give her space. He climbed the bank and took a seat high above the pool, in the warmth of the dawn light. She needed freedom; that was the essence of fishing.

But he also needed to get a grip. Waves of longing and desperation and regret had begun sweeping through him, each causing him to lose his train of thought, and some to lose his sense of balance. The first bad one had come on the drive up. The second as he watched her step into her waders. But since landing the boat, he'd had three more—each as disorienting as an epileptic event. He hadn't slept but four hours in two days and she was leaving him at dark. God or not, she was leaving him. A force as predictable as the river itself.

The river. From this angle, it had that liquid metal look, cellular undulations of blue and gold. Her fly sent broad wakes across the metallic surface, the neon fly line arcing toward shore, a force all its own. She would leave him tonight, and then what would this place be?

God or not, she would stay gone too, he knew it. Because what could he offer her but a bridge to some distant past that she didn't want? As a child, she had been part of his story, while he'd been the entirety of hers. Now, though, he realized the truth: He was only a tiny part of her story, and she was the entirety of his.

He couldn't go back to the way it had been, their connection reduced to the painful anonymity of the Internet image search. Their connection. There she was as a two-year-old, at the Rock Creek cabin, nestling into his neck, her long dream breaths like fluttering feathers against his skin. He couldn't bear it, the gaping divide between that warm past and this stark new reality. A reality of half-truths and selective disclosures. Of stilted authenticity and charitable interest.

What he wanted to give her, what he wanted in return—the soul-deep and simple connection they'd had in those years—wasn't even a possibility anymore. So what was left? Ipsyniho was too slow for the woman she'd become, and the Eastern world was too fast for him. Maybe she could call him, maybe she could ask his advice and invite him for visits and send him pictures of her new life, maybe she could share herself, her raw and true self. But between here and there spanned a ravine of unspoken resentments.

There was another memory from Rock Creek, little Riffle upset about Hank lifting the plate of cookies from her reach and putting them in a cabinet. She pounded on his leg with both her fists, wailing wildly, and then collapsed to the floor. Had he finally given her those cookies? Had she waited until he wasn't looking and climbed up and gotten them herself? Or had she eventually acquiesced to the unfairness of it all and wandered off in search of something her own?

She was nearing a prime bucket at the end of the pool, and Hank hurried down to be near her while he still could. "Just a smidge of technical advice," he called, pointing to the seam where she should drop the fly. "You'll need a downstream reach cast. As the line straightens, extend your arm like this."

She did as he said.

But could she hear between his words and understand his intention? Did she know that this is how men say they're sorry when they can't find the proper words? They talk passionately about something else. "The fish will come up that rapid right there; it's the obvious migration route. And they'll slide into that holding lie to recover energy."

"Lie," she said, throwing an excellent cast. "A lie."

A question? "Yeah, there are many kinds of lies: transition lies, staging lies, holding lies. Each is approached differently. A holding lie is a place where a fish dodges the main current, usually immediately above and below a substantial rapid."

"Holding lie," she muttered. "How long does a fish hold its lie?"

"Well," he stumbled, "how long depends. An hour or a day. But if the water levels drop, the fish can be trapped there indefinitely."

"Indefinitely," she said.

He laughed, not knowing how else to handle this queer exchange. "But eventually all rivers rise."

*

THEY FOUND THEIR first steelhead in the fifth run, a wild six-pounder that rose to Hank's dry fly five times before finding the hook. He brought it quickly to the shallows and unpinned it, and Annie hovered over his shoulder as he let it go. Even now, forty-five years after landing his first one, the experience brought a rushing sense of euphoria: an intoxicating cocktail of gratitude, hope, and faith rewarded—the indelible reality of one little resolution in this world so dead-set against them.

And for a moment, anything was possible. "I love you, Annie."

"What is it about steelhead?" she asked, maybe without hearing him. She had asked this question before, her first day after arriving.

"They're the sun," he said. "Everything in this valley orbits them. Always has."

"That doesn't mean anything. There must be something," she continued, "something about them that made this life of yours—of

214

Caroline's and Danny's and everybody else's around here—orbit them, as you say."

Hank rinsed the slime from his hands. "The river is washing the land's nutrients downstream to the ocean; steelhead and other anadromous fish are the vehicle that returns those nutrients to the headwaters. Without them, the land withers and eventually dies."

She considered this, staring at the passing water, so calm here compared to above. "But why are you drawn to them? I get they play some important role in the watershed. That makes sense. But so do trees, and I don't see you climbing a big fir every morning." She wasn't hiding the bite of these questions.

He fumbled for an answer, finally settled on one. "The word the native Ipsynihians used for salmon meant ancestor."

"Danny says," Annie surprised him, "that every population of steelhead is unique, that every stream has—or had, really—its own genetically distinct group. Big fish, small fish, red fish, green fish, fish that enter in spring, others that enter in fall. He says it's the stream's unique features, the power of its rapids and the length of its course and the temperatures and shit that make them what they are."

He thought of Danny as a fire-haired boy, pointing to a spawning redd in the tailout of a hidden tributary. The conclusive clank of grown-up Danny disappearing through the fly shop's back door. "It's true. Every generation, they become better at living in this world."

"But that's my confusion," Annie said. "That answer is really just another question: Doesn't every species operate this way? So what's the point? I mean, I'd understand if you were all addicted to gambling or something . . ." She trailed off, seemingly having thought better of this.

"I don't know what to say." Rosemary had once called fishing "harvest gambling," a "disease worthy of a twelve-step."

"So we're back where we started," Annie said. "What makes steelhead so special that you all would sacrifice your lives for them?"

Sacrifice their lives? It was Rosemary's logic, and he could have broken a rod over his knee.

"Because," he said instead with inflated confidence, "they're the river and the river isn't going anywhere."

But maybe, he realized now, it was because they were a safer fight to lose.

*

THE MORNING PASSED and they were four hours closer to her departure, and they'd all but stopped talking.

She was exploring, he reminded himself, stepping on stones she'd never before walked. Maybe that was why she remained pensive, because she was so taken by this place.

When he looked her way, when he saw her blue shirt stamped against the white rocks, he felt nothing but her absence. So many years had passed since little Riffle left, but the feeling remained like a smell that the deepest folds of memory can't forget. Now, though, there was something else too. She wasn't simply the tearful girl anymore—she was also the cold and confident grown-up driving her child self away.

They had lunch on a sun-drenched slab of basalt, a hulking thing the size of an A-frame home. The river swirled below over a bottomless blue hole. Juvenile steelhead were rising freely in the eddy. Caddisflies, it looked like.

He laid out the wraps and the lox and the flatbread and the pistachios and a bottle of pinot he'd brought as a surprise, but Annie wanted none of it. "I'm not hungry," she said. He took a few bites, but burped fire and put the food down.

She had taken off her waders and was now lying beside him. She had her arm over her eyes. It was like she was on this rock all alone.

A breeze came up the canyon now, a breeze stronger than the typical afternoon thermal. He opened a hand to it, feeling its chill, feeling the potential in its gusts. "We should probably get a move on." Winds, if they became too strong, could strand a drift boat, the river ferrying one way, the wind ferrying the other. In those cases, an oarsman could have real trouble lining up on a rapid.

She didn't sit up. A moment passed and he started packing up the food. Then, "How should I do it?" she asked. "How do you find the courage? That's what I need to know."

"Courage?"

"Yeah, I mean, that's what it boils down to, right? Thad is a kind man, and he's never done me wrong, but I can't go on with him. It's bleeding me."

"Bleeding you?"

"I don't know," she sighed. "Maybe I'm just too young to be married. Or maybe I'm just not made for marriage. I'm thinking it's that one."

He lit a cigarette, thought of that ring in his pocket, the other one on her thumb. He understood something of this. He remembered what it was like to feel shackled by a relationship. And he also realized what this was: a last chance. "I wasn't made for it either," he said. "But then something changed in me."

She sat up, and found her sunglasses, and looked off downstream. "Did you come to know yourself better? Is that why you realized you needed it? Maybe if I understand myself better, I'll see why Thad and I should stay together?"

He sat up a little straighter as if that might facilitate honesty, and said, "I came to realize how selfish I'd been. How I'd disappointed the most important people in my life. That I'd blown it. And that made me not want to blow it again."

She rose and walked to the edge of the rock and looked down at the water below. The wind was tossing her hair. Her toes were inches from the lip. "Are you saying I shouldn't leave him?"

He pointed at her feet. "Step back from there, sweetie."

She didn't seem to hear him. "It's the courage that I need. I know what I'll say. But I need the courage to say it. God, it is just so much easier to sabotage a relationship than to exit one properly, isn't it?"

He was desperate to give her some morsel of advice that would put the whole situation in context. And yet, he had nothing. "Sabotage is no good."

She blocked the sun with her hand. "I almost cheated on him once. That's what a coward I am." She had turned and looked right at him at the word "coward." "I always sabotage the relationships that matter."

"Don't do that, don't cheat." Again, he pointed at her feet. "Step back from there, Riff. It's a long way down."

"Annie," she corrected. "That's my name."

A gust lifted the flatbread and carried it off the rock and out of sight.

"How did you leave?"

He steadied himself with a long even breath. "Listen, Annie, I've never left anyone. They leave me. I've been left so many times . . ."

"Because you cheat." It didn't sound like a question.

He stood, smudged the remainder of his cigarette on his wading boot. "I want to have all sorts of fatherly wisdom, I want to be that man, I'm trying. But I'm a wreck and I don't know shit about how to live in this world. Except you've got to be straight with him. If you're honest, he might come to understand. If you're not, he'll despise you forever. That's all I know."

She was staring at him with a scary coldness. He put the remaining food back into the cooler. When the wine wouldn't fit, he nearly threw it across the river. "We really should get going."

"Please stop it," she said. A horsefly buzzed them, and she swatted at it aimlessly. "How long are you going to hold your lie?"

He saw that the ring he'd given her wasn't on her thumb any longer—it was in her hand.

"When Thad's father died, I realized how little I really knew. About you, and about me. Can't we finally be honest with each other? If not now, then when?

"There's been this lie between us forever," her voice shook. "You paint yourself as the victim, and you hide behind that. But please. I'm here because I want to start fresh and I want to do right and I want you in my life. Please, stop hiding from me."

He chuckled, because he wanted to say the perfect thing but was lost trying to find it.

She took his hand and placed the ring he'd given her in his palm. "I can't take this. I can't pretend any more. I love you, Dad, but I don't want a ring. I want the truth."

The ring felt as light as paper, as flammable too. He closed his hand around it so he wouldn't have to see it. "What do you want to know?"

"Start with then. Start with why Mom moved away."

"You want to know what happened, Annie?" The anger in his voice surprised him. "Your mom got a bug up her ass that this valley wasn't cosmopolitan enough for her daughter, and she packed the house and put you in the car and drove you away from me forever."

She turned away from him.

The ring in his hand: "And you'd do the same thing right now."

She didn't turn back. She wasn't even facing him.

He sidearmed the ring. A shard of light against shade. "'Sacrifice your lives.' Shit. Where do you come off?"

A long moment passed, and she said nothing, until, "Okay, Hank. Maybe you're right. We should get a move on. As you say, this wind is picking up." She was gathering her things, and he realized how straight the line was from this rock to tonight's airplane.

He reached for her. "Forgive me. That wasn't fair."

She pulled away, as if to scoff, *Was any of it fair?*

He lit another cigarette. And was struck by a memory of his own father lying prostrate in his coffin, that fuckup of a man who dodged them with a bottle and manipulated their mother and left the remnants of his cheating in the back of the family car, struck by what he felt in that moment when he was supposed to feel rage or pity. Confusion. That was what he felt. *Am I like you?*

"You hold on to all these theories and myths about yourself," she said, "and you don't pay any attention to what you've really done. We're the same that way. And that scares me."

"We're not the same. You're better." He took her hand in his, and remembered what he always wished his own father would have said to him. "Annie. I blew it. I fucked up and I ruined everything. And I wish every day that I'd done things differently. I wish I'd been a better man." She turned from him. "But you're not like me. You have what I'm missing. I can see it—"

"Stop," she said. "Just stop."

His own father never admitted the cheating, even after Hank found him with some woman behind a bar. *We were looking for her necklace,* he had said. Looking for her necklace, as if his father assumed him dumb enough to believe that. Part of the man's myth: that every human being, including his own children, was a peripheral character in *his* story.

Just stop. "I cheated, okay? That's why she left."

She wasn't saying anything, so he kept going because this is what she wanted. "We were going through a rough patch, your mom and me, and there was this kayaker from Portland, I can't remember her name, but we really connected, and this led to that."

Annie put a hand to her sternum, as if standing before a mirror and seeing a terrifying reflection.

"And later," he continued, "there was a woman from town, a waitress. That one was off and on."

"For how long?"

"Several . . ." He almost said weeks. "Years."

Caroline was right; he loved whichever woman was appreciating him most. He'd never left a woman, but he'd cheated on almost every one of them. It wasn't the sex he was after, though maybe he thought it was in the moment. But now he knew it was the intimacy. To linger in a moment with no past and no future, a moment of contraction and expansion that so overwhelmed the dark loneliness haunting him. The cheating was something he felt bad about, but not something he dwelled on. Back then he considered it part of who he was, a man with needs, a force—just like the river will always return to the sea.

Back then. Who was he kidding?

Because he'd cheated on Caroline. Only two years before. He'd come clean to her, which he'd never done with anyone before. She'd told him to "fuck off and never call again," as he deserved. But he hadn't let her go. For once, he hadn't quit. Caroline was different, and he was different then too; O'Connell had died because he told him to stand on that wet ledge. Hank sent her notes with flowers and brought her meals when he heard she had caught the flu. For months it kept up like this, him trying to amend this crime. After she let him back, though, she had always maintained a barrier between them. She might invite him for a night, they might share a bed, but she never again offered what he wanted most: to share her life.

He told himself she was just that way, and found evidence in her past to support this deduction. But really, he knew, didn't he? He'd caused this. He and no one else. She had offered him everything, and he'd consumed it all and gone looking for more.

"But why"—Annie's eyes were wet now—"did you let me go? Why didn't you fight for me? Why have you never, not even once, fought for me? Why only call on my birthday? Do you know what that's like? Do you know how it feels when your father doesn't make an effort? What's wrong with me? Please, tell me?"

He took her in his arms. "Oh god, there's nothing wrong with you. Hear me, Annie: These years, I haven't come to you because I haven't wanted to face *me*."

A minute passed, and she pulled away and looked him in the eyes, and he was afraid of what she might say next, so he spoke first. "This wind."

"Yeah. This wind."

*

THE WIND CARRIED the roar of the Falls up the canyon, the thunder of water mashing against rock. The gusts were so strong now that he had to turn the boat around and oar downstream to make any progress, and as they neared the rapid, he saw why. The canyon walls opened here, catching the wind and funneling it through the river channel.

He remembered arriving home to Rock Creek after an afternoon of lustful but insular sex. He remembered lifting Riffle and twirling her in the air and avoiding Rosemary's eyes, especially when Riffle said, "Where were you, Daddy?"

Annie now sat in the front of the boat, the hood of his coat pulled up and blocking any sight of her. He heard echoes of *Cornell '77. Born in the desert, raised in the lion's den.*

Just above the Falls, he backed the boat onto a small patch of gravel and shouted against the wind, "I'm going to scout a line!"

Annie stayed in the boat, unmoving.

There was a Chinese proverb Caroline had told him once, something about water always overcoming. Place any obstruction in the path of water, and it will find a way around. More than that, it will eventually devour the obstruction. "Think of Wikkup Canyon," she had said. Water always appears to be surrendering, and yet it never surrenders. Water always arrives because of its willingness to bend.

The water here had no options but to rush down the chute, bending left first, then dividing around a cabin-sized boulder, before rejoining and bending hard right and dropping over a lip into a gravy train of head-high waves.

He was here partly to scout the line, but mostly to find Annie a way around. He didn't want her in the boat, not with these gusts. As the boat rounded the boulder, it would be blasted with the full force of the wind, a wind powerful enough to shear the tops of the waves, as it was doing now, and blow them upstream. He'd have to keep his line and push forward at the precise moment if he was to make it off the wall. If he hit that wall, he'd never straighten in time for that last drop. This was too much risk for his daughter.

And yet, he couldn't find a way around the cliffs, not in a half hour of scaling up and down. He even hiked back upstream checking for a gap in the canyon rim. There was nothing that didn't require ropes and anchors.

"You were gone a long time," she hollered when he returned. He could tell by the sound of her voice that she'd been concerned. If he was gone, how would she get out of here?

The world was huge and rolling and his mouth was bone-dry. He'd fucked up and broken his routine and run a section he shouldn't have run and here was his daughter hating him and in grave danger. "It's fine. I've run it before. It looks worse than it is."

He thought of the ring out there somewhere, tumbling in the current. His daughter was safer when she was out there somewhere living her own life—the farther from him the better.

He turned his attention back to the rapid and tried to force out all the doubts, all the self-loathing, all the pain of her contempt. She was a client. He owned these oars. He knew this water. And he knew the secret, that every rapid is run the same, one move at a time: Straighten at the top, push, push, ship the oars through the first squeeze, push, push, push, quarter left, pull, pull, straighten, and ship—they would smack there against the rock and the wind would strike—push then quarter right and pull into position, push like hell and hope the boat makes it over the waves and around that wall and then line up for the drop. If they made it to there, he'd just have to stay straight and the gravy train would carry them through and into the pool. It would happen fast, but it would happen. He'd done it before, and he'd do it again.

Besides, this worry was a good thing, the body's natural caffeine; it was giving him the fast reactions and powerful strokes he would need to keep them in line and upright.

Double-check the floatation bags and bowline. The oar locks. The extra oar. The vests. He tightened his own, then reached a hand to Annie. "Here, pull that strap." She did, and then he lifted the vest as he'd done when she was a child to be sure it wouldn't come over her head.

She was looking at him now, and he couldn't make heads or tails of her face. "What?"

"You're nervous."

"So are you."

"But you're the guide."

He took his seat and stretched his shoulders and loosened his neck and spit in his hands and worked his grip on the oars. He was good at one thing in life, and this was it.

They were halfway to the lip when he called, "I'll get you out of here. Don't worry."

She turned and hollered, "What?"

"Nothing, forget it." There wasn't time now.

They were between gusts, thankfully, and the boat was keeping its line. More important than any single move, he reminded himself, was keeping the oars working in power position, at shoulder level and within reach. Form before stroke.

The current caught them and pulled them over the lip: like being released from a slingshot.

*

Blackness and ringing and cold and bang bang bang. Who was there?

You're fucked now, Patrick O'Connell said. His voice riding a darkness spawned from the roar. You shouldn't have brought her here and you shouldn't have gone left around that boulder, and now you're fucked.

What happened?

Live by the sword . . . Really, though, it's your kid that I'm feeling for.

There she was, running through the grass toward him after he'd failed to come home the night before. Summer morning, the dew climbing the sunlight, an ethereal veil just out of reach. She did a cartwheel, and yelled, "See Daddy! See what Mommy taught me!" That's when he felt it.

O'Connell's voice: A cubic foot of water weighs sixty-four pounds. If you were forced to hold only the H_2O that exists in the column of atmosphere between your person and the limits of space, only that thin slice of airborne water, you'd be pressed into a wafer of flesh.

But this was far heavier than water. What he was holding was the weight of his failure, the weight of fractured succession: He hadn't cheated Rosemary as much as he'd cheated Riffle.

There's only one thing that matters in this world, Hank. You know that. And you knew it then too.

⸱

A SANDALED FOOT on fingers. Cold steel against skin. And bang bang bang.

He could feel it like a distant memory: the rush of wind in his face, the pillowy bounce of the boat riding curls of *white water*, the feeling of unstoppable momentum. He could feel it, but he couldn't place it. Or himself. And where the hell was O'Connell?

Gagging, and rising. A dark figure grunting. Punching the oar at something. His mouth tasted metallic and this boat was leaning and there was the river coming right at them, surging over the gunwale. He must have lost his footing (had he been kneeling?) because then he was on the bottom again, coughing at a lung load of water.

Trapped. Pinned against a rock. And Patrick O'Connell was doing his best.

Hank tried to say, "Faster," but he heard nothing of the sort. He looked up to see Caroline dropping the oar into the lock and pushing hard on one stick. They were moving again, and he could tell they weren't straight to the current because the boat was wobbly, but there was the unmistakable freedom of the drift—and he heard a voice much like his say, "Straighten out!"

"How!"

How to straighten a boat. How. It was so simple, and yet there were no words.

And then terrifying speed and the floor rising up and punching him in the face. They were slowing, slowing, slowing up a wave, and he knew they weren't straight by the pace of the climb and he knew they were in trouble. But then they were accelerating again and a wall of water broke over the gunwale, so much that he was floating inside this boat which was floating on some river, and he turned to see the sunlight illuminating her.

Riffle was at the sticks. It was Riffle oaring this boat. She had come back to him.

*

AFTER THE FUZZ cleared, there was the nausea. "You've lost a lot of blood," Annie said. She was poking at the tear above his ear. He could feel the pressure, but none of the pain.

"What happened?"

She shook her head. "I don't know. All of a sudden you were on your back and the oar was gone and we were broadsiding into the cliff. Everything was fine, and then it was like so fucked."

"You got us out of there."

She was looking at his wound, not his eyes. "You'll need stitches."

He'd been knocked silly by oars before and he'd been razored open a time or ten too, and this would be fine. He just needed a few minutes here, in the sun, to shake out the remaining clutter.

"Was there someone else with us?" he asked. "I feel like there was someone else with us."

"We need to get you to a doctor."

"No doctors." He could feel blood dripping from his elbow now, and he looked to see if he'd been cut there too, but he couldn't find a wound.

"It's coming from this laceration," she said, pointing at his ear. "Listen. We need to get you to a doctor."

*

"LEFT HERE." HE pointed at the gravel driveway with the hand that wasn't holding a shirt to the wound. Annie was driving. She had loaded the boat too, only requiring the slightest guidance. Now, she

226

fumbled with the gears—grinding, roaring, a jolt—and they rushed up the steep hill. The nausea was still there. Not concussion nausea, he knew that well enough, this was different. It wasn't how-the-fuck-did-I-get-here nausea, it was the-stars-are-creeping-closer nausea. He hadn't eaten lunch, and now he'd lost a lot of blood.

Rita was coming out the door before the truck was even stopped. Slung over her shoulder was a blue case with yellow reflection strips on it. "Nice work, Hank." She was smiling, which meant this couldn't be too bad. "Take my hand. Let's sit you right here. You dizzy?"

Annie had explained everything on the phone on the drive down. She'd brought that BlackBerry after all.

Rita was flashing a penlight across his eyes. "What day is it, Hank?"

He waved her off. "I'm fine, I'm fine. Really. It's just a cut."

"Well then, tell me what day it is."

He told her.

"Can you tell me the time of day?"

He had to think about it. But he could see the sun through the trees. "Around three."

Rita pulled on a pair of purple gloves. "You're going to need sutures. Probably seven or eight of them." She told Annie to grab a glass of water. "Cabinet above the sink." After Annie had left, "So where did this happen?"

Rita had this way about her, this calm voice that was like aloe to a sunburn. It had been that voice, and the unflinching confidence behind it, that had attracted him so profoundly all those years before. And there, clearer than anything, was the look on young Bridge's face when he showed up that night to have it out over what had happened. "You were running a hard boat through the Falls? With Annie?"

"I've made mistakes, Rita."

She was pulling back the suture's foil packaging. "I'd say."

Somehow they'd gotten through it. Somehow, Rita and Bridge had worked it out, and Bridge forgave him. How had that happened? How had they gotten to where they were now?

"How do I fix this?" If anyone would know, she would.

"No, Hank, I do the suturing."

There was a sharp pain, then another one. The needle and pain-killer. "How did we fix what we did?"

Rita held a gauze pad to the wound, and leaned so that she could see his eyes. "You'll be okay, Hank."

"No, I know. I mean. You know, between you and me and Bridge. How did we fix that? How did we get here?"

She went back to the laceration, and he could only see her shoulder, her silver hair riding the breeze. "I haven't thought about that in decades."

Annie was coming through the door with that glass of water. "That's what I mean. I need to know."

"Maybe we didn't fix it. Maybe we just moved on. Who knows? Maybe we decided we were too valuable to lose."

*

AFTERWARD, ANNIE INSISTED on driving. "I'm not putting my life in the hands of a dizzy man."

"I'm not dizzy anymore." His head was pounding now though, and the gauze wrap was pulling hairs every time he turned to look at her. "Give me the keys."

She was holding open the door for him, not saying any more. Like her mother, she knew the best way out of an argument was to stop talking.

They were already on River Road and halfway home when he said, "I'm sorry, Annie. I shouldn't have taken us there. It was a mistake. I shouldn't have put you in that position."

She was quiet for a long minute, and he didn't know if she would ever talk to him again. Then she said, "There is something else I want to say."

From the tone of her voice, he understood this was serious.

"If I say it to you, I won't be able to pretend it didn't happen."

"I'm here," he said, turning to see the tears on her cheeks.

"I did it even after I saw what it did to Mom. Does that make me worse? It does, I know it. Some ethicist."

He wiped her cheek with the back of his fingers. "What happened?"

"I cheated on Thad. I did it. I connected with someone and cheated because I knew it would sabotage everything."

It was Danny she had cheated with; he knew as much without even asking, though it hardly mattered. "You're wrong," he said. "You're not worse. But now you should tell Thad, and you should tell him why you did it." He'd learned that much, if nothing else.

THEY SAID GOODBYE where they'd said hello, under the rustling oaks in his driveway. It would be a hot day tomorrow; these breezes weren't wet coastal northwesters, but dry southerlies. He told her as much, said, "You're lucky to be leaving tonight."

She was freshly showered and dressed again in long supple pants and fancy flip-flops and oversized sunglasses—she looked cut from a fashion magazine he would see in the checkout of the grocery store. "I always trusted you had your reasons for not calling or coming." A tear slipped loose under those glasses. "I just hope it wasn't something I did."

"No, not it at all."

"For years when we spoke, I walked on eggshells, afraid to say the wrong thing and drive you farther away. Even when I got here, I was so nervous." She laughed, though there was no humor. "I vomited in the airport."

He took her in his arms because he trusted his arms. "This isn't a good answer," he began a moment later. "It isn't an answer at all. But it's the truth. I put off calling you after you left here the last time because I regretted what happened between us. Then I regretted not calling you, which only made me put off calling you longer. It's no excuse, but that is what happened. Regret, maybe, is the strongest current."

And he thought then of his own father, escaped into his death, escaped from all Hank had to say to him, and all he was owed in return. A simple "I should have been the man you needed" would have gone so far. Just eight words might have set him free.

He took Annie's hand in his and tried to say a million things, but all he could muster was, "You deserved better. You've always deserved better."

"I was so cruel the last time I was here," she said.

"You were seventeen."

He reached into his pocket and handed her a worn photograph, the very photograph he'd kept on his person for twenty-something years: the two of them together on a sunlit beach, her five years old and river tanned and gleaming wet and holding a crawdad to the camera, and him lean and brown-not-gray and beaming at his little girl—buoyant and hopeful at the promise of all the years together to come. "I want you to have this."

She seemed hesitant to touch it, but she finally did, holding it to the light. "Do you have a copy?"

He put a hand to his heart. "Right here." Maybe she would cherish it as he did, or maybe she would tuck it away and never look again. Either way, he wanted her to have it; he wanted her to remember. "You've always been here with me."

A moment passed with them standing just out of reach, and he realized this was it.

She checked her watch. "I should—"

"Of course."

But she hesitated. "Daddy?"

"Annie?"

She looked to the ground between them. "I'm sorry about the ring."

He smiled. "It never fit you right."

"Maybe it was a little big, but you couldn't have known my size. I'm sorry."

He extended his hand and said, "Here."

She looked and muttered, "How . . . when did you . . . ?"

"Do you want to know? I'll tell you if you do."

She touched the ring in his palm as if it might be made of vapor. Then she checked for the inscription. "When alone, remember these arms reaching." He'd had it made months ago for Caroline, but now he realized he'd written this inscription for Annie.

"Don't tell me," she said, sliding it on her thumb. "I might be a grown woman, but I still need magic."

They both turned toward the sound of a truck climbing the driveway, Caroline's green Tundra. He'd left a message on her answering machine inviting her to come say goodbye, but he wasn't sure if she would show up. He wasn't sure if she would ever come again. But there she was, slamming the door behind her and holding a Tupperware container. "Just some smoked salmon and filberts and stuff. Figured you could use some grub on the flight."

Annie thanked her with a hug and a kiss to the cheek, and said, "Take care of my daddy, will ya?"

Caroline smiled and took Hank's hand in hers. They stood shoulder to shoulder now, and watched as Annie put the food and her purse in the rental car. "She's so beautiful," Caroline whispered.

Hank turned to see Caroline's eyes welling up, and he knew what she was missing, out there in the world somewhere. "She is."

Annie said, "Well?" and stepped toward him and they embraced. She wasn't letting go and neither was he. "You'll do better," he whispered, and she pressed her tear-wet face against his neck.

Chapter Twenty-Seven

HANK SCRATCHED AT the patch stuck to his arm as he drove up River Road, the shotgun in back. It was a Winchester Camp Defender, a short-barreled twelve-gauge with an improved choke. He'd bought it used years ago, to ward off bears when he, Rosemary, and baby Riffle lived up Rock Creek, in the hippie house. He'd only shot it at the quail that frequented the hilltop, often hitting three or four with a single blast. They'd eaten a lot of quail in those days.

Walter was out front at the picnic table tying flies. His glasses were low on his nose, his cap tipped back on his head, and he was looking withered and white, and Hank was pretty sure from the look of him that he hadn't slept much the night before. He didn't look up from the vise when Hank approached. Instead, he said, "I nailed it, finally. Look at this fucker." He cut the thread and dropped the fly from the vise and tossed it to Hank. He'd wrapped the moose hair so densely that it felt like a solid object, and he'd trimmed it to produce a concave nose. "It'll cast easy with that small head, but it should chuck water like the best of your poppers. Took ten years, but I got it."

Hank leaned the shotgun against the table and studied the pattern. It was a spectacular tie.

Walter only glanced at the shotgun. "You and your curiosity theory. I was a hard sell, wasn't I? Not true, I guess, what they say about old dogs."

Hank pinned the pattern to the table's wood. "When are we going to fish it?"

Walter handed him a fly box—his fly box, the wooden one he'd carved himself as a young man. In it were twenty-five or thirty of the flies in two colors and in two sizes. "Stayed up most of last night tying. Fish them, tell me how it goes." He nodded toward the shotgun without looking at it. "Did you bring me any shells?"

"Sorry."

Walter spit. "That was mighty selfish of you."

Hank had two old bricks of double-ought and a newer box of sixes, but he'd left them in the closet, and not because he thought he'd someday use them.

"I'm sure I can round one up," Walter said. "Better not take two."

Hank flinched away, this was all too much. Walter's drift boat was pulled out, and dozens of rods were slanting up from it, their tips fluttering in the hot midday breeze. "Did you fish today?"

"Take that shit, Hank. I want you to have it."

Hank scoffed. "Come on, Walt."

"I don't have no use for it. Sure as shit ain't oaring that old beast again. You better not leave here without it."

"I'm not taking your tackle. Come on. We got to get you up and on the water."

"Don't get your waders in a bunch. I kept out my seventy-one fifty-two. I'm done grocery shopping, but I ain't done fishing." He maneuvered a leg out from the picnic table, cringing against the pain as he did. "If something there don't meet your highfalutin standards, give it to Danny. That kid knows quality when he sees it."

Walter started to stand from the table, but sank back before he'd come up halfway. Hank slipped his arm under Walter's and helped him rise and lift his other leg over the bench. It was then that he saw Walter had pissed himself. The rate of Walter's descent left Hank without words.

Walter swung around the wading staff and leaned onto it, and pushed back at Hank. "Get off me. I ain't feeble." Walter didn't seem to notice the urine on his pants, that or he was pretending not to.

Hank stuttered. It was all he could do.

"Help me to the truck. Bring that thing." He gestured at the shotgun.

Together they walked, Walter leaning on his wading staff while Hank kept him steady, across the yard to Walter's old pickup. "I named Mindy my heir. Only seemed fair that she get this house after all I put her through. Not that there'll be much left after the mortgage is settled. But I want you to have the truck. Sell it if you want, but don't let her get her hands on it. I got my reasons, old reasons. Don't let her have it. You hear?"

"Yes sir."

"I got the title all signed over to your name. Put your squiggles on it, and send it on to the DMV. Do it today."

Hank looked out over the valley. In this moment, he felt like a stranger here, felt like he'd never really known this man named Walter. Part of it was how fast he was failing, how fast death was taking him. But there was something else too.

Last night, Bridge had shown up at the house, coming by to check on Hank and make sure he was doing all right with that head wound and all. They'd shared a couple beers on the porch, listening to the river between the road noise, Hank talking a little about Annie, about her life back East, then about Walter, about how suddenly this cancer was getting him. Bridge sighed, "Fucking shame." For a long few moments, they'd been quiet, sipping together and considering. Bridge had been the first one to speak. "Not sure if you know this or not, but my daddy always had his suspicions about Walt, you know, that maybe he was the one who shot Jackson up at Altitude Ramp." He seemed to think better of this topic after he'd voiced it, but Hank pressed and

Bridge eventually went on to say, "He was the one that found the body and all." Which was news to Hank. And which seemed like the kind of detail Walter would have mentioned. Should have mentioned.

"What is it, Hankle?" Walter now said. "Pull that broom out your rear and speak your mind."

Hank put his arm under Walter's, gestured toward the truck. "Let's get fishing."

"Fuck off. You only look like that when you got something to say. Speak up, don't got time for your pussyfootin'."

"It's nothing."

Walter swung his wading staff and clocked Hank's shin, hard enough to leave a weeklong bruise. "Man up, son. You're running out of chances."

Hank reached for a cigarette, and only then remembered the carton in the trashcan, the goddamn patch on his shoulder. "Jackson's murder. When you told me about it, you didn't say you were the one who discovered his body. Seems like a detail you'd relate."

Walter shrugged, hawked up some phlegm, and spit. "Long time back."

"True enough." He shouldn't have asked. He didn't really want to know. He'd known Walter forty-something years, and he had a clear sense of the man, and he wanted it to stay that way.

Walter was poking at the ground with that wading staff.

Hank tried to bail him out. "Should we hit Red Gate?"

But Walter didn't look up; he was chewing his cheek and cursing under his breath. Finally he muttered, "He's the one giving me cancer. I know it."

"Who?"

Walter was shaky now on his wading staff, too shaky to be standing. "I didn't go up there planning on anything. I just went up there to stop him from snagging those fish, that's all. It was a warm day and I knew the winter fish would be on the redds. You know the day, short sleeves in March. And there that bastard was, throwing trebles."

"Here, sit down, Walt."

Walter didn't move, he just kept teetering there. "I'll tell you because I know you'll stick by. I only ever told Mindy."

"You don't have to tell me." He didn't want to know, and yet he did, more than anything.

Walter took a breath, and stared hard at a point in the dust like he was aiming to snap-shoot it with a pistol. "We're pushing at each other, that's how it starts . . . and I got my rifle out, shouldn't have done that, but there's the rifle . . ." He was breathing hard now, like it was happening at this moment. "I don't know how, but there it was, and we're pushing and pop, the thing goes off. We were pushing at each other, Hank. I didn't mean to, I just meant to scare him, if I meant anything at all. And that's god's truth."

Walter staggered a couple steps and sat on the tailgate of the truck. It was there that he seemed to change, the wide eyes narrowing into cold slits, the heavy breathing replaced by calm, almost imperceptible inhalations. His voice changed too, flatter now. "You'd be surprised what a man's body does when he catches one in the neck. You'd be surprised how the sight of that stays current."

Hank took a seat on the tailgate too.

"He was snagging those fish though," Walter continued a few moments later. "It happened because he was up there. He shouldn't have been up there. He should've been doing his job. That's why it happened. Gotta be in good with the river. I was just the messenger. Can't feel shitty about that, right? If it hadn't been me, woulda been somebody else. The river made up its mind."

The breeze slowed to a stop, and the day felt that much hotter. Walter passed his sleeve over his brow. "What? Stop looking at me like that."

A moment passed and Walter pointed at the boat. "I gave you the reels for those rods, the lines too. Hank? Are you going to tell anybody?"

Was he? Could he? Could he not? "Do you want me to?"

That's when Hank noticed the fear. He wasn't afraid of Walter, he was afraid of his reasons. Afraid that Walter's logic might be lying dormant in him too.

Walter shrugged. "It was a long time ago. Nobody cares anymore. Jackson didn't have no sober kin."

Walter took the shotgun, racked the action. "Christ, Hank, don't you ever clean this? This here powder looks like it's from the Carter era."

Hank was thinking of Morell, of that wading staff leaning against the truck. Metal, stiff, and heavy enough to crack a skull. This man he'd known forever, this stranger. Capable of anything.

Walter pointed at Hank's truck. "You should get on. Hook up the boat and put those rods in your rig and fuck off. Last thing I need is somebody around here looking at me like that. You and Mindy. I'm in good with Lady Ipsyniho. That's all I need."

Hank didn't know what to say, how to leave Walter—or how to remain near him. He knew this man better than he'd known his own father, and yet, there he was, old and dying and guilty as all hell and more wicked than anyone he'd ever known.

"I'm a part of this valley, Hank, I'm part of her. It's her juice in my blood, and my bones is her gravel, and I've only ever done what's best for her. Sure, I've fucked up. But I've never worked against her. That's got to count for something."

"It counts," Hank said, though he didn't know if it did. "Counts as much as anything."

"Stop thinking I did it," Walter said. "I can see it in your eyes. The river killed that kid."

Hank backed away, sure now.

"The river killed him. You know it."

Hank turned and walked to his Bronco, forgetting everything except the wickedness. Even the firs looked menacing, their limbs crooked and reaching and knowing. They'd known all along.

Walter called, "Don't forget this title. Sign it like I said. Get it in the mail today. And for fuck's sake, rig up that boat and get it out of here."

Hank was already at the Bronco.

Walter pointed the wading staff at him. "Hank? There's fifteen G's worth of tackle there."

But he needed out of here.

Walter stood, and Hank thought he was going to holler at him. But instead, he tried to crack a joke. "Hope you ain't expecting this scattergun back."

The Bronco rumbled to life, and he dropped it in gear.

"Hank?"

His foot was still on the brake, and there was Walter calling after him—calling after his only future.

This old man looked nothing like the man who'd shown Hank the way. He looked poisoned and prehistoric, and Hank wanted none of that for himself. Yet he knew all the same, *this* was his precedent.

He turned the engine off and kicked open the door and walked back. Walter was handing him the truck title, and Hank folded it without a glance and tucked it in his shirt pocket.

Hank put his hand on Walter's shoulder, as close to an embrace as Walter would allow. "You've been damn good by me."

Walter whispered, "Is that enough?"

Hank shrugged. "Come by my place. Let's pack a bag and you stay a few days."

"No." Walter shook his head. "You ain't a nursemaid, you ain't what I need. I'm nobody's burden."

Hank tried to take his hand and lead him to the Bronco, but Walter pushed away. "Go on."

When Hank didn't move, Walter grew angry. "I said get. Leave me be. I ain't no charity case. To hell with your pity. Take my things and get on. That's the way it's done."

"I'm not leaving."

Walter heaved up the empty shotgun and, tears swelling his eyes now, leveled it on Hank. "I'll do it, Hank. I will."

Hank considered pushing past the shotgun. Or staying put until Walter relented. But in the end, he backed away for the same reason he'd brought Walter the gun in the first place. "I'll come up first thing, Walt. Tomorrow we'll fish, okay? First thing."

Walter held fast.

And he was still holding fast when Hank reached the end of the driveway and turned downstream, nearly blind with the knowledge of what he had lost.

Chapter Twenty-Eight

HANK HEARD DANNY'S truck pull up the driveway just after dark. He finished putting Annie's bed sheets in the washing machine and met him at the door, wiping the sweat from his beard with a towel. It must have been in the nineties still, and these patches weren't worth a shit. "Good to see you."

Danny looked like he always looked, substantial and determined and capable. His sunglasses hung around his neck and there was a band of sweat darkening his baseball cap. He'd been on the river today. "I got some bad news, Hank."

"First," Hank interrupted. "You got to know that nobody, not Caroline or Walter or me or anybody else on the inside, has been talking behind your back. That was just me at the shop, me being stupid."

"Walt," Danny said, his face canted, but his eyes square on Hank's. "Hank, he's dead."

Hank reached for the doorjamb. He'd known it, and yet it still hit him like he hadn't.

"Some joe found him just an hour ago in the Campwater. Carter located his truck upriver. A note on the seat. He floated some miles, I guess."

He'd left Walter leaning and broken. That wasn't the way it was supposed to go. He should have been there.

And yet, how else could it have gone?

The crickets were buzzing like a bad headache. "What did the note say?"

"Classic Walt," Danny said, as close to a laugh as one could get given the circumstances. "Something like, 'I'm killing myself 'cause I got my reasons and don't go blaming nobody. Walter P. Torse.'"

Hank pointed at the porch chairs, and they both sat and stared out into the dark woods. "There had to be something else. That can't be all the note said."

"Goddamn shame." Danny pulled free his hat and set it in his lap. "He'd been looking pretty sorry, but I didn't reckon on this. Not now."

They just sat there, together, figuring the world now that Walter wasn't part of it. And then Danny surprised him. "Hank, I know why he did it. I know why he killed himself."

He turned to see the moonlight in Danny's eyes. "Do you."

Danny wiped the sweat from his forehead and said, "He's the one, Hank. He's the one that did it."

Danny explained what Andy had told him the day Morell went missing, that Andy had been driving upriver to fish that day when he'd seen Walter's rig hidden on an overgrown spur road, a place he'd never seen anyone parked before. He parked just up the road, and dropped down to the river, assuming that Walter must have some secret walk-in location. What he saw was Walter coming back through the woods, without a rod. "He was torn, Andy said. Real messed up. Andy called to him, offered to help, but Walter hurried off through the woods, all crazylike. Andy thought he'd had a stroke or something. It was only later that he put it together. Walter was coming up from Whitehorse just about the time Morell would've been going through."

There were a dozen possible explanations. Walter did have a lie down there, one that nobody fished, a spot that produced on hot days. Maybe he'd ditched his rod when he saw Andy. And maybe he'd hurried off because he didn't want to be recognized.

But even as Hank worked this out, he knew better.

"I don't know what to do," Danny said. "I mean, you saw Morell's mom and sister. You saw what they're going through."

Hank turned to the man beside him, this man he'd known from diapers. This man he'd helped make. "You're thinking you got to tell Carter what you know?"

Danny turned to him. "I don't know what to do. Fuck Carter. But Morell had family. They deserve to know everything, don't they? But then what about Walt? I mean, what he did—if he did it—was wrong, but he did so much else that wasn't. And if people think he's the one, well, they'll be quick to forget everything else." Danny leaned over his knees, and stared straight into the porch below him. "What's right here?"

It was true, everything he said. If people learned what Walter had done, his legacy in the valley would evaporate. If people knew about Morell, what was worthy of example would be lost. Morell's family would gain for sure, but the valley would lose.

"The family deserves to know," Danny said. "But would they want to know? I mean, by now, they must have figured it was an accident in the rapid, right? And wouldn't you rather think, if you were that mom, it was an accident that took your son, not some pissed-off old man? I mean, no parent wants to know that someone hates their kid. Tell me I'm right here."

Hank thought of Annie settling in back at home. He wondered if Thad was at this moment hating her, or if he was still living in the dark.

"Hank?"

He thought of Annie walking on eggshells all those years, afraid to call and say the wrong thing.

"I'm mean, I guess I'm looking for some guidance here."

And he thought of Walter, living his lonely life in that house, devoting every authentic part of himself to the river, and why? Because he could know right by the river. And because he could keep the river at a distance.

"We don't hold this one," Hank said. "We tell that mother what we know. And if she tells Carter, well, that's the way it'll go."

Danny turned to him. "I didn't think you'd say that."

Hank felt the stitches above his ear, the fluids oozing from the wound. "If you disagree, speak up."

"I don't disagree."

Chapter Twenty-Nine

FALL **ARRIVED LATE** that year, toward the end of October, the first freshets clouding the river and filling it with drifting leaves. Shimmers of yellow and red and orange fluttered through the tea-stained pools, spun endlessly in the eddies, and carpeted the cobbled shores. Cool coastal gusts rushed upriver, ripping still more leaves from the trees and carrying them upstream in an inverted reflection of the river below.

Everything was waiting for the fish. The bears sat on the beaches, their berry bellies shrinking with each passing day. Bald eagles circled their roosting trees, long whistles echoing upstream. Ospreys streaked through the airborne leaves then the water-soaked ones, trying to snatch those few young trout cruising the eddies. Anglers too waited, in their hotel rooms, in their tents, in the fly shop. No one dared ask the question everyone was pondering: *Might this be the year the fish fail to return?*

Hank found Caroline at her gate. Samson and Delilah stayed behind, barking and chasing each other in circles. "Beasts," Hank said, as Caroline pulled shut the door.

"We all got our bark," she said.

Since Walter's memorial service, they'd only seen each other a few times, evenings when Hank had driven up to spend the night. They'd both been working steadily, though their clients hadn't been catching many fish. Which meant they had been working harder, staying out longer, covering more miles. Both of them felt a responsibility to do all they could to get a sport into at least one fish. A dude who touched a steelhead was a citizen willing to fight Cherry Creek Timber.

But soon the year would slow and they'd have time again, time for themselves and each other. That was part of this life Hank appreciated most, the fluctuation between the seasons, the rush and then the calm, their own version of the week and the Sabbath. The original version, maybe.

Caroline asked if he'd heard from Annie, and he told her he had, though he hadn't exactly "heard" from her. They'd been exchanging e-mails, one or two a week, which seemed an easier way for her to stay in touch. He disliked the distance of it, how he couldn't hear her inflections to tell if she was joking or not, but he was grateful to have these updates, to be part of her life. She and Thad were living in separate apartments now, though neither had filed for a divorce. "Thad is so forgiving," she had written one day, and "maybe I'm willing to try."

"I'm going to build a sauna this winter," Caroline said. "Off the bedroom. I got a line on some fallen cedar. Good stuff. Bridge said he'll mill it for me." She was wearing her weathered work pants and her wading jacket and her fishing cap, her hair in a ponytail out the back. Despite the rain, she was wearing sunglasses, the low-light version. You could always spot riverfolk, Hank thought, because they never leave home without their polarized; they might miss a chance to see past a reflection.

"I'd be glad to help," he said. "You know I like wearing a tool belt."

"You and that tool belt are why I'm building the thing."

They parked at the ridge and Hank handed Caroline the dry bag and lugged on the backpack, and they started down the trail to Pine Basin Springs. From all the leaves on the trail and grass hanging across, it looked like no one had walked here in some time. Maybe since Hank and Annie.

They cleared the needles and cones from the base of the cliff, right below the patch of young rock, and Hank carefully placed the pictograph so that it faced the pool. Its image was of one person holding the hand of another, a parent and a child maybe or just two adults, it was hard to tell, and there behind and before them were the salmon.

They backed away a few steps and surveyed the whole sequence, unbroken again, the story intact if not complete. They didn't know whether to read it from left to right, or right to left, or whether its originators meant it as a single story at all. But, nonetheless, there it was, before them, offering.

Hank left a kiss on Caroline's temple, and she pulled him close.

After a time—the rain pattering the pool and the trees sifting the winds—she whispered, "How's this done?"

Hank opened the dry bag and removed the urn. "We write it as we go."

They both held the container and tipped it toward the pool, and watched as Walter ghosted over the water and joined the currents that flowed toward the lip. A small trickle left the pool there, a creek that descended two thousand feet through a forgotten ravine before joining the Ipsyniho, which descended another three thousand feet through canyon and farmland and estuary to the join the Pacific. "Everything runs downhill," Hank whispered.

"Except salmon."

For a time, they were quiet, and then in the lee of the cliff's story, Caroline began humming "Brokedown Palace" and Hank joined in and their voices merged with the pattering rain and the breathless wind, and that seemed words enough.

Acknowledgements

NOVELS ARE CRUEL projects. Early mornings, late nights, the precious hours between—their epiphanies slip away if they're asked to wait.

And so, first, thank you to the singular person who made *Holding Lies* possible: Ellie Rose. I hope the finished story is worthy of all you sacrificed on its behalf.

And to my enchanting daughters: may you remember everything you came into this world knowing.

A novel also demands readers and critics who care enough to take the story's hand and lead it where it means to go. So thank you, Lilly Golden, who, like the finest doctor, inquired, diagnosed, and healed. And thank you, Nick Lyons, who first offered encouragement and later advocated on the manuscript's behalf.

And thank you to Wayne Harrison, Ted Leeson, Alison Ruch, Rachel Teadora, and Joshua Weber, who each highlighted fissures where I saw none.

And thank you also to those who supported the writing of the story: Tom Christensen, Tracy Daugherty, Jay-Roy Jones, Nate Koenigknecht, Jim and Elaine Larison, Ted and Sarah Larison, Steve Perakis, Scott Powell, Sarah Rushing, Rob Russell, Marjorie Sandor, and Keith Scribner.

Also thank you to the English Department at Oregon State University for its continued support.

And to those inspired souls and organizations dedicated to winning the good fight, including Lee Spencer at the Refuge Pool, Bill Bakke and the river stewards of the Native Fish Society, Dylan Tomine and Rich Simms at the Wild Steelhead Coalition, Guido Rahr and Jay Nicholas at the Wild Salmon Center, and the thousands of volunteers across the West working to save wild salmon. May others learn what you know: that salmon are more than this coal mine's canary.

I am indebted to each of you.